"I think we need to cut to the chase."

Folding his arms along the edge of the table, Rhys leaned closer and held Jacquie's gaze by sheer force of will. "I'm not sure what's going on, but I am sure I'm tired of playing games. Why are we here, Jacquie? What do you have to say to me?"

She drew a deep breath. "You asked me why I left without saying anything."

"Yes."

"Well, there is no husband. I invented him because I couldn't come home as an unwed mother with an illegitimate child."

Setting down her coffee, Jacquie looked Rhys straight in the eyes. "*Your* child, Rhys. My daughter, Erin Elizabeth Archer, is your child. The only proof you'll need is a single glance at her beautiful face."

Dear Reader,

I taught myself to ride a horse when I was in junior high school...with a scarf looped around the bedpost, me mounted on the footboard and a volume of the *Encyclopedia Britannica* open on the mattress for instruction. Yes, I really was that crazy about horses. But in time I grew up, gained a husband and children and let the horse dreams fade.

Then my younger daughter, aged twelve, began pestering me to go riding with her friends. I'm not quite sure how it happened, but now we own four horses and spend most of our time outside school hours "at the barn."

The Fake Husband is a story about people who love horses. Jacquie Archer and Rhys Lewellyn are brought together the first time by their competitive equestrian careers. And when all-too-human concerns tear them apart, it's the horses—and one very special child—that bring them together again. I think the nobility of the horse draws out the best in us humans, and I thoroughly enjoyed spending time with people who respond to that call. I hope you'll do the same.

Happy reading!

Lynnette Kent

lynnette@lynnettekent.com
or PMB 304
Westwood Shopping Center
Fayetteville, NC 28314

The Fake Husband
Lynnette Kent

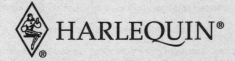

HARLEQUIN®

TORONTO • NEW YORK • LONDON
AMSTERDAM • PARIS • SYDNEY • HAMBURG
STOCKHOLM • ATHENS • TOKYO • MILAN • MADRID
PRAGUE • WARSAW • BUDAPEST • AUCKLAND

ISBN 0-373-71177-8

THE FAKE HUSBAND

Copyright © 2004 by Cheryl B. Bacon.

To the friends I've found "at the barn"

Kelly and C.J., Kim, Beth,
Karen and Julie and Kelly K. and Laura,
Dr. Garrett and Dr. Brian

Your laughter, your tears and your teaching
will always be with me.

Books by Lynnette Kent

HARLEQUIN SUPERROMANCE

Don't miss any of our special offers. Write to us at the
following address for information on our newest releases.

Harlequin Reader Service
U.S.: 3010 Walden Ave., P.O. Box 1325, Buffalo, NY 14269
Canadian: P.O. Box 609, Fort Erie, Ont. L2A 5X3

CHAPTER ONE

RHYS LEWELLYN ARRIVED in the "sunny South" on New Year's Day, just in time for the worst snowstorm to hit North Carolina in eighty years.

"Damn snow wasn't supposed to reach this far till tomorrow," he growled, switching the windshield wipers to maximum speed. "And we should have been here two days ago."

"Two flat tires and five horses make for slow traveling." Coming from the back seat, Terry O'Neal's brogue was as thick as the day he left Ireland thirty years ago.

"Tell me something I don't know." Rhys shifted his weight from hipbone to hipbone and flicked the switch for the seat heater to high. The escalating ache in his back measured exactly how much effort he'd put into this trip and how much stress he'd undertaken.

"All right, then." Terry rattled the map. "Your turn's coming up on the left."

"Thank God." A glance toward the passenger side showed his son's posture unchanged, head turned to look out the window at the white blanket shrouding trees and road alike. No sign of interest, or fatigue, or anything remotely resembling enthusiasm had slipped through Andrew's guard since leaving New York. He might as well have declared himself a hostage.

Perhaps he was—a hostage to his father's failure.

For now, though, the struggle was not father against son but man against nature. Rhys eased his foot onto the brake and felt the tires skid.

"There has to be six inches of snow on this road, over a layer of ice. Have these people ever heard of snowplows?" With the weight of the trailer behind him, he needed all the traction he could get—which appeared to be none, as the truck continued to slide despite antilock brakes and four-wheel drive.

Rhys muttered a string of curses. "I can't stop the damn thing."

"Just take the corner," Terry advised, leaning forward between the seats. "Wide as you can."

Teeth gritted, Rhys didn't have time for another smart answer. He turned the steering wheel gently to the left, avoiding thoughts of what would happen if the trailer behind him twisted or, worse, capsized. Holding his breath, he glanced at the rearview mirror to see the rig behind him come into line. All he had to do was straighten up a bit and they'd be headed down the lane, none the worse for their little skating adventure.

Then the truck's front tire jolted into a deep hole on the right side. "Oh, Jesus," Terry groaned. "What now?"

The rear wheel followed. Before Rhys could brake, the trailer's double wheel, loaded with two and a half tons of horse, dropped into the pit and stuck fast. Their forward progress skidded to a shuddering, lurching stop.

Swearing, Rhys released his seat belt and jumped down into the snow, wincing as the impact jarred his back. His first glance at the trailer showed him the worst—a forty-foot conveyance tilted to the side of the road at a steep angle, containing five animals known for their tendency to panic at the bite of a fly.

Terry charged past him. "Got to get them out," he muttered through the fog of his breath, "'fore they go hurting themselves."

"And how are we going to tie up horses in an empty field in the middle of a snowstorm?" Rhys joined the older man in letting down the back ramp and opening the double doors.

"God knows."

"And we're waiting for divine revelation?"

"Better revelation than a broken leg."

Three horses were loaded side by side at this end, facing forward and trying to keep their balance on the sloping floor. An ominous thumping came from one of the berths at the other end of the trailer.

Rhys put a hand on Terry's shoulder. "You unload here. I'll start at the front end."

"You can't bring that stallion out by yourself."

"I'll get Andrew to help."

"That'll be a trick."

Contrary to Terry's pessimism, Andrew had sized up the situation and solved one of their problems already. As Rhys headed to the center door of the trailer, he saw that his son had found a pair of trees off to the left and was stringing a line between them to which the horses could be tied.

"Good idea," Rhys called across the snowy

ground. Andrew didn't hear, or chose not to. Either way, he didn't react.

But within the trailer, Imperator had heard his master's voice. His shrill whinny ratcheted the anxiety of the other horses up several notches. Rhys got the ramp down and the door open just in time to see the big Thoroughbred hunch, elevating his hindquarters. With the sound of a cannon shot, both hooves impacted the wall of his stall.

"Jesus, Mary and Joseph." Beside the trailer, Terry hung on to a lead rope as the bay gelding on the other end, taking exception to Imperator's display, attempted to rear. By the sound of it, the horses still in the trailer with Imperator were on the verge of outright revolt. "Down, Abner. Down."

Rhys climbed into the trailer to stand spread legged in front of his stallion. "Okay, big boy, we got the message. You want out. Can you be halfway cool about this?"

Eyes wide, nostrils flaring, Imperator was anything but cool. His winter coat of thick black hair was streaked with sweat. He didn't travel well at the best of times, and this morning's tranquilizer had worn off a couple of hours ago—the scheduled time of their arrival before the intervention of the storm.

"Settle down, son." Rhys stroked a hand along the arch of Imperator's neck. "Just a little uneven ground, here. You're the best there is over hills."

The horse pawed the floor with an impatient hoof, barely missing the toe of Rhys's boot.

"Get you out, is what you're saying. Right. Just don't kill me in the process." He untied the lead rope from the ring on the wall and stepped back as Imperator lunged against the padded breast bar keeping him in the stall.

"No." Snapping the rope taut, Rhys put steel into his voice. "Back up. Back up," he ordered, pressing his fist into the stallion's chest. "You heard me. Back." Imperator brought his own stern will to the argument, refusing to retreat. Snow blew into the trailer, along with a cold wind that froze Rhys's rear end and stiffened the tense muscles in his back.

Giving in, however, would destroy what control he might possess over this powerful animal. He jerked the lead rope once more, pulling the horse's head down until they met eye to eye. "Imperator. Back. Now."

After a moment, Imperator conceded and shuffled back a step, then another. Rhys let him stand there for a few moments, submissive, to reinforce the lesson. "Okay. Now we'll try again." He released the breast bar. "Slowly. Walk on, Imperator. Walk."

The horse stepped to the door of the tilted trailer and hesitated at the top of the ramp, staring out at the white world swirling around him. Snowflakes matted his mane and eyelashes immediately. Imperator snorted and shook his head.

"Yes, we were leaving this weather behind, weren't we? The point of coming south was to get warm, right?" Rhys felt for his footing in the soft snow. "Among other things. Walk on."

Steadily Imperator moved down the ramp. Once on the ground, a combination of fresh air and the prospect of freedom energized the big horse. Head high, eyes wide, he surveyed his new surroundings, shifting his body to take in a three-hundred-sixty-degree view.

Though he obviously would have preferred to gallop across the field to the trees where Abner was already tied up, Rhys held him to a walk on the unknown ground and tied him at the other end of the line from the bay. "You two be gentlemen. We don't need any other complications this afternoon."

When he turned back to the trailer, he saw Andrew trudging through the snow leading the two mares, Daisy and Lucretia, followed by Terry with Felix, the black-and-white pinto yearling.

"So," he said as they came close, "we've got five horses to move down this lane in the snow. Any reason we can't ride three and lead the other two?"

Terry shrugged. "Whatever we're going to do, let's be quick about it. I'm freezing my cheeks off out here."

Rhys nodded. "I'll take Abner and lead Imperator. Andrew can mount Daisy." He gave the gelding a pat. Daisy and Abner were brother and sister, though a year apart in age, and shared the same even temperament. Riding either horse was like relaxing in a favorite armchair.

But Terry stopped him with a hand on his arm. "I'd advise against riding her after all the upset. You can never tell what will cause a mare to drop her foal too early."

"Damn." Daisy was pregnant, and Terry was exactly right. But Felix was far too young to carry a rider. "That leaves us a mount short."

Andrew looked around, his eyes bright. "I'll ride Imperator."

Rhys shook his head. "No."

"I can. He—"

Keeping a firm grip on his temper, Rhys explained the obvious. "All we need is an Olympic champion running wild with you on his back, through a snowstorm, over unfamiliar, unseen ground. The way things are going today, both of you would end up with broken bones."

An insolent—even contemptuous—sneer curled Andrew's mouth. "I'm not the one who fell off him last."

"That's enough of that," Terry said sharply. "Keep a civil tongue in your head, boy."

Rhys swallowed against a surge of emotion he didn't want to classify. "I have more weight to use and twenty years of experience to my advantage. That makes me a safer bet." Avoiding the sullen outrage on Andrew's face, he turned toward the truck. "I'll lock up the rig."

First he tried to pull the trailer wheels out of the hole again, thinking that without the weight of the horses, he might actually succeed. But the traction just wasn't there. Even in low gear, the truck's wheels spun uselessly against the weight behind it.

In the tack room of the trailer, he slung Imperator's bridle over his shoulder and pulled saddle pads off the racks. He'd seldom ridden this horse bareback—Imperator needed the discipline of a saddle to keep him focused.

Then again, the last time he had been on Imp's back, a saddle hadn't kept either of them from disaster. For a moment, Rhys stood with his eyes closed, fighting back the memory of that last fall, his own sense of helplessness as the world literally spun around his head.

But that was the past. Today, he was making a start on his future. *Their* future, his and his son's.

When he rejoined Terry and Andrew, they'd fashioned their horses' halters into bridles without bits. Rhys gave them blankets and turned toward the stallion. Again Terry grabbed his sleeve. "I'll ride him, if you want," the Irishman said in a low voice. "You've no need to take such a risk, with your back still tender."

"I'll be okay," Rhys assured the trainer, and himself. "Give me a leg up." As they walked to open ground for mounting, Imp tossed his head and capered, obviously wanting a brisk run.

"Are you sure?" Terry asked once more.

"What do you think?" Rhys brushed the snow from Imp's back before slinging the saddle pad across.

"That you're a damn lunatic, just as I have said since you were five years old."

"Well, at least I'm consistent. Ready?" He closed the reins inside his left fist.

Terry bent his back and held out his clasped hands for Rhys to put his knee into. "If you say so."

Then, with three bounces on his right foot and a toss up from Terry, Rhys found himself, for the first time in two months, astride the great Imperator.

"All right?" Terry said, as Imp sidled and shied.

What other choice did he have? He could either admit he was all but puking with fear…or else sit here and ride the damn horse.

Rhys drew a deep, shaking breath. "All right."

The Irishman retained Daisy's lead rope as he ploughed through the deepening snow—at least eight inches by now—to Lucretia, a gray Thoroughbred named for the wicked glint in her eye. Andrew, again wearing his mask of indifference, had already mounted Abner.

As he had for the past week, Rhys ignored his son's attitude and his own inability to make a connection with the boy. "Let's get this parade underway."

Heading Imperator toward the lane, he kept a firm hand on the reins, restraining the stallion's desire for speed. The asphalt road surface was solid under the snow, but treacherous nonetheless, thanks to that layer of ice.

"How far do we have to go?" he called back to Terry.

"Five miles, or thereabouts."

"Terrific."

Five frozen miles to a cold house and barn he'd leased without seeing them, on a horse he had failed the last time they rode together. Imperator didn't trust him any more than he trusted himself. Not exactly the perfect start to a new life.

"Happy New Year." Rhys blew out a frustrated breath. "Happy New Year, indeed."

COVERED WITH SNOW and laughing with no breath left to do so, Jacquie Archer staggered into the warmth of her kitchen and leaned back against the door to prevent her daughter from coming inside.

"Let me in!" Erin pretended to pound on the window. "Little pig, little pig, let me come in."

Jacquie grinned at the recollection of childhood stories. "Not by the hair of my chinny chin chin."

"Then I'll huff—" Erin pushed at the door "—and I'll puff—" she pushed again "—and I'll blow your house in." She gave one more push, just as Jacquie stepped away from the door and allowed it to swing open. With a cry of surprise, Erin stumbled across the threshold and into her mother's arms.

They collapsed against each other, still laughing. Hurry, their Australian shepherd, came in behind Erin and danced around their feet in exuberant canine fashion, panting and jumping up at them in an effort to join the game.

"Now I remember why we named her Hurricane," Jacquie said, rubbing the perky ears. "We'd all better get dried off before we end up standing in a puddle of melted snow."

Minutes later, their ski jackets and bibs hung from the shower curtain rod in the back bathroom. The snow caked on their boots melted into the tub. Erin toweled Hurry's long, black-and-white coat to a reasonably dry state and gave her a snack of dog food mixed with warm water while Jacquie heated water for tea.

"Orange spice, lemon, or English breakfast?" She turned off the heat under the whistling kettle. "Honey or sugar?"

"Lemon and honey," her daughter decided. "And gingersnaps. Yum. What movie should we watch?" She set out the tin containing their remaining Christmas cookies.

"You decide. I need to look at my schedule for next week and check the machine before I sit down. After spending the morning outside, I figure I'll be asleep in seconds."

"'Kay." Erin took a plate of ginger cookies and her mug into the living room. Jacquie sipped at her orange spice tea and finished off a couple of cream-cheese cookies before turning to the answering machine. Sure enough, the light was blinking. She gathered her pen and appointment book, then pressed the button.

"Hi, Jacquie, honey." Her mother's sweet Southern accent always made her smile. "We enjoyed having y'all over yesterday to watch the games and share our New Year's Day. Looks like the snow won't last too long—the weather channel says the temperatures will be in the fifties the first of next week. You be careful driving around, though. We'll look to see you at church on Sunday. Let me know if you want to come here for lunch."

Message two was from her friend Phoebe Moss, who lived down the road. "Happy New Year, Jacquie. How about this snow? You should see my horses kicking up their heels out there. Speaking of which, we're due for a trim. Give me a call and we'll set up an appointment."

Jacquie was still writing a note to call Phoebe when message three started. "Ladysmith Farrier Service? This is Rhys Lewellyn. I'm leasing Fairfield Farm…"

She heard nothing else. A black cloud swirled in front of her eyes and the room tilted under her feet. For the second time in her life, Jacquie thought she might actually faint.

Holding her mug in two shaking hands, she went to the kitchen table and sat down with her back to the answering machine. What she couldn't see wasn't there, right? Rhys Lewellyn didn't exist. Keeping her mind deliberately blank, she reached the bottom of her mug and the little pile of sugar that hadn't dissolved.

Erin padded into the kitchen in her socks. "Hey, you're eating all the cookies. No fair." She rummaged through the tin and pulled out another gingersnap. "Last one. I'm watching the last half of the asteroid movie. Are you coming?"

"In a little while."

"'Kay." Unaware of looming disaster, her daughter returned to the simplicity of a world threatened merely by destruction from outer space.

Reality presented a much more immediate and complicated menace. Feeling colder than when she'd been playing outside, Jacquie returned to the answering machine and pressed the button to repeat the last message.

"Ladysmith Farrier Service? This is Rhys Lewellyn." His voice hadn't changed in fourteen years, the words still crisp and clean, the tone light and yet somehow rich. A voice that horses listened to, obeyed. A voice that a woman might savor like the ripple of silk against her skin.

"I'm leasing Fairfield Farm—we arrived yesterday in the middle of the storm. I've got three horses which lost shoes in the snow. If you have time, I need a farrier as soon as possible." He left his number and hung up. Decisive and direct, just as he had been all those years ago.

"Mom, you're missing the movie." Erin leaned around the door frame between kitchen and living room. "They're already at the space station." With her black hair cut short and her slight frame, Erin looked like Peter Pan, mischievous, adventurous, untamed. Straight brows slanting over icy blue eyes increased the effect. On horseback, in a helmet that disguised her feminine chin and mouth, she might have been a boy. She rode like one. Or, to be more precise, like a young version of the man she resembled so closely…her father, Rhys Lewellyn.

"Mom?" Erin came to the table, put a hand on Jacquie's shoulder. "You all right?" Then she glanced down at the appointment pad and gasped. "Rhys Lewellyn? The Olympic rider? He called you?"

Jacquie hadn't realized she'd written down his name. "I—"

"You're going to work for Rhys Lewellyn? Awesome." Erin bounced across the kitchen and back. "Is he gonna be here for a while? Or is he just passing through? He used to winter in Florida. This is kinda out of the way for driving to Florida, though. Isn't it? Oh, please, say he's staying here at least till spring."

"He—he said he's leasing Fairfield Farm."

"How cool is that? I could ride across the Allens' land and the Brentwoods' and be there for lessons." She threw herself on her knees at Jacquie's side. "Mom, you gotta ask him if he'll give me lessons. I couldn't stand it if he was this close and I didn't get to ride with him. He probably charges, like, a hundred dollars, but I'll earn the money, I promise. Please, please, promise you'll ask."

Jacquie pulled herself together. "We don't know if he's teaching, Erin. Let's get the facts first." *Like the fact that you're his daughter. And he doesn't know you exist.*

"When are you going out there? Can I come? Fairfield has that great stone barn, doesn't it? And I bet he's brought Imperator with him. That's his Olympic ride, you know. They took the gold in eventing at the last games. Oh, man. I gotta go with you.''

''I have to call back to set an appointment, Erin.'' And she would make sure to choose a time when her daughter was otherwise occupied. ''You're missing the movie.''

''Who cares, when I can ride with Rhys Lewellyn? So incredibly awesome. I'm gonna go find that magazine with the big article on the Olympics. They spent pages and pages on him and Imperator.''

Erin dashed to her room. Jacquie folded her arms on the table and buried her head in them. She'd never read an article on the man, not so much as a paragraph over all these years. She hadn't needed pictures to see the resemblance to his daughter, of course. That was as much a reminder of her time with Rhys as Jacquie had been able to bear.

If she failed to return his call, he would find another farrier. She could lie to Erin and tell her that Rhys wasn't teaching, only training his own horses. Which might be true.

But if Rhys was going to teach, Erin would hear about it from her friends. And he would most likely be riding at the shows and events scheduled in the area, including the prestigious Top Flight HorseTrials coming up in April. Erin planned to compete there. From what she knew of him, Jacquie would be surprised if Rhys did not.

No matter who rode where, chances were good that she and Erin would encounter Rhys Lewellyn somewhere during the next few months. The horse world around the town of New Skye just wasn't that big. Thinking of running into him, confronting him with a daughter he didn't know he had in front of her friends, clients, and plain old nosy strangers, churned Jacquie's stomach worse than any amusement park ride Erin had ever forced her to take.

She made it to the bathroom before she lost her tea and cookies. Washing her face, Jacquie decided she would have to take control of the situation if she expected to salvage her relationship with Erin. Her only concern was that her daughter suffer as little as possible. She didn't care what happened to Rhys or herself or anyone else involved, as long as Erin came out okay.

"Mom, they're about to set off the nuclear warhead," Erin called from the living room. Jacquie sighed as she went in to watch the last ten minutes of the film. She didn't need to witness an explosion.

As far as she was concerned, Rhys Lewellyn had already blown her world apart.

SHE CALLED THE NUMBER Rhys had left in his message while Erin was out at the barn the next morning.

"Fairfield Farms." That Irish brogue was immediately familiar. Terry O'Neal had worked with Rhys's father on their farm in Wales and had moved with the family to New York when Rhys was eight years old. He'd been an integral part of the riding program during the time Jacquie trained there, fourteen years ago.

"This is Ladysmith Farrier Service, returning Mr. Lewellyn's call." She wasn't about to give them her name in advance. And she was pretty sure Terry wouldn't recognize her voice. After all this time—and, no doubt, a long string of women—Rhys wouldn't, either.

"Good to hear from you, ma'am." Terry was brisk, businesslike. No ghosts from the past for him. "We lost another shoe in the muck this morning. When can you be here?"

She had carefully checked Erin's schedule. "We'll have someone out there tomorrow morning at nine, if that works for you." Erin was spending the night at a sleepover party and wouldn't be home until afternoon.

"Not today?"

"I'm afraid that's the earliest free slot we have." Untrue, but she was lying for Erin's sake.

"I guess it'll do. We're not working in this slush, anyway. We'll look for you at nine on Saturday." He sounded rushed, now, and in the background she heard voices shouting, apparently at each other. One, she easily recognized as Rhys. She almost grinned—he could be hard on any of the help who didn't give one-hundred percent to the horses. And he was always hardest on himself.

Fortunately, for her peace of mind, Erin didn't think to ask about the appointment until lunch. "When are we going to Fairfield Farms?"

Jacquie kept her gaze on her soup. "I'm going tomorrow morning, while you are probably still asleep."

Erin slapped her hands on the table. "Mom, why didn't you wait until I could go? Or go today? We don't have anything to do today and it's too messy to ride."

"They were busy today." Another lie. "Tomorrow was the earliest we could schedule."

The girl pouted over her grilled-cheese sandwich.

"You'll ask him about lessons, though, right? The snow'll be gone soon and we can get to work."

Jacquie managed to change the subject without making a definite commitment. And she managed to keep Erin diverted for the rest of the afternoon, until they arrived at the party. "Have fun," she said, giving her daughter a kiss on the forehead. "I'll see you tomorrow afternoon."

Erin grabbed her sleeve as she turned. "Don't forget to ask him about lessons."

Erin's friend Cathy, the hostess for the night, was standing with them on the front porch of her house. "Ask who about what lessons?"

Jacquie groaned silently.

"Rhys Lewellyn," Erin said. "You know, the Olympic rider?"

Cathy frequently rode with Erin. "You mean the guy who won the gold?"

"Yeah, and he's moved here, can you believe it? My mom's going to ask him about lessons. Maybe you can come, too."

"That would be so cool. I've got these pictures of him…" The girls closed the door, chattering away about Rhys and his exploits. His riding exploits.

Instead of going home to an empty house where she would have too much time to think, Jacquie went to a loud, explosive movie at the New Skye Cinema and then shopped for a month's worth of groceries. She'd learned quickly and well how to divert her thoughts from Rhys. She wouldn't think about him again until she had to.

Deep in the night, though, she found herself awake and wondering if he would recognize her at all. How dreadful would it be if she met him and he didn't know her? Her name, though, would remind him...wouldn't it? Surely Rhys hadn't been with so many women that he didn't even remember her name.

Tears threatened at the thought, but she drove them back. She'd stopped caring about Rhys Lewellyn a long, long time ago—the day, in fact, that he went back to his pregnant wife.

Now, protecting Erin was her only concern. She had to figure out when to tell Rhys about their daughter, and how she would expect him to deal with the situation. Nothing else mattered in the least.

In the morning, she dressed in her usual jeans, T-shirt, and sweatshirt, then braided her strawberry-blond hair, so different from her daughter's. Adding makeup was a reasonable defense, she thought. To stay in control, she needed every weapon she could muster.

Hurry jumped into the truck as she opened the door. Jacquie shook her head at the dog. "You're coming, are you? Want to watch the fireworks?"

Would there be fireworks? Or just a terrible discomfort as she did her job on his farm for the first and only time? He wouldn't ask her back, once he knew who she was.

Across country, as Erin had pointed out, Fairfield Farm was a short ride away from her own place, Archer's Acres. By road, the trip took twenty minutes. Jacquie pulled through Rhys's stone-arch entryway exactly at nine and parked near the massive barn. A black-haired man walked out of the door as she shut off the engine. She swallowed hard, tense beyond breathing. As he came closer, though, she realized this wasn't a man, but a boy. A boy with black hair, black, slanting eyebrows, and ice-blue eyes, the same ones she'd looked into every day of the last thirteen years. The eyes in her daughter's face.

Rhys's son had inherited his father's strong shoulders and long, powerful legs, beautifully built for wearing riding breeches. "Can I help you?" he said, politely enough, in his father's voice.

"I'm the farrier." She cleared her throat. "Jacquie Archer."

He tilted his head. "Andrew Lewellyn. You want to park at the door to the barn? We can tie them in the aisle."

"Great." A few minutes' delay would give her a chance to collect herself, settle her nerves.

By the time she'd backed the truck up to the double door of the barn, there were three men and a horse standing in the aisle. Terry O'Neal she identified by his silhouette—stocky, bushy-haired, bowlegged. Andrew was about the same height, and shorter by a head than the third man…the man he favored…his father.

"Stay," she told Hurry. No sense having the shepherd underfoot. Deploring her own weakness, she glanced in the rearview mirror before getting out. What good would makeup do, anyway?

Then, with her heart in her throat, she opened the truck door and jumped down. She'd forgotten her hat, and wisps of hair had escaped to blow around her face in the cold wind. She tucked them behind her ears as Rhys stepped from the shadows of the barn into the weak January sunlight.

He took one look at her and stopped dead. His hand, already extended to shake hers, dropped to his side.

For a moment—an eternity of frozen silence—no one moved.

"Jacquie?" The word was strangely rough. "Jacquie Lennon? What the hell are you doing here?"

After a paralyzed moment, he covered the ground between them with quick strides, then grabbed her by the shoulders and shook her, not gently.

"More important...why, in the name of all that's holy, did you disappear without a trace?"

CHAPTER TWO

JACQUIE'S EYES WIDENED, and Rhys heard his own words with horror. In front of his son and his best friend, he stood on the brink of revealing a secret he'd kept from everyone in his life, except this one woman.

But how the hell was he supposed to remain calm when the missing piece in his existence had just reappeared after a fourteen-year absence?

He took a deep breath, fighting for control. Under his hands, Jacquie moved her shoulders, and he realized how tight his grip was.

"Sorry." He released her and took a step back. "I'm...surprised...to see you. I had no idea you lived in this area."

"Yes, I—I came back home. When I left New York." She avoided his eyes, looking past his shoulder to where Andrew and Terry stood with Imperator. "Is this your champion?" She walked to the horse, stood close enough to let Imp get her scent. "He surely is gorgeous. Which shoe does he need?"

Business, Rhys reminded himself. *She's here on business. She's the damn farrier.*

"Right fore," Terry supplied. "Good to see you, Jacquie. You were quite the rider when you were with us. Thought you'd go all the way."

She smiled at him and shook her head. "I decided

to pursue a more dependable income. But farrier work doesn't always give you access to the great horses like this one.'' When she extended her hand, Imperator allowed her to stroke his face—not a privilege he offered to many people. "You're a big beauty, aren't you?" Jacquie crooned. "I'll bet it's like riding the wind, being on your back.''

Rhys watched her commune with the horse, earning Imp's trust in the way she'd always had with animals. They trusted her and, in turn, performed for her, meeting her demands with as much talent as they could command. He'd been harder on her than any of his other students, simply because she was so damn good.

Or maybe because he'd fallen in love with her the first time he saw her smile.

"Okay," she said, turning from the horse to the bed of her truck. "Do you want me to trim him, or just replace the shoe?''

"Does he need a trim?" Rhys asked, knowing the answer perfectly well.

Jacquie eyed Imp's hooves from a distance. Then she approached the horse, talking to him softly, running her hands over his shoulders to his chest and down his forelegs, picking up each in turn. Imp was usually a handful for any kind of examination, but he stood quiet for Jacquie, of course. He gave her a little more trouble about the rear legs, but she talked him through it and managed to look at each hoof closely.

When she came back to the truck, she glanced at Rhys and cocked her head. "As you no doubt know, he's been trimmed within the last three weeks and doesn't need it now. Do you have the shoe he pulled off?''

He grinned at her, relieved that she'd passed his test. "No, it's somewhere on the lane between here and the highway."

Tying on her farrier's leather chaps, she didn't grin back. "What were you doing riding on the road?"

"Long story."

"Here to the highway is a long ride."

"That, too." He held her gaze for a moment, felt the shock as awareness kicked in, bringing with it memories he'd worked for years to bury.

Judging by the way her face froze, so had Jacquie. She jerked her head back and forth, a very definite rejection, and turned her back to him. "I've got the shoe he needs."

Fast and efficient, she shaped the shoe on her anvil and fit it perfectly to Imperator's hoof, then nailed it with a minimum of fuss and filed the ends off the nails. "I checked the other shoes," she said, straightening up from her farrier's crouch as easily as a child. "They look sound. You shoe him on the usual five-to-six-week schedule?"

"Unless there's a problem."

She nodded. "Then he should be good for another three weeks, at least."

Rhys glanced at Terry and got his nod of approval. "Glad to hear it. Andrew, bring Abner out here. Imperator can go into the paddock for a run."

The shoeing process went as easily with the other three horses. At the end of an hour, Terry and Andrew resumed the schedule for the day as Jacquie put away her tools and took off her chaps. "If that's all, I'll write up a receipt."

Leaving the door open, she climbed into the seat of

her truck. On the passenger side, a black-and-white Australian shepherd sat up, panting with pleasure at having company once again.

"Nice dog," Rhys commented, hoping he sounded more relaxed than he felt.

"We...her name is Hurry." She didn't look at him, or the dog.

He went around the hood of the truck and opened the passenger door to pet Hurry. "I've still got Sydney. Her arthritis is pretty bad, so she stays inside when it's cold."

The hand holding the pen faltered. "She was just a puppy."

"Fourteen, now." And an Australian shepherd, same as this one, which unnerved and pleased him, at the same time. "Would you like to come in and see her?" Jacquie was tempted, of that he had no doubt. And he would use any weapon he could find to reach her. "I bet she'd remember you."

"Thanks, but I've got another job in a few minutes." She handed him the receipt. "The total is one hundred dollars. My address is on there, if you'd like to mail me a check."

"No, I'll pay you now." Trusting that she wouldn't disappear while he went into the house wasn't easy, but at least he had her address on the receipt. He could find her, this time. No private detectives, bringing back only dead ends.

On the driver's side again, he handed her the cash. "Sure you won't come in? We've got hot coffee and cold cinnamon rolls."

"Tempting, but no thanks." The corner of her mouth twitched, as if she wanted to grin. She tight-

ened her fists around the steering wheel. Neither hand
bore a ring or any sign she usually wore one.
"So...are you here for the winter? Moving back to
New York with warmer weather?"

He'd take any interest she displayed and be glad for
it. "Probably not. The New England winters aren't
worth the summers anymore." That was part of the
truth, at least.

"And your family is down here with you?" Her
flat tone suggested that she didn't really care and
asked only out of courtesy.

He tilted his head and gave her a bitter smile with
the truth. "If you mean Terry and Andrew, yes. Olivia
and I were divorced—finally, officially and forever—
twelve years ago."

"Oh." Jacquie looked stunned for a second but recovered quickly. "Will...will you be teaching?"

"Definitely. I'll get advertising in place soon, and
I'm planning a schooling day when the weather gets
warmer, just to let people know I'm here. Meanwhile,
if you've got any clients who'd like lessons, send
them my way."

"Sure. Welcome to the neighborhood." She said it
without looking at him.

"Thanks." Rhys decided to push her a little. "You
didn't answer my question, you know."

"What question?"

"Why didn't you get in touch when you left?"

"I—" For a moment, she looked cornered. "You
know why. He's mucking out stalls while we're talking."

The old anger grabbed him. "You didn't even say
goodbye."

"What was the point? You were going back to your wife. I needed to clear out fast." Her deep breath shook. "And now I'm going back to my own life. Thanks for the business. William Innes is a good farrier, next time you need somebody." She cranked the engine, put the truck in gear and drove away—once again—without saying goodbye.

Rhys held up his receipt. "Oh, no, my dear. I've got a farrier already, by the name of Ms. Jacqueline Lennon." He glanced at the paper, then did a double take. The sheet read "Ladysmith Farrier Service, Jacquie Archer, Farrier."

"Archer? *Archer?* Just what the hell," he demanded aloud, staring at the black truck now leaving his property, "does that mean?"

SINCE HIS FALL during a competition in New Zealand last November, one chore Andrew's dad didn't do was cleaning stalls. Most mornings, Andrew got that task all to himself, though occasionally Terry helped. Like today.

"So they knew each other before?" he asked the trainer, when he was sure his dad had gone into the house. "She was a student?"

"Yeah." Terry dumped a forkful of dirty shavings into the bin. "One of the best he's had. She was Olympic material if I've ever seen it."

"What happened?"

"Not for me to say." Terry pitched another load and then glared at Andrew. "And I wouldn't ask, if I were you, boyo, unless you relish getting your nose snapped off and your ears singed."

The old man cast a glance at the three stalls he'd

cleaned to Andrew's one. "Guess you've got work to do." Hanging up his fork, he stomped out of the barn toward the house.

Andrew gave him—no, both of them—the finger while they weren't looking, then turned back to finish Imperator's stall. When *didn't* he get yelled at around here? Whatever went wrong came down on him, like crap flowing downhill.

Privileges, now, those he had to steal. Yesterday, Terry and his dad had ridden Abner and Lucretia back to the highway to fetch the truck and trailer, leaving Andrew to keep an eye on the place. He'd kept an eye out, all right—just long enough to be sure they got out of sight. Then he'd saddled Imperator and gone for a ride.

The lady farrier was right—being on the big stallion was the absolute best. One side of Fairfield Farm bordered a horse preserve with miles of trails and acres of open ground for riding. Andrew intended to take Imp there one day soon, but to begin with he'd stayed in the pastures behind the barn, knowing his dad would literally kill him if he let Imp get even slightly injured. The horse was as crazy for freedom as Andrew, and enjoyed every second of their stolen gallop. By the time the truck and trailer pulled in at the gate, Imperator was cool and calm and back in his paddock with no evidence to suggest he'd ever been anywhere else.

Today they wouldn't get such a break. All Andrew could do today was his job—finish the stalls, empty, clean and refill all the water buckets, and sweep the cobbled hallway of the stable. Finally certain that nobody could yell at him for something he hadn't done—unlike yesterday, when his dad had blown up over the dirty buckets—he went to sit on the fence of the paddock where Imperator waited.

The stallion came over to investigate Andrew's down vest and pants and shoes. "No fun today, Imp." He combed his fingers through the thick mane. "Maybe I can sneak out tonight, after bedtime."

But the weather had warmed up and the snow was melting—how insane was that, in January? Wet, soft ground with patches of snow and ice would make riding in the dark too dangerous. He put his forehead against the horse's neck. "Or maybe not."

All he wanted—in fact, all he'd asked for as a Christmas present—was to ride this horse in practice every day. He put up with his dad's impossible demands and Terry's grouchy moods, was willing to take lessons and submit to training like a beginning rider, though he'd been on horseback practically since the day he was born—the birthday he shared with the fantastic horse. Whatever his dad and Terry required, Andrew would agree to, if he could just make Imperator his horse.

A door slammed at the house. Imp startled and hopped away, leaving Andrew no choice but to fall forward, off the fence. He landed on his feet and was straightening up when his dad arrived at the paddock.

The great Olympic rider stopped and stared for a minute, stone-faced. "What are you doing?"

"Nothing."

"Were you thinking about riding him again?"

"N-no." He couldn't help asking, "Again? What are you talking about?"

"You rode him yesterday while we were gone."

Not a question. *Shit.*

"Don't bother to lie." His dad leaned his elbows on the top rail of the fence, his gaze following Imperator as he trotted around the paddock. "I did laundry this morning. You had his hair on the legs of your jeans."

"I was careful. He didn't get hurt."

"Believe it or not, I'm thinking more of your safety than his. He's too much for you."

"I had him under control the whole time."

"That's what he allowed you to think."

"I'm not stupid."

"No, you're just not experienced with top-level horses."

Andrew managed to resist stomping his foot. "You're the one with the experience. You're the one who got dumped."

His dad's mouth tightened into a straight line, and his eyes glinted like cold steel. "Exactly. If I can be unseated, what chance has a novice rider got against a horse like Imperator? Stay off of him. Or I'll ship you back to your grandfather." Turning on his heel, he stalked to his office in the barn and let the door bang shut behind him.

Now that was a threat worth listening to. Compared to his grandfather, his dad looked like Captain Kangaroo.

Andrew climbed through the fence and straightened up to give Imperator one last pat over the rail.

"Nothing around here ever changes," he told the horse. "Same shit, different day."

ANY HOPE JACQUIE HARBORED that she would be given a respite before dealing with the problem of

Rhys Lewellyn died the very night after she'd visited his farm. Her phone rang at eight-thirty and Erin answered, using the polite manners her grandmother had taught her. "May I say who's calling?"

With a gasp, those manners vanished. "Wow, Mr. Lewellyn, it's so cool to talk to you. My name's Erin Archer and I've been a fan of yours ever since I can remember. I've got all sorts of pictures of you and Imperator at the Olympics. That has to be just the most awesome feeling, taking him over fences."

Erin stopped for a moment, and Jacquie came to get the phone, but her daughter waved her off. "Yes, sir, I've been riding since I was little. I'm almost fourteen and I compete at third-level dressage with my Thoroughbred gelding, Mirage. We're working on training level in cross country and show jumping so I can ride in the Top Flight Horse Trials this spring." Another gasp. "I would love to take lessons—I was talking to my mom about that when she said she was going to shoe your horses. That is just so amazing. When can I start?"

Caught between horror and despair, Jacquie turned her back to her daughter. Her pulse pounded in her fingertips, her throat, her ears and head. Hadn't she already paid for her mistakes? Why had retribution come twice?

"Mom?" Erin tapped her on the shoulder before she was ready. "Mr. Lewellyn wants to talk to you."

She reached for the phone over her shoulder. "Thanks." When Erin didn't leave the room, Jacquie cleared her throat. "Privacy, please?" Once alone in the kitchen, she shut the door and put a chair against it to prevent unexpected reentry. "Hello?"

"Hi, Jacquie." His voice in her ear was like a sip of sweet harvest wine, spicy and intoxicating.

Jacquie collapsed into a chair at the table. "What can I do for you, Rhys? Is there a problem with one of the shoes?"

"No, not at all. I just wanted to ask…" He paused, then cleared his throat. "I was confused, that's all. But I guess I've already got the answer."

"To which question?"

After another hesitation, he gave an uneasy laugh. "There's no way to say this gracefully. I didn't expect you to be married, that's all, so I was confused by the name Archer on your receipt. But obviously, since you have such a delightful daughter, there's a…dad…in the picture, too."

Oh, how she wished that were true. How easy this would be if she could trot out a husband and trail him under Rhys Lewellyn's nose.

Jacquie sighed. "I'm a widow." Even that was a lie. But at least it was a lie everyone she knew, including Erin, believed.

"Ah." The confidence returned to Rhys's voice in that one syllable. "I'm sorry you lost your husband."

"Thanks. Is there anything else I can help you with?"

"Well, it sounds like we need to set up some lessons for your daughter. She's enthusiastic, to say the least. Is she as good as she says she is?"

A mother's pride would not be denied. "Better. Better than I was at her age, too."

"Definitely a student I'd enjoy. Why don't you bring her over tomorrow and we'll do some schooling?"

"I can't." No hesitation about that answer. "We have church and dinner with my family afterward."

"Then when would be a good time?"

"I—I'll have to call you back. My schedule's pretty full next week. And school starts Monday."

"Yes, I reminded Andrew of that depressing fact today. He'll be going to New Skye High School—with Erin, I presume."

"That's right." And she would not offer to carpool with them.

So, of course, Rhys did. "I would be glad to drive her to school along with Andrew. As soon as I figure out how to get there, of course."

His rueful tone tempted her to smile, and Jacquie had the sensation of clinging by her fingernails to the edge of a crumbling cliff. "Thanks, but I like to drive her myself. We get a chance to talk."

"Which can be a blessing, or a curse." He was silent for a moment. "Then if you can't come for a lesson and I can't drive your daughter to school for you, I'll have to go the direct route. Will you have dinner with me next week? Say, Friday night?"

He might as well have punched her in the stomach—her reaction was pretty much the same. "Why?"

"For old times' sake?"

"Our old times aren't something to celebrate, Rhys."

"Why not?" He sounded genuinely confused.

"You were married, remember? What we were...what we did...was adultery."

"Olivia and I were separated, Jacquie. More than halfway to a divorce."

"Until you went back to her. End of story." She was breathing as if she'd run a five-minute mile. "I have to go, Rhys. Good night."

"Wait, Jacquie—"

But she hung up on him. She knew too well the power of his voice, its effect on her will and her good intentions. If ever a girl had been talked into a man's bed, it was young Jacquie Lennon.

Erin banged the door against the chair. "Mom? What's going on? What in the world are you doing?"

"Nothing." Jacquie moved the chair and opened the door herself.

"Did you talk about lessons? When do I start?"

"We didn't set a time, Erin."

"Mom! Why not?"

"Because there's more to my life than your whims and fantasies," Jacquie snapped, unfairly, she knew. "Like earning a living to keep a roof over our heads and food in the horses' mouths. Riding lessons with overpriced, big-ego trainers are just not at the top of my list right now, okay? I'm going to bed. Good night."

She aimed a kiss at Erin's head and did an about-face, heading for her bedroom. Behind a closed door, she drove her fists into her pillow until her hands were too heavy to lift, her arms too weak to try. But she'd killed the fear. For now, anyway.

THE EXTENT TO WHICH Rhys's arrival would disrupt her life became obvious when Jacquie arrived at her parents' house for lunch on Sunday.

"Hey, sweetie." While putting the lid back on a

steaming pot of green beans, her mother tilted her cheek up for a kiss. "Where's Erin?"

"She saw Daddy outside and went to talk to him."

"She's Grandpa's girl. How was your week?"

"Same as usual." And if that wasn't a lie, what would be? "How about you? You got your hair cut? I really like it."

"It is nice, isn't it?" Becky Lennon gave a self-conscious pat to her short blond hair, then smoothed her hands over her plump hips. "I bought this dress, too. I had to get out of the house for a little while. Your daddy was underfoot most of the time."

"I bet you put him to work."

"What choice did I have? I can't have him bothering me all day long." She bent to the oven and pulled out two trays of golden biscuits. "He put up those shelves I've been needing in the sewing room and then installed a new shower door in you girls' bathroom." Neither Jacquie nor her sister Alicia had lived at home for ten years, but that was still their bathroom. "Jimmy came over on Friday and the two of them moved the furniture out of the living and dining rooms, gave the carpet a good shampooing."

"Which is a nice way of saying you let him come over to give his wife the day off." As farmers, neither her brother nor her dad knew what to do with themselves when confined to the house by ice and snow.

Her mother winked. "Sandy did the same for me yesterday—had your dad come over and help Jimmy put together the furniture for the nursery. We look out for each other."

"She's due next month, right?"

"February tenth is her due date, but the doctor says he thinks she'll go early, from the size of the baby. Though in my experience, most first babies are late. Except Erin was early, wasn't she?"

"Ten days."

Becky nodded as she poured creamed corn into a serving bowl. "That's why I didn't get to be with you for the delivery."

Jacquie winced at the unspoken reproof. Erin had been born in Oklahoma, far from family, with only her mother and a midwife to welcome her into the world.

In the front of the house, a door slammed. "That'll be them, coming in from church. Alicia said she'd ride with Jimmy and Sandy. I'd better get this meal on the table."

"What can I do?"

"You carry the vegetables into the dining room while I get the chicken." Becky Lennon organized her Sunday dinners with the efficiency of a marine drill sergeant. In moments, the whole of Jacquie's family was seated around the table.

As soon as her grandpa had given thanks for the food and the melting snow, Erin started talking. "Grandma, guess what? I'm getting riding lessons this week with Rhys Lewellyn. Is that amazing, or what?"

"That's nice, honey." In the middle of serving herself a slice of chicken, Jacquie's mother looked across at Erin. "Lewellyn? Isn't that…?" Her frowning gaze moved to Jacquie.

"That's right." Jacquie spoke over the gallop of her heartbeat. "I trained with him in New York. He's just moved down here with his horses, and Erin's dying to get his help with her riding.''

"More than just training,'' Alicia said. "As I recall, you had a huge crush on Rhys Lewellyn. Every phone call was about how handsome he was, how he smiled—''

"You're exaggerating,'' Jacquie said, though her impulse was to scream *Shut up!* "I liked him a lot. He's a good teacher.''

"And gorgeous?'' Alicia prompted.

"Okay, yes. Still is, for that matter.'' She hoped her appraisal came across as casual.

Erin's eyes were round with surprise. "Mom? You and Mr. Lewellyn went out together?''

"No.'' They'd never gone on dates because he'd been married. "No, Erin, we didn't go out together. I was young, he was attractive and older and paid attention to me because I rode well. End of story.'' More or less.

"Except that the next thing we knew, you'd moved halfway across the country, married Mark Archer and were having a baby.'' Alicia shook her head. "You always were crazy, but that year had to be one of the craziest.''

When Jacquie glanced across the table, her mother's frown hadn't eased. So much about that time in her life had gone unexplained, she wouldn't be surprised if Becky Lennon's suspicions were easily aroused.

Damn you, Rhys. Damn you for showing up to ruin my life yet again.

Desperate for distraction, she turned to her sister-in-law. "Sandy, I hear you got your nursery set up this week. Have you finished sewing the curtains and quilts? When can I come see?''

Listening to Sandy's glowing description of ruffles and rainbows, Jacquie recalled the ''nursery'' she'd arranged for Erin almost fourteen years ago—a thrift-shop crib in the corner of her one-room apartment over the barn, with worn baby sheets borrowed from the family she worked for and a yellow blanket representing her first and only attempt at knitting. Crooked and lumpy, the yellow blanket had been Erin's ''friend'' until she went to kindergarten, and rested safe now at the bottom of their family keepsake box.

Alicia took over the conversation at that point. Jacquie tried to relax and enjoy her baked chicken, but her stomach was fisted tight. Thankfully, she got her plate scraped off and into the dishwasher before her mother noticed. And she got Erin out of the house before the subject of Rhys Lewellyn could come up again.

Her daughter had left most of her homework until the last day of vacation, of course, and they struggled through the rest of the day with an English paper and an algebra worksheet. Jacquie could help with the writing assignment, but algebra had never been her strong point.

''Alicia got all the math genes,'' she told Erin, when they'd both worked on a problem and failed to get the correct answer. ''She's the brain and Jimmy and I are the brawn of the family.''

''Can we call her and ask her to come over? It's still early.''

''According to whom? It's after nine o'clock. Alicia's ready for bed by now. She gets up at five to walk, remember?''

"She could skip her walk and drive me to school."

"I'll drive you to school. I'm having breakfast with Phoebe tomorrow morning."

"Can I go, too? Maybe Phoebe could do my math."

Jacquie sighed and shook her head. "You're going to have to ask your teacher for help, Erin."

"But, Mom…!''

Between a troubled night's sleep and the usual early-morning scramble to find school clothes and make lunch, Jacquie felt she'd lived through a whole day by the time she drove into New Skye and dropped Erin off at the school door.

Across the street from the school, however, was Charlie's Carolina Diner, where she knew she could get good food and a healthy helping of friendship. Kids at New Skye High School had been hanging out at the Carolina Diner after class and on weekends since long before she and her friends took up the tradition. Many of them still came back as adults—to catch up with each other and the latest news in town, or, like Jacquie, for a chance to unwind.

"It's only eight-thirty," she said, sliding into the booth where Phoebe Moss waited for her. "And I'm already exhausted."

"I know the feeling. What's going on?" Phoebe flipped her long, ash-blond braid behind her shoulder and cupped her hands around her mug of tea.

Jacquie caught a glimpse of a sparkle on her best friend's ring finger. "I'll tell you in a minute. First, let me see that rock you're carrying around."

Grinning, Phoebe stretched her left hand across the

table to show off a diamond engagement ring. "We got it in New York while we were there over the holidays."

"Fabulous. I love the emerald cut. Where did it come from?"

"Tiffany's."

"Oh, wow." Jacquie sat back in awe. "Adam really does things with style, doesn't he?" Adam DeVries, Phoebe's fiancé, was a childhood friend of Jacquie's and a fellow graduate in the class of 1989. Elected mayor in November, he would assume his office in a matter of days.

Phoebe's grin turned into a dreamy smile. "We had the most wonderful time—skating at Rockefeller Center, a carriage ride in Central Park in the snow, museums and restaurants and shows..." She sighed. "Everything was simply perfect."

"And now you're back home, stepping out as the fiancée of the new mayor of New Skye. Are you ready?"

Her friend gave a mock shudder. "Just organizing the swearing-in party has me going crazy. But tell me about you and Erin. What's going on that's making you so tired?"

She toyed with her napkin. "The holidays were great. We loved the snow, of course, since we don't get much. But..."

"But?" Abby Brannon arrived at their table with coffee for Jacquie and fresh tea for Phoebe. As the owner's daughter, Abby had worked in the diner since she was a little girl. Not much happened in the town of New Skye she didn't know about. More important, she'd been Jacquie's close friend all during high school. "Something wrong with the horses? With Erin? Your parents? Your sister-in-law's not due till February, right?"

"Oh, no. Everybody's fine." She shouldn't have started this, Jacquie realized. How much could she say without revealing the truth she'd never told a soul, not even her best friends? "There's a new trainer in town, Rhys Lewellyn."

"The Olympic champion?" Phoebe kept horses, and would know his name.

"That's the one. Erin's crazy to take lessons from him."

"And he doesn't teach?"

"Yes, he does."

Both Abby and Phoebe looked puzzled.

"It's just…I worked with him, back before Erin was born. And we parted on bad terms. So having him as her teacher would be…difficult."

"You don't have to socialize, right?" Abby shrugged. "Just take her to the lesson and drive away when it's done." A bell rang behind the counter along the back wall. "Your breakfast is up. I'll be right back."

Phoebe nodded at Jacquie. "I agree. Write the check and don't talk to him any more than you have to."

If only it were so easy. "You know Erin. She thinks everybody should be friends. And she'd take a lesson every day, if I said okay. But I…" Her excuses sounded so weak. And the fear inside her was so strong.

"You…?"

Jacquie tried to tell the truth. "After what happened

between us, I can't bear the thought of seeing him that often.''

Not the whole truth, of course. Not the part about how being within a few feet of Rhys had been enough to set her pulse to pounding, just as it had when she was eighteen years old. How she'd caught herself wanting to trace the lines on his face with her fingertips, to rub the pad of her thumb over his lips. How, after years of banishing every wisp of memory, last night she'd dreamed of the past and all the lovely hours she'd spent in Rhys Lewellyn's arms.

Phoebe swallowed a sip of tea. ''Sounds to me like there's more to this than you're telling.''

''Well...yes,'' Jacquie admitted, folding the napkin into crisp, even pleats. ''I had a crush on him at the time. So it's hard to meet him again as an old-widow woman with a kid.'' How hard, she wasn't prepared to say.

Her friend nodded. ''I can see how that would be awkward. You could just tell Erin 'no,' right? She would survive.''

The only way to keep Erin and Rhys from seeing each other would be to forbid her to have anything to do with horses altogether. ''I don't think that would work.''

''Well, then, just concentrate on the bad and try to forget the good stuff.'' She narrowed her eyes, thinking. ''He's probably insufferable, anyway. Arrogant and callous.''

That wasn't fair. ''Only when someone doesn't give him their best effort.''

''And peremptory,'' Abby added, setting down

their plates. "Always ordering people around." She leaned against the side of the booth.

"He can be," Jacquie admitted. "But—"

Across the diner, the bell on the door jangled as another customer came in. Jacquie glanced at the new arrival, then looked again and felt the blood rush to her face.

"What's wrong?" Phoebe had her back to the door, but she could, no doubt, read the trouble in Jacquie's flaming blush. "*Who* is it?"

Abby gave a long, low whistle. "Speak of the devil. My guess is that Mr. Rhys Lewellyn just walked in. And we left out his most obvious character trait."

Eyes wide, Phoebe looked from Abby to Jacquie. "Which is…?"

"He's gorgeous," Abby said. "With a capital G."

Phoebe turned in her seat to get a quick peek. Flushing, she sat back again, facing Jacquie. "Oh, yes."

Beside Jacquie, Abby straightened up. "And he's heading this way."

CHAPTER THREE

OTHER THAN THE CHANCE to pick up a cup of coffee for the twenty-minute drive back to Fairfield Farm, Rhys hadn't expected anything out of his visit to the diner across the street from Andrew's school. Finding Jacquie inside was a stroke of good luck he was sure he didn't deserve, but one he intended to take full advantage of.

She had friends with her—a plump, chestnut-haired beauty standing by her shoulder and a cool blonde seated in the booth. They reminded him of watchdogs. If he didn't behave, he had a feeling they were prepared to chase him off the premises.

"Good morning," he said as he approached the table. "Is this where weary parents come to recover from the struggle of getting teenagers out of bed before noon?"

Jacquie grinned. "There's a special pot of double-strength coffee set aside for those of us who need it." Then, as if she'd suddenly remembered she didn't want to talk to him, the grin faded. "Let me introduce you to some of your new neighbors. This is Abby Brannon." She nodded to the woman standing beside her. "She and her dad Charlie run the Carolina Diner. Phoebe Moss," she said, gesturing to the blonde, "lives just down the road from me, and when she's not taking care of rescue horses, she works as a speech therapist. Abby, Phoebe, this is Rhys Lewellyn.''

"I'm glad to meet you." Rhys tried out a smile on each of them, without much success. Phoebe's gray gaze seemed to possess X-ray powers with which she intended to expose his every sin. If Jacquie had shared the details of their personal history with her friend, then there were a hell of a lot of sins to be found.

"Would you like anything else with your coffee?" Abby had a commercial interest to protect, he understood, which forced her to talk to him. "Doughnut, biscuit, piece of pie?"

"Just coffee, thanks." When he smiled again, she lifted the corners of her mouth slightly, but he wasn't sure that counted as progress.

"I'll bring it out right away. Can I get y'all anything else?" She looked at Jacquie and Phoebe, who shook their heads, before hurrying off to the kitchen.

"This seems to be a popular place for breakfast," Rhys commented, trying to keep the conversation going. No one, he noticed, had asked him to sit down.

"And lunch and dinner." Jacquie looked around the room instead of meeting his eyes directly. "Most people in New Skye probably eat at the Carolina Diner at least once a week."

"Some of them eat here every day," Phoebe said, as the bell on the door jingled yet again. "Like my fiancé. Adam?" She lifted her hand and waved to the dark-haired man coming in the door, who quickly joined them.

Rhys stepped closer to Jacquie as the newcomer bent to give Phoebe a kiss. "Good m-morning, s-sweetheart, I didn't know you'd be here. I'd have c-come in s-sooner.''

Phoebe's smile was gentle as she laid her palm along the man's jawline. "I came for breakfast with Jacquie."

"S-sorry, Jacquie." The guy straightened up and grinned. "I didn't m-mean to ignore you."

"That's okay—you have your priorities right." She winked at him, with a camaraderie Rhys envied. "Let me introduce you to Rhys Lewellyn. Rhys, this is Adam DeVries, Phoebe's fiancé and, incidentally, the mayor-elect of New Skye. Adam, Rhys moved in during the snowstorm."

"W-welcome to the area." DeVries extended a strong hand. "Where are you c-coming f-from?"

"New York."

The mayor-to-be laughed. "Well, if you were hoping to escape the sn-snow, don't worry—we don't usually get this m-much. Every f-few years we'll have a fr-freak storm, but m-mostly we see an inch or two that melts by m-morning."

Relieved at the absence of undercurrents, Rhys smiled. "I'm glad to hear that. The horses thought we'd done all that driving for nothing."

"Horses?" DeVries sat down beside Phoebe, who scooted over to make room. "This is a good part of the country f-for horses. I know Jacquie's been riding since she could walk—did the two of you know each other before you arrived?"

Rhys looked at Jacquie and found her staring at him, her eyes wide with alarm. He turned back to DeVries. "Jacquie came up to train at my barn, quite a few years ago. But we haven't been in contact—it's just my luck that she's in this area."

Abby returned just then to hand him a large foam cup with a cover. She saw Adam and gave a genuine smile. "Morning, Mr. Mayor. What'll you have?"

"'M-morning, yourself, M-Miss Abby. The usual will be great." DeVries looked up at Rhys. "Can you s-sit down with us?"

"I—" He would have refused—Jacquie obviously didn't want him here. But, still without looking at him, she moved over into the corner of the booth, which left him no other option. "Sure, I'll sit down for a few minutes."

DeVries was a personable man, and a politician, so the conversation flowed easily enough for the next few minutes, until Rhys thought even Jacquie had begun to relax beside him. At least she'd eaten some of her breakfast. His awareness of her was like sitting near a blazing fire on the winter's coldest night—the burn along that side of his body created a penetrating warmth that reached all the way to his core. Only as the ice began to melt did he realize he'd been frozen for fourteen long years.

"Have you met Erin?" DeVries asked, then smiled at Abby as she set his breakfast plate on the table. "Jacquie's daughter is every bit as horse crazy as her mother was at that age. And from what Phoebe tells me, she's really good."

"I've talked to her on the phone. Jacquie and I are supposed to set up some lessons, I believe." Rhys risked a glance to his left and found Jacquie's gaze focused on the napkin her fingers were busy folding into a fan. "I'm looking forward to that."

"Do you have a family, Rhys?" Phoebe Moss had evidently decided to suspend hostilities...or else she planned to come in under his radar.

"I'm divorced. My son Andrew lives with me."

"How old is Andrew?"

"Going on fifteen." Beside him, Jacquie stiffened for a moment, then relaxed again.

"Just a little older than Erin. Does he ride?"

"He could hardly help it, given the family business. Our branch of the Lewellyns has trained and sold horses for a couple of centuries, now, in Wales and the U.S. But Andrew does love it, thank God. He's aiming for the Olympics."

Phoebe buttered a piece of toast. "Like his father?"

DeVries looked up. "The Olympics?"

"Rhys has been to the Olympics twice," Jacquie said. "He took a gold medal last time in eventing."

The other man quirked an eyebrow. "I apologize. I didn't recognize your name."

Rhys shook his head. "No reason you should. Equestrian events aren't as widely publicized as, say, track-and-field."

"And what is eventing, exactly? I'm still being initiated into the horse world."

"Eventing—held at what we call horse trials or three-day events—is a competition designed to test the endurance, athleticism, and discipline of horse and rider. The first day's test is a dressage performance, in which we execute a complicated series of figures on flat ground within a ring of specified length and width."

The mayor-elect nodded. "Right. I've watched dressage."

"On the second day, horse and rider compete in the speed and endurance section, which includes several elements of fast work. The most impressive is the actual cross-country run, over seven kilometers or so on a course which includes obstacles ranging from simple fences to water hazards, even buildings to ride through. Each ride is timed, and any refusal or fall pretty much eliminates the pair for the entire event."

"The jumps are massive," Phoebe added. "Four feet high, or more, and at least that wide. Or in a series, where you make two or three jumps, one right after the other."

Rhys grinned at her. "Right. And those jumps are fixed in place—they don't come down if they're hit."

"Painful," Adam DeVries commented.

"Can be." Rhys cleared his throat, forced his thoughts past that inevitable memory. "On the last day, the horse and rider compete in stadium jumping, another timed event, over painted wooden fences which do come down if knocked hard enough. Cross-country and show-jumping times are combined, and the dressage score figured in to determine the overall winner."

"And you do this on a regular basis?"

"The season runs spring to late fall. The big four events are Burghley and Badminton, in England, Rolex in Kentucky, and the Adelaide Horse Trials in New Zealand. And the Olympics, every four years."

"So what brings you and your horses to this part of Carolina?"

"I was looking for a change of pace—and weather." He grinned and got Adam's smile in return. "An old friend lives in the area and suggested I try it out for a season. We're thinking of doing some breeding together, and so I thought I'd take her advice.''

"Horse breeding?" Jacquie asked, with a sidelong glance.

"I don't breed dogs," Rhys said, with a wink.

"And are you already looking forward to the next Olympics?"

Rhys chose the polite answer rather than the truthful one. "That's the ultimate prize. And Imperator is the horse to do it twice, if anyone can. You all should come out to see him one day. He's quite the showman." Realizing that he still held his unopened coffee in his hand, he slid out of the booth. "Just drive out to Fairfield Farm whenever you have the time. I'll be happy to give you a tour."

"I'll do that." DeVries got to his feet and offered a firm handshake. "It's good to have you in town, Mr. Lewellyn."

"Rhys."

"And I'm Adam. I'll look forward to seeing you again soon. If there's anything I can do, feel free to call."

"Thanks." Turning to the table, he finally managed to catch Jacquie's eye. "Call me about those lessons."

Her serious expression was not encouraging. "I'll think about it."

He had to let it go. "Good to meet you, Phoebe. Abby." Jacquie's friends unbent enough to nod. As he crossed the diner, he heard the conversation pick up behind him, heard a woman's laugh and would have sworn it was Jacquie's. She hadn't laughed or even smiled since that first grin when he arrived—not a good omen for any future companionship.

After fourteen years, though, whatever had been be-tween them that summer should really remain in the past. They'd been young, and he'd been on the re-bound. With hindsight, he could see how doomed the entire relationship was from the beginning. Even if Olivia hadn't returned and begged him to cancel the divorce, he and Jacquie would surely have burned out their passion and gone their separate ways.

Rhys climbed into his truck, turned on the engine and took a sip of lukewarm coffee. That theory was all well and good. But the fact remained that seeing Jacquie again had jump-started his imagination, his memories...his libido...as nothing else had in four-teen years. She'd brushed him off twice, so far, and would have sent him to hell today if she could have brought herself to be so rude. She hadn't, though.

And he wouldn't leave her alone unless she forced him to.

SCHOOL WAS PRETTY MUCH SCHOOL, Andrew thought, wherever you went. These Southern kids he'd been dumped in with weren't nearly as cool as they thought they were. But by lunchtime, he'd decided they were probably easier to get along with than the nerds and snobs in his last school in New York.

The courses he'd taken at home put him a grade ahead at New Skye High School, and he'd hung around with tenth-graders most of the morning. But all students ate lunch at the same time in the big caf-eteria, where there were sections labeled for each class. Andrew figured he'd play it safe and sit at a ninth-grade table. He didn't want to argue with some territorial freak over being in the wrong place.

So he watched from the empty end of a bench as the usual groups formed—the guy jocks, the cheerleaders, the popular girls who weren't cheerleaders, the smart kids, the girl jocks, the losers. He found his eye drawn to a girl in the popular group, maybe because, in a bevy of suntanned blondes, her short black hair and pale skin singled her out.

Cute, definitely. Wearing jeans and a sweater under a leather jacket, she was worth a second glance, even a third. He'd think about asking her out, if there was any possibility his old man would let him go on a date.

Since there wasn't, Andrew went back to his sandwich. Next thing he knew, somebody was standing across the table.

"Hi."

He looked up to find her standing in front of him and smiling. "Hi, yourself."

"You're new to school, right? I'm Erin Archer."

"Andrew Lewellyn."

Her pale blue eyes got big. "Lewellyn? As in Rhys Lewellyn?"

"No, as in Andrew. Andrew Lewellyn."

"But Rhys Lewellyn is…your dad?"

"Yeah." He watched with resignation as she sat down on the opposite bench.

"How cool is it to have Rhys Lewellyn as your dad? Does he give you riding lessons every day? Do you get to watch him ride Imperator? Were you there at the Olympics when he won the gold?"

"Do you always talk so much?"

She laughed. "I guess I do. Do you want me to leave?"

He'd noticed the glances coming their way from the jock table. "No, that's okay."

"Do you work with Imperator every day? Are you planning to ride him at the Top Flight Horse Trials in April? There are a couple of smaller shows coming up before then, too—"

He held up a hand. "Slow down, why don't you? Nobody rides Imp but my dad, unless I steal him. So he's not in shape to jump and probably won't be by April and Top Flight. Which means he won't compete."

"What are you talking about? Why not?"

"My dad doesn't ride much cross country these days."

"I remember, he fell at the Adelaide Horse Trials, didn't he? But that was months ago. He must be well by now."

"His back still bothers him sometimes." Andrew decided against explaining the rest. "So if he doesn't ride, Imp won't run."

"You've got three whole months to get him in shape. I bet he'll let you." Her eyes got even bigger. "Or, maybe…I'm gonna get my mom to let me take lessons with your dad. Maybe he'll let me ride Imperator."

Andrew snorted in disbelief. "You think he'd let you ride Imp when he won't let me? That's a bunch of crap."

She stiffened up. "It is not. I'm riding in the Top Flight trials. I could handle Imperator, even on my first lesson."

"In your dreams. My dad doesn't put lesson riders on Imp."

Her chin went up. "Maybe he just hasn't had any-body good enough."

"Like I'm not?" He got to his feet. "You are so full of—"

"Hey, Erin." Two of the blondes she'd been sitting with earlier walked up. "You're going to the algebra-help session, right?" one of them asked her.

"Right." Erin swung her legs over the bench and stood up with her back to him. "Let's go."

"Hi." The blonde sent a smile in Andrew's direction. "Are you new? I'm Cathy Parr."

"Andrew Lewellyn."

"Rhys Lewellyn's son?" Cathy's jaw dropped a little. "Awesome." She stopped there, which won her major points as far as Andrew was concerned, and glanced at her friend's frown. "What are you mad about?"

Erin hunched one shoulder, still without turning around. "Nothing. Let's go, okay?"

Cathy shrugged. "Okay." As she shifted her books in her arms, she looked at Andrew, then Erin, and back again. "Gee…you two kinda look alike, you know? Must be 'cause you both have black hair."

"And those same light blue eyes," the other blonde added. "You could be, like, twins. How cool is that?"

Erin snorted. "Then I'll be a redhead by tomorrow morning. Come on, we're gonna be late." She stalked away and, with an apologetic tilt of her head, Cathy followed.

"Good riddance." Andrew squashed the leftovers from his lunch into the brown bag, aimed a three-point shot at the trash can…and missed.

Muttering to himself, he walked over to pick up the

bag before some teacher yelled. "Give me a break, Miss Erin All-Star. You're gonna ride Imperator like I'm gonna play for the NBA."

Erin bounced into the truck Monday after school. "Did you call Mr. Lewellyn today? When can I have a lesson?"

Jacquie steeled her nerves and shook her head. "No, honey. I haven't talked to anybody since breakfast. Two urgent calls came in this morning and I've been working nonstop since then."

The momentary silence was deafening. "I can't believe you just blew me off." That wide lower lip, so like her father's, stuck out in a pout.

"I didn't blow you off, Erin. I have a job to do, that's all."

With an exasperated sigh, Erin flopped back in the seat. "Great. Just great." She sulked for the rest of the afternoon, sullenly doing her homework as she sat in the truck and refusing to get out at the two farms Jacquie had to visit. As they drove home in the dark, though, she sat up a little straighter.

"Can we stop at the drugstore? I need some notebook paper. And pens."

Thankful that Erin was still speaking to her, Jacquie was glad to cooperate. At the first opportunity, she swung the truck into a shopping center parking lot. "Want me to run in?"

Erin shook her head. "I'll get it."

Jacquie handed her a ten dollar bill. "Why don't you get some chips to go with dinner tonight? And maybe some cookies."

"Um…" Erin's brows drew together. "I might need more than this."

"For chips and cookies and paper? I doubt it." But she dug into her wallet and came up with another twenty. "That should do it."

With a nod, Erin walked briskly across the parking lot to the big, brightly lit store. Jacquie had started allowing little solo trips like this as lessons in growing up for both herself and Erin. Still, her breathing stayed fast until she saw her daughter reappear on the sidewalk and start back to the truck.

"Here's your change." Erin handed over a surprisingly small jumble of bills and coins as she settled into her seat.

"That much for chips?"

"I realized I needed some other stuff."

For the sake of peace, Jacquie accepted the explanation, though she suspected the bag Erin carried held more along the lines of makeup, maybe candy, than school supplies. Pushing for details seemed like a bad idea when they were already at odds.

But when, with an early good-night kiss, Erin disappeared into the bathroom as soon as her homework was done, Jacquie felt certain of her hunch. The shower turned on and off, and there was an extended period of blow dryer noise, followed by silence. She only hoped the new look wasn't too extreme to wear to school.

Early the next morning, when she got her first glimpse of Erin's makeover, the wooden spoon Jacquie was using to stir oatmeal slipped from her fingers to the floor.

"What…" Her voice squeaked like a rusty gate.

"What in the world have you done? Your hair is...is...red!" A deep, dark, unmistakable red.

"I know." Erin's pixie grin hadn't changed. "Isn't it just totally awesome?"

"I..." Jacquie rubbed her scratchy eyes. "What possessed you to dye your hair?" At her feet, Hurry picked up the fallen spoon and carried it to her private space under the kitchen table for an episode of devoted licking.

Erin went to the mirror beside the door and fluffed the red strands. "I...I just thought it would look cool."

"And you didn't think you needed to ask my permission first?"

"It's my hair." She avoided Jacquie's gaze in the mirror.

"You're my daughter. That entitles me to an opinion about what you do with your appearance."

"Come on, Mom. The color washes out in a couple of months."

"A couple of months during which you won't look like yourself." Crossing the room to stand behind Erin, Jacquie turned the girl to face her. "I'm not happy about this, Erin. Why would you change the way you look?"

"I just wanted to be different."

"From what?"

Erin fidgeted with the honey bowl on the counter. "Well, see, there's this guy..."

"You dyed your hair to make some boy notice you?" Her throat closed on panic. "Who is this person?"

"No, Mom, it's not like that. I met him yesterday

at lunch. Andrew Lewellyn, Mr. Lewellyn's son. And he was so obnoxious, I couldn't believe it.''

From upset to panic to horror...Erin had met Rhys's son on his first day at school. ''And...?''

''He said his dad wouldn't let me ride Imperator even if I did take lessons.''

''That's probably true.''

''But I'm good enough. I know I am. Anyway, then Cathy said we kinda look alike—we both have black hair and blue eyes. So I said I'd be a redhead by today, so I couldn't possibly look anything like such a jerk.'' She posed her hands on either side of her hair. ''And—ta-da!—here I am.''

Oh, dear God. An unobservant teenager had noticed the resemblance between Erin and Andrew. It would only be a matter of time until more perceptive people commented. Jacquie saw her worst fears cascading toward her like an avalanche.

At least Erin's red hair might give her a little extra time. But only a little. Somehow, she had to deflect this disaster.

And Rhys would have to help her.

SLOUCHED IN A CHAIR Tuesday night, half asleep and half intoxicated, Rhys considered not answering the phone's insistent ring but, at the last minute, changed his mind. ''Fairfield Farms, Lewellyn speaking.''

''Rhys, it's Jacquie.''

The glass between his fingers slipped to the floor, spilling the dregs of his fourth...or fifth?...brandy. ''Damn,'' he muttered, awkwardly getting down on his knees to rescue the leased carpet.

"I beg your pardon?" Her voice was as stiff as his mother's starched tablecloths.

"Sorry, I didn't mean that for you. I spilled a drink." He blotted the wet spot with the sleeve of his sweatshirt. "I didn't expect to hear from you again. Ever."

"I know. But...I've thought about it, and I think we should meet. Dinner will be okay, if you're free. Friday night?"

Rhys eased back into his chair. "Why does it sound as if you're facing the guillotine?"

"I—I don't know what you're talking about. Does seven work for you? At the Starting Gate?"

"I assume that's a restaurant. You'll have to give me directions."

She did so in a hurried, distracted voice that told him she couldn't wait to get out of the conversation, and Rhys didn't push her. Whatever was wrong, he had a feeling she would offer the explanation Friday night. If she didn't offer, then he would push.

HE ARRIVED EARLY at the restaurant just for the pleasure of watching her come toward him across the room, and the experience didn't disappoint him. She wore her hair loose, glinting like strands of soft, rosy gold draped across her deep blue sweater. In dark pants and boots, her walk wasn't a feminine sway but the strong, direct stride of a strong woman. Rhys shifted in his chair, thinking he really was too old to be turned on by a woman's looks.

But then, this wasn't just any woman.

He stood as she reached the table and went around to pull out her chair. "Hello, again. I'm glad to see you.'' She took her seat without answering, or even meeting his gaze.

The waiter appeared at his elbow. ''Drinks, sir? Or wine?''

With a tilt of his hand, Rhys deferred the question to Jacquie. She shook her head. ''Could I have some coffee? I got chilled on the way here,'' she explained, when the waiter had left. ''I'd really like to warm up.''

''Your fingers do look frozen.'' Rhys reached out to touch her, just a stroke of his fingertips, and was startled when she jerked her hands off the table, into her lap. His patience, which stretched much further for horses than humans, suddenly snapped.

''I think we need to cut to the chase.'' Folding his arms along the edge of the table, he leaned closer and held her gaze by sheer force of will. ''I'm not sure what's going on, but I am sure I'm tired of playing games. Why are we here, Jacquie? What do you have to say to me?''

The waiter, with impeccable timing, returned at that moment with their coffee. And then wanted to take their orders, which required consulting the menu. But with all those details taken care of, tension still bracketed the table, isolating them from the other diners.

''Well?'' He took hold of his coffee mug with both hands. ''I'm waiting.''

Jacquie's eyes widened, as they had on her first day at his barn in New York when she'd arrived at the riding ring two minutes after the scheduled lesson time. For a second, Rhys relived his own immediate attraction to the girl with the sunny green gaze, which made him even more brusque. ''Come on, Jacquie. You were never one to avoid a fence.''

"You're right." Her voice was steadier now. "Although this one's been a long time coming." She drew a deep breath. "You asked me why I left without saying anything."

"Yes."

"You came to my room that night, in New York, to tell me your...wife...had returned. She was pregnant, you said, and the man she had been living with didn't want your baby."

Hearing her relate the memory brought all the anguish rushing back. "I remember."

When he didn't say anything else, Jacquie continued. "I was hurt, of course, that you'd chosen your wife over me. And furious that you'd slept with her so recently before we..." She picked up her coffee and took a sip. "But I knew your decision was the right one, and I couldn't stay to make the situation more difficult."

"Where did you go?"

"Oklahoma. I got a job as a nanny for a family with horses, so I taught lessons, as well."

"And you met this Archer and married him?"

She stared at him for a long time, her lips pressed together. "I...no. There is no husband. I invented him because I couldn't come home as an unwed mother with an illegitimate child."

Setting down her coffee, Jacquie looked him straight in the eyes. "*Your* child, Rhys. My daughter, Erin Elizabeth Archer, is also yours. The only proof you'll need is a single glance at her beautiful face."

His breath left him, just as it had after his fall from Imperator. He could only manage a whisper. "Say it again."

"We were going to have a child together. I was pregnant."

"Dear God." She was a virgin, their first time together. He didn't have to wonder if there'd been others.

Their waiter, timely as ever, brought a dinner that neither of them touched. Rhys pushed his plate away first. "You could have written, or called. I would have helped."

Jacquie stared for a second at the green bean on the end of her fork, then returned it to the plate. "I didn't want to hear you suggest an abortion."

"I wouldn't do that." He hoped he wouldn't have done that. But he had been an arrogant young man.

"And I didn't want to be bought off with your family's money."

"That's not what I meant."

"If your parents had gotten wind of my condition, they would've done whatever they thought would protect their precious son. They might have tried to take my baby away altogether."

Her bitterness ran deep, with justification. His parents had not treated her with respect. "They aren't bad people."

"Just people with money who are used to getting their own way." She didn't smile, made no effort to take the sting out of the comment.

"So you handled the situation, you supported yourself and *your* daughter without help." He took a perverse satisfaction from her wince. "What's the point of telling me now?"

He'd forgotten—or had he ever known?—that Jacquie possessed a temper, too. "Don't be stupid.

You're here, in our backyard. We live and work in the same world—horses. And Erin looks just like you. There's no way this secret is going to keep. I'm concerned about how to protect my little girl against being hurt."

Rhys shrugged, pretending not to care. "You could run away again." But Jacquie's stare made him ashamed. "Sorry. You've had fourteen years to adjust to this whole mess. Give me at least fourteen minutes."

As the waiter bustled over their uneaten food, a different face flashed in front of Rhys's eyes. When they were alone again, he looked at Jacquie. "Andrew. Do you think they'll see the resemblance?"

She nodded. "One of their classmates already has. It's only a matter of time."

They declined the waiter's offer of dessert but accepted a refill on coffee. Rhys gave him a credit card without looking at the bill, just to make the man go away. "So they have to be told, as soon as possible."

"No. Absolutely not." Her eyes had hardened, and her fist hit the table. "That's what I wanted to be sure you understand. No one is to know. Absolutely no one."

"You just said—"

"She looks like you. And there are thousands of guys all over the world making money because they look like Elvis. If we don't give people around here a reason to believe there's a connection, there won't be one. So you have to promise me you won't say a single word about this to anybody, ever.

"But—"

"And I want you to stay as far away from me and my daughter as you possibly can."

CHAPTER FOUR

THEY ARGUED for an hour, over cold coffee, until Rhys finally conceded that he wouldn't say anything *for now*. He would wait to see what happened in the first weeks of school.

A month's reprieve, at best. Jacquie counted herself lucky that he'd agreed to even that much. He could have insisted on his parental rights, and she doubted she could have stopped him. Rhys Lewellyn usually got what he wanted. Sitting across the table from him, watching him smile, studying his face and his hands and remembering…

No. She wouldn't put herself through the torture. That part of her life—their time together—must stay completely in the past. For sanity's sake.

One step outside the restaurant's front door, the vicious whip of a cold wind sent her staggering backward. Rhys stood just behind her, and for a second they were pressed together, back to front, his hands gripping her shoulders, his chin resting on the top of her head. Like a shower of sparks, awareness drenched her from head to toe.

She moved away as fast as possible and turned to face him. "Call me," she instructed, with as much distance as she could put into her voice, "if something happens. Erin might not say anything."

"Andrew's not likely to confide in me, of all people. But we'll see. You can only take one jump at a time."

Instead of standing where he was, Rhys moved with her into the parking lot. To her frustration, he appeared prepared to walk her all the way to her own driver's seat.

"Some of these jumps are water hazards," Jacquie grumbled, "with a stone wall before and a hill with a drop-off behind." She stopped at the tailgate of her truck. Cars had parked on either side of her, and she didn't intend to be confined in such a close space with this man. "I'm too old for that kind of ride."

His gaze moved beyond her, assessing the situation. He must have agreed with her, because he took a step back. "If you need to get in touch, I'm usually at the farm. Except for tomorrow—the rest of my horses are flying into the Raleigh airport about noon and I'll be driving them down."

"Imperator doesn't fly?"

"Not if given a choice." He smiled, for the first time that evening, and her stupid heart fluttered in response. "We try to keep his flights to a minimum, because he gets so rattled that it can take weeks to settle him down to work. And we came here to work."

"So first we have a snowstorm, and now you're in the middle of a personal disaster. You must be thrilled with this decision."

Rhys looked at her for a long moment, his face unreadable in the dark. "It's not all bad," he said quietly. "Good night."

He stood by the back of the truck until she got the engine started, then gave her a brief salute and went to the other side of the parking lot for his own vehicle. Jacquie wondered if he always drove a truck, or if he still indulged himself with the wickedly fast sports cars he'd owned fourteen years ago. She couldn't quite visualize the great Rhys Lewellyn at the wheel of a minivan with a car seat in back.

Or maybe she could, she realized as she headed home. The image of Rhys carrying a toddler in his arms made a very appealing picture.

And that was very bad news, indeed.

JACQUIE FOUND that she couldn't just sit down over Saturday lunch and chat with Erin as if nothing important had happened. She had become so caught in a web of lies, she feared she might blurt out the truth without thinking about it.

"Let's go for a ride," she suggested, instead. "We'll load up Mirage and Nina, drive over to Rourke Park and spend a few hours on the trails." The land for the riding preserve ran along one side of Fairfield Farm, but Rhys had said he wouldn't be home this morning and most of the afternoon. No danger there.

Erin glanced out the window. "Mom, it's looking kinda gray. We might get caught in the rain."

"No way. Maybe it'll snow a little. Riding in the snow is fun, right?"

"Snow means temperatures around thirty-two degrees. That's cold, Mom."

"Oh, come on. It's the weekend. Let's live a little."

"Okay. I guess." After giving her a puzzled look, Erin addressed her tuna sandwich. "I hope I can find my gloves."

She did find her warm riding gloves, and by the time the horses stood in the trailer and Hurry had been locked in the house, she'd found her enthusiasm, too. They sang with the Christmas carols still loaded in the CD player as they drove, ending with ''The Twelve Days of Christmas.''

''My favorite carol.'' Erin sighed happily when they'd finished. ''I remember watching you decorate a really tall tree with bows and hearing you sing that song.''

''You remember that? You were only two when I did the tree with the bows.'' Discounted ribbon had been all she could afford that year. ''That tree was about four feet high. You must have been on the floor looking up.''

''Seemed really tall to me. And I remember getting a fashion doll with a fancy red dress and shoes.''

''Which you promptly took off.'' Not the name-brand doll, of course, but an inexpensive version. ''That poor woman never wore clothes again.''

''After a while, her head got lost.''

Jacquie grinned. ''You were playing doctor, I think.''

''That's one way to cure a headache.''

They laughed together, and Jacquie tried to take a mental photograph to save against the time to come.

The wind was brisk and cold, the sky heavy with clouds as they unloaded the horses. Jacquie shivered as she swung into the saddle on Nina's back. ''Cold leather against your rear end. What a great feeling.''

Erin rolled her eyes. ''You're weird. Let's go.''

The trails in Rourke Park ran through a forest of longleaf pine trees and leafless hardwoods, over small rises and shallow dips, with the occasional fallen trunk to jump over or find a way around. Patches of snow lingered in the shade, but the trees cut the wind.

"See, it's not so cold." She caught up with Erin at the edge of an open ride, after a good long trot.

"That's why your breath is hanging in the air with icicles dripping off, right?" But Erin grinned, happy and energetic, the way she always was on horseback. "Can we gallop here?"

"Be my guest." Erin took off across the field on her dappled gray, a study in the close communication possible between horse and rider.

Then Jacquie glanced down at Nina and gave her glossy brown neck a pat. "Ready, girl? We can match that, right?" When she looked up again, she thought for a second her eyes had crossed.

Two horses now moved in profile against the sky. Other trailers had been parked at the entrance to the park, and other riders were using the trails, so the sight wasn't unexpected...until you noticed the quality of that second horse. The fluid movement, the perfect form, the exquisite arch of a proud neck, said "champion" louder than words ever could.

Even so, there should have been no reason for alarm. This part of North Carolina boasted plenty of fine horseflesh, fielded more than its share of winners. Yet Jacquie knew, with a certainty that chilled her to the marrow, which horse she was watching. Imperator.

"Damn you, Rhys Lewellyn." Blaming him made no sense—he hadn't known they would be out today. But she had to blame somebody. She urged Nina into a trot, and then a fast canter, in deference to the uneven footing. "Damn you."

Her mare Nina was a big girl, and covered ground at a fast clip. Soon enough, they reached the crest of the hill where she'd seen the other horses. Mirage and Imperator now cantered down the far slope side by side, their riders as alike as dolls off an assembly line. Then she realized the truth. This wasn't Rhys astride the champion horse, but his son Andrew—the last person Jacquie wanted Erin to spend time talking with. Other than her father, of course.

With no hope of being heard if she shouted, all she could do was charge after them, trying to catch up with horses bred and trained to race across country just like this in record time. Nina's giant heart gave everything she had, though, and Jacquie closed the distance between herself and her daughter.

Hearing hoofbeats behind them, Erin and Andrew reined in their horses and eased to a stop. When Jacquie arrived, the two kids turned their heads in unison to look at her. In boots and breeches and parkas, wearing helmets buckled under their chins, boy and girl were virtually indistinguishable.

Erin spoke first. "Mom, this is Andrew Lewellyn. Mr. Lewellyn's son."

Jacquie nodded. "I met him last Saturday. Hello again, Andrew."

"Mrs. Archer." Even their voices were similar, and both resembled Rhys's smooth tone.

"And Imperator," Erin added. "Isn't he gorgeous?"

"Amazing," Jacquie agreed. She looked at Andrew. "And I'm even more amazed your dad allows you to ride him. He's a handful, isn't he?"

As if to prove her right, the champion sidled, attempted to rear, then kicked out at the wind with his back legs. Andrew admirably held on to his seat.

Since the boy obviously rode quite well, Jacquie's only real concern was getting away before any tricky questions could be asked. "Erin, we need to head back. The horses will get chilled." With a nod to Rhys's son, she turned Nina toward the pine forest. "Take care, Andrew."

The distant shrill of a horse's call—panicked, or maybe angry—echoed unexpectedly across the open hills. Nina startled and shied, and for a moment Jacquie had her hands full calming her own horse. When she could, she looked to see Erin handling Mirage just fine.

Andrew, however, could only cling like a burr to the back of his out-of-control stallion. Imperator reared, bucked and hopped, then kicked out with both front and rear legs. The boy hung on and, when all four hooves hit the ground again, attempted to exert control.

Not a chance. With the bit literally between his teeth, Imperator took off again, galloping madly in one direction, wheeling, then dashing at a different slant. During one of those abrupt changes of angle, Andrew finally fell off. The horse vanished over the next hill.

Jacquie reached him first and slid off Nina's back, praying the mare wouldn't choose to bolt, since there was nowhere nearby to tie her. Erin trotted up and started to dismount, but Jacquie held up one hand, reaching into her pocket for her cell phone with the other.

"What you need to do is follow that stupid horse.

Don't try to catch him. We just want to know where he is. The park is fenced and he can't get out—well, unless he chooses to jump the fence and then we're all screwed.'' A million-dollar horse, loose on the road. ''Maybe you can herd him—from a distance—back this way. Just keep him in sight.''

Erin nodded and headed Mirage in the last direction Imperator had taken. Jacquie made her report to the emergency services number, receiving an assurance that help was on its way. Then she turned to get a good look at Rhys's son.

Unconscious, he lay on his back as he'd landed, breathing but not otherwise moving. His helmet had stayed on, which was for the best, and she thought the angle of his neck looked normal. She'd been warned not to move any part of his body, but she prodded gently, without finding obvious breaks. He wasn't wearing a protective vest, as both she and Erin did in country like this, so there might be internal injuries. At the very least, he had a concussion—a common enough occurrence for those who worked around and with horses. She only hoped that was the worst of his injuries.

The day dimmed as she knelt beside the injured boy; the wind picked up and the temperature dropped. Andrew didn't regain consciousness. Jacquie covered him with her parka, terrified that he would go into hypothermia before the rescue squad arrived. Protected only by her vest, sweatshirt, turtleneck and long johns, she was soon shivering uncontrollably. Thank God, she still had her gloves and helmet. And that Erin had worn hers.

She looked at the countryside around them, peering

through the darkening twilight. Where was Erin? And where the hell was that diabolical, son-of-a-bitch horse?

Sirens alerted her to the approach of the ambulance, and then her phone rang—the driver asking for specific directions. The flash of lights at the top of the rise brought tears to Jacquie's eyes and startled Nina into a trot which, fortunately, did not take her too far away. Two ambulances descended the slope and stopped at Jacquie's shoulder. A swarm of EMTs emerged, one of whom offered her blankets and a cup of hot tea and handed her parka back. The rest completely ignored her in their concern for Andrew.

Jacquie downed the tea and gave the EMTs Rhys's phone number, reassured that they would take the boy straight to the hospital. Wrapped in the welcome warmth of her coat, she went to Nina and loosened the reins she'd knotted to keep them off the ground, put her foot in the stirrup and launched herself once more into the saddle.

The leather was much colder now than when she'd complained earlier in the day. How good would it feel to get home, take a hot bath and curl up under a heavy layer of quilts? After this adventure, she and Erin might sleep their way through Sunday, dawn to dusk. But first...

First, she had a horse to catch.

"HE'S NOT HERE," Terry announced, coming back to the stable from the house.

"Imperator's not in the stable." Rhys walked Ricochet, who'd arrived only a couple of hours ago, out of the trailer and into his stall. "I told Andrew I'd send him back to his grandfather if he did this again."

"You shouldn't make threats you can't follow through on."

"I know." He'd accepted his incompetence as a parent long ago. "I guess we'll just wait until he rides in and have another showdown. Want to watch?"

"I'll pass, thanks. But when you're finished, I'll take my turn."

"Have at it."

By the time their work in the barn was done, the horses settled and the sun setting, the truants had not yet returned. Rhys conceded to the worry that had gnawed at him for the last couple of hours. "Something's happened."

Terry nodded. "Probably."

"I'll call the hospital, just in case."

"Good idea."

But he was saved the trouble by the blinking light on his answering machine. "Rhys, it's Jacquie. Andrew took Imperator out this afternoon in Rourke Park, the riding preserve that runs along your western property line. He got thrown and knocked unconscious. I called the rescue squad and they're here with him now, taking him to the hospital. Erin's supposed to keep an eye on that damn horse of yours, and I'm going to try to catch him. You go to Andrew. I'll get the horse home if I can."

There were other messages, but Rhys was out the door before they started playing. Terry dug up a map with the directions to New Skye Hospital, and they made the fifteen-mile trip in under ten minutes.

Rhys stood in line for an endless stretch of time,

awaiting his turn at the emergency room information desk. "My son was brought in," he stated, keeping his voice under control with his clenched teeth. "Andrew Lewellyn. He fell off a horse."

The receptionist consulted her clipboard. "I'll let the doctor know you're here." She turned away, reaching for the phone.

"Wait. Do you have any information? Is he all right?"

"I don't know, sir. The doctor will be able to tell you."

Fists on the counter, Rhys growled in frustration. Terry took his arm and drew him out of the way, to a pair of free seats in the corner.

"Sit yourself down," he counseled. "They'll be with you as soon as possible. Complaining won't change things."

Terry would know. He'd sat in a waiting room often enough through the years, while Rhys got a broken arm set or an ankle x-rayed, a concussion observed. And just two months ago, with a broken spine as a possibility...

"Parents of Andrew Lewellyn?"

"Here." Rhys got to his feet. A vise had closed down on his chest, his gut.

The doctor, a young woman, looked Terry up and down. "I'm afraid I can only allow parents with the patient."

"I'm his mother," the Irishman said gruffly.

She winked and smiled. "That's okay, then. I'm Dr. Singh," she said, leading them down the long white hallway. "Andrew's going to be okay. He lost consciousness for quite a long time, but did come to in the ambulance on the way to the hospital. We've been waiting for your signature to do a CT scan.''

Rhys took the clipboard she offered and signed at the *X* without a second thought. He remembered this routine well.

"His mental functions are normal and his physical exam is fine, so we don't expect problems. And here he is.'' She drew back the curtain on a cubicle, closing it behind them as Rhys and Terry stepped inside.

Andrew lay with his eyes closed, looking small and afraid. Rhys couldn't speak through his closed throat so he simply waited until the boy finally lifted his lids.

Terry gave a grunt. "Hoping we'd think you were asleep?''

"Guess it didn't work.'' His voice was little more than a whisper.

"Not likely,'' the Irishman said with a snort.

Rhys cleared his throat. "I warned you about this.''

Andrew shrugged, then winced. "Yeah, you did.''

Moving closer, Rhys extended a hand to touch his son's tight fist. "What were you thinking?''

"That I'm not afraid.'' After a second's pause, he added, "Like you.''

Anger and hurt froze solid inside him, preventing Rhys from saying anything else at all. He let his arm fall to his side and backed away from the bed.

"That's enough of that.'' Terry cuffed Andrew lightly on the shoulder. "You're luckier than you deserve, boyo. We'll talk about it when you get home. They're coming for some tests, but we'll be around. See you later.''

A steel grip on Rhys's arm dragged him down the hallway, through the doors and into the waiting area, where Terry pushed him into the same chair he'd occupied before, then settled beside him.

"Pay no mind to what the boy said. You know he's trying to goad you, avoid the tongue-lashing he deserves."

Rhys nodded slowly. "Sure."

"He idolizes you, always has. That fall of yours shook him up as much as any of the rest of us."

"No doubt."

"He's wanting you to get back to form for his own sake. Just cut him a break." The Irishman's weathered hand rested on his arm for a second. "Cut yourself a break."

Rhys leaned his head back against the wall and closed his eyes. "Why not?"

Minutes...or hours...later, he heard his name called again. "Rhys, I got here as soon as I could. How's Andrew?"

He looked up to see Jacquie directly in front of him, eyes wide and worried, face pale, teeth chattering. He got to his feet and took her hands, noticing how cold they were. Noticing that she didn't jerk away this time.

"He's going to be fine. They're doing tests to be sure, but he's conscious, alert, smart mouthed as always." He turned them both around and urged her into the chair he'd just left. "I can't begin to tell you how grateful I am that you were out there, that you took care of him. He's not supposed to ride Imperator, but that's obvious, isn't it?"

Terry got to his feet. "I'll get some tea," he said, as Jacquie continued to shake. "And blankets."

Jacquie shook her head as he headed down the hallway. "It's reaction, I think, as much as anything. I found the horse...well, Erin found him, and I found her. She had no trouble leading him across the park to your barn. I guess he got all his fidgets out."

For the first time, Rhys became aware of the girl standing to his left, just behind his range of sight. He called on every ounce of willpower he possessed and turned his head to look at her directly.

Only to find himself gazing at an image from his past, a portrait of himself at fourteen. Or of Andrew, yesterday. The tousled hair might be disguised by red dye, but the pale blue eyes and impatient jawline were a feminine version of his own.

With her mother's cute, pointed chin.

After a couple of tries, he found his voice. "Hi, Erin."

Her eyes sparkled like blue diamonds. "Hi, Mr. Lewellyn. It's so cool to meet you." Her smile faded for a second. "I mean...I am sorry Andrew got hurt."

"I know you are. And I owe you my thanks for taking care of the horse. He's more trouble than he's worth, sometimes. And he's worth a good deal."

"One point three million," she agreed. "That's what I read."

"Right. He's not vicious, though. He just doesn't have good impulse control. We're working on that."

"I would love to ride him. I watched the video of your cross-country run at the Olympics yesterday afternoon and it was just incredible to see him take those walls like they were little crossbars on the ground. I'm doing four-foot jumps with my Thoroughbred, Mirage, but I'm not sure how high he'll be able to go. He's fifteen hands—"

"Erin." Jacquie stood up and put an arm around her daughter. "Mr. Lewellyn has much more to think about right now than your riding questions. We'll ask him another time."

Rhys knew that statement for the lie it was. At dinner last night, Jacquie had been quite clear about her intention to keep Erin as far away from him as possible. No lessons, no contact, no chance for anyone—especially Erin—to notice the resemblance and comment.

But this was his daughter, for God's sake. Did Jacquie really expect him to ignore that fact?

"I'd like to see you ride," he said to the girl. "Do you have a free afternoon this week? I'd be glad to give you a lesson."

Erin's pixie face glowed. "That's…that's awesome. Monday? Would Monday be okay?"

"I think Monday afternoon is open." He'd cancel everything on his schedule, if not. "I'll see you about four o'clock?"

"Oh, yes!"

"Excuse me." The harsh tone bore no resemblance to Jacquie's usual soft Southern drawl. "Do I have anything at all to say about this arrangement?"

THE SIMILARITY of the two faces that turned to her—wearing identical expressions of surprise—was almost more than Jacquie could bear.

"I am the one who does the driving," she said, fighting to keep her voice steady. "I'm the one with a job that takes me from one end of the county to the other, morning till night, shoeing horses to make ends meet. I'm the one who has to balance the budget, and

I'm pretty sure high-priced riding lessons would tip us right into the manure pile.''

Lifting one arrogant, questioning eyebrow, Rhys crossed his arms over his chest as he looked Jacquie up and down. "I think I owe Erin at least one free lesson for bringing Imperator back safe.''

"Mom, maybe I could work off some of the payment at Mr. Lewellyn's barn.'' Erin stepped close and put her hands on Jacquie's arm. "He'll need somebody to clean stalls and stuff while Andrew gets better. I'd be glad to do some of the work in return for lessons.'' She looked at Rhys. "Would that be possible?''

"I don't see why not.'' The glint in his eyes challenged Jacquie to disagree.

She looked at her daughter. "You have stalls to clean at home. Horses to be cared for and exercised. Homework.''

"I can get it all done, I promise. It's just a couple of days a week.''

"Whoa, there. We're talking one lesson, here. Not a couple of times every week.''

"But you know how much better I'll get with that kind of training, Mom. Mirage needs the work, if we're going to be ready for the Top Flight Horse Trials in April. And Mr. Lewellyn—''

"Mr. Lewellyn,'' Jacquie said desperately, "doesn't have that kind of time.''

"Sure, I do. Two days a week sounds good to me.''

She threw him a dirty look.

"Please, Mom. Please?''

Before she could gather the gumption to devastate her daughter in public, a woman in a white coat joined their group. "Mr. Lewellyn, I've got the results of Andrew's tests. If you'll come back with me, I can discuss them with you." After a curt nod at Jacquie and a quick smile for Erin, Rhys followed the doctor across the waiting room.

"That's it. Let's go." Jacquie grabbed Erin's wrist and headed for the door."

Erin resisted her pull. "Don't you want to know how Andrew is?"

"I'll call tomorrow and ask."

"We didn't settle about lessons."

Jacquie didn't answer, for fear she'd lose her temper in the middle of the E.R. waiting room. She tugged harder on Erin, forcing her to follow through the automatic doors and into the parking lot, where Erin dug in her heels.

"Mom!"

Breathing hard, Jacquie faced her daughter. "Don't start with me. I don't want to talk about Rhys Lewellyn, riding lessons, or anything else. I'm tired, I'm cold, and I want to go home. So just get in the truck."

Erin pouted all the way home, which gave Jacquie the silence she'd asked for. Once in the house, they went to their separate bedrooms without even a goodnight kiss. Jacquie emerged briefly to let Hurry outside for her nightly patrol, but was soon back in her bed, lying tense and angry in the dark.

About two in the morning, she heard footsteps in the hallway. "Mom? Mom, are you awake?"

Jacquie turned over to face the door. "What's wrong, Erin?"

The door opened. "Can I come in?"

"Of course." She sat up.

Erin came to stand by the bed, just beyond touching distance. "I'm sorry I bugged you about the lessons. I don't have to—" she drew a deep, shaking breath "—to take lessons with Mr. Lewellyn. I'm doing great with you as my teacher."

Until that instant, Jacquie hadn't even considered that Erin might think there was a professional competition between her and Rhys. "Erin, I'm not jealous of you taking lessons with somebody else. There are plenty of riders out there who know more than I do." She leaned forward enough to catch Erin's hand. "Come here, baby."

With a grateful sigh, Erin sank onto the bed and let Jacquie hold her. They sat in a peaceful silence for a few minutes.

"Then what's wrong?" Erin rubbed her head against Jacquie's shoulder. "Mr. Lewellyn is one of the very best."

There couldn't be a more perfect moment to tell the truth. In the cool darkness, with a winter moon shining through the window, she should give Erin her birthright, plus the chance to know her father and benefit from his presence in her life.

Jacquie took a breath, preparing to speak.

In the next instant, she recalled what else Erin would learn from that moment of truth—that her existence was a "mistake." Her conception had come at the worst possible time for everyone concerned. The father she had believed in for fourteen years, the man she thought had loved her before he'd ever seen her face, was a fallacy. Her mother had lied to her every day of her life.

How would that knowledge improve Erin's life in the least?

Smoothing her daughter's hair, Jacquie wove yet another thread into her fabric of truth and lies. "He is the best," she assured her daughter. "I know he could teach you some important skills. I was stressed tonight, with Andrew's fall and the missing horse. I'll talk to Mr. Lewellyn on Monday and see what we can work out." *For one lesson, and one lesson only.*

"Thanks, Mom." Erin sighed happily and snuggled closer. Gradually they eased into bed and under the covers, with Hurry at their feet. Holding her sleeping girl in her arms, Jacquie knew she'd made the right choice.

And she would make sure Rhys Lewellyn agreed.

ERIN SLIPPED OUT to the barn early Sunday morning, where Mirage greeted her with his breakfast-time whicker. She put his grain in the bucket, then stood beside him, stroking his shoulder, while he ate.

"We're gonna get lessons," she told him. "From one of the best. Won't that be awesome?"

Then she thought about last night, and her mom's deep sighs. "Mom's not happy, though. Mr. Lewellyn upsets her. He seems nice to me, but she was as nervous as a cat around him. What do you think?"

Mirage, busy with his grain, didn't answer. "I know, you think all humans are strange. Maybe you're right." She hugged her best friend, resting her cheek against his warm neck. "Sometimes I think I should have been born a horse. They make more sense than people, any day."

AFTER A NIGHT of observation in the hospital, Andrew had been sent home Sunday afternoon with instructions to stay in bed on Monday. Rhys gave him a pass on his daily chores and left him lying on the sofa with a stack of movies to watch. Homework would have been a better idea, but why start off the day with an argument?

He had finished mucking out the ten stalls on one side of the barn and had started on Imperator's impressive overnight deposits when he heard the sound of an engine outside, soon cut off. The slam of a truck door was followed by the quick thud of boot heels on the brick floor of the barn aisle. Having little doubt about who his visitor would be, Rhys threw a forkful of manure into the wheelbarrow just outside the stall door, to let Jacquie know exactly where to find him.

She faced him across the almost full barrow. "The great man cleans his own stalls?"

Rhys braced the pitchfork upright in the stall bedding and propped his elbow on the end. "Good morning to you, too. Andrew's fine, thanks."

Even in the dimness of the barn, he saw the flush stealing over her cheeks. She glanced toward the outside door, like a caged animal wishing for escape.

"I'm sorry," she said after a minute, bringing her eyes back to his face. "I'm wrong on all counts. You never ordered anybody to do work you wouldn't do. I'm glad to hear Andrew's okay—I should have asked about him first." She kicked at the tire of the wheelbarrow with one toe. "But, dammit, Rhys, what were you trying to do to me, Saturday night at the hospital?"

Now it was his turn to avoid a direct confrontation. He forked up a pile of droppings to add to the barrow. "I suppose you mean about lessons for Erin."

"What else? I told you I didn't want you seeing her any more than was absolutely necessary. You said you understood. Encouraging her to think about taking lessons from you is not my idea of cooperation."

"She wants to train with me."

"And I wanted an Olympic medal. Some things just aren't meant to be."

"You could've had a medal, if you hadn't run away."

"Oh, right, that would have been so cute—you and your wife and I, all setting up housekeeping together. Except polygamy is illegal in New York."

"So you ran off, created this fake husband for yourself, and never bothered to let me know you were pregnant."

"There was nothing you could do about that. What was the point of telling you?" She stared into the empty stall beside her, hiding her face from him for a second. "Look, Rhys, we don't have to rehash the past. Just understand that I won't have Erin hanging around with you. I'll give her the one lesson, tomorrow, because I have to work this afternoon. We'll trailer her horse over, she can ride for an hour, and then we're going home. Period." Pivoting on her heel, she marched toward the end of the barn.

Rhys eased past the wheelbarrow, into the aisle. "Erin is my daughter. You said so."

Jacquie stopped in the doorway, where early-morning sunlight struck glints of gold in her braid and silhouetted the slimness of her hips, the straightness of her shoulders. She did not turn back. "What's your point?"

"I can't just forget she exists. Believe it or not, I care about her, even though I just met her for the first time Saturday night."

"No, I don't believe it." Her fists clenched at her sides. Still, she didn't face him. "And even if it were true, it'll be better for both of you if we call a halt right now, before anybody gets more involved. I'm not asking you for anything, Rhys. Not money or time or even the damn riding lessons. Just get on with your life. And stay out of my daughter's."

"The hell I will." With a few quick strides he came up behind her, put a hand on her shoulder and pulled her around. "What do you think I am?"

Even in anger, the physical connection between them caught fire, as it had all those years ago. Rhys felt the heat in his blood, saw the awareness in Jacquie's eyes…until fury rose up to drown it.

"I don't care what you are or what you like. My job is keeping Erin safe. Deal with it." She shook off his hand and walked away again. This time he let her go, because he knew she would be back tomorrow. With Erin.

And by then, he would have his plans in place.

CHAPTER FIVE

SITTING ALONE at lunch on Tuesday, Andrew kept his eyes on his sandwich—except when the cafeteria door opened and some girls walked through. He wasn't looking for anyone special, of course. Just looking.

Halfway into the break, Cathy Parr arrived, surrounded by the same crowd she'd been with every day last week. Carbon-copy blondes, all of them...except for one redhead. A redhead with ice blue eyes.

As she had every day last week, Erin Archer walked by him with a sniff and a lift of her chin. Andrew replied with a shrug, though it took a real effort not to turn and watch her walk down the room to the food line. She'd been cute with black hair, but that red tone gave her an edge he kinda liked. Now that he'd seen her ride, he wouldn't mind getting to know her better. Even if she was a pain in the butt about Imperator.

The girls took their trays to a table within his range of sight and sat down to eat. Erin made sure she had her back to him, which suited Andrew just fine. Who wanted her around, anyway?

"So." Three guys from the jock crowd sat down, one beside him on the bench and two across the table. "You're new, huh?" The one at his shoulder did the talking, while the other two stuck out their beefy hands and nabbed his potato chips.

"Yeah." This encounter would not improve his headache.

"What's your sport? Football? Basketball? Soccer?"

Andrew sighed silently. *Been here, done this, didn't want a T-shirt.* "Horses."

The guys across the table laughed. "Horses? What does that mean?"

"I ride horses."

"You mean, like the girls do? In those fancy pants and shiny boots? With your butt stuck up in the air?"

Andrew didn't deign to answer, and got an elbow in the ribs for his effort.

"Answer me, boy. That's the kind of horse riding you do?"

He shrugged. "At least my fancy pants aren't all shimmery, like your football duds. And I go up against a thousand pounds of sheer animal adrenaline without wearing a bunch of sissy padding. When I fall, I hit the ground, not some other guy's equipment."

Suddenly he was on his feet, courtesy of the fist wrapped in his shirt by the short-tempered guy he'd been sitting next to. "Listen here, you wussy little—" Andrew took a deep breath, centered himself, then sliced down with the side of his hand. Giving a sharp cry, the bully stumbled backward holding his arm against his chest.

"I forgot to mention, I'm also into judo." Andrew gathered his trash. "Comes in handy now and then." Again he pitched the bag toward the trash can. This time, thank God, he made his three-point shot. He walked away looking like a winner.

And he didn't miss Erin Archer's stare following him as he left the room.

The day went downhill from lunch, though, mostly because the football thug turned him in for that chop. Andrew refused to go into details with the assistant principal, who assigned him detention for the rest of the week. That required a call home to tell Terry to pick him up an hour later than normal, which would earn him one lecture when he got into the car, and another when he reached home. Too bad he couldn't give one of his dads to somebody else.

When he walked into the barn that afternoon, the great Lewellyn was standing in the doorway to the office. "How was your day?"

He didn't really want to know, so Andrew shrugged and reached for a pitchfork.

"That's not much of an answer. How do you feel?"

If he shrugged again, he'd get yelled at. "Okay."

"You were in a fight at school?"

"A guy was bugging me about the horses. I had to make a point."

There was a moment of silence. When he glanced at his dad, he was surprised to see a slight smile on his mouth. "Enough said. Erin Archer will be here for a lesson in about ten minutes. Tack up Imperator."

Andrew felt his brain explode. He threw the pitchfork against the wall of the stall and stamped down the aisle toward the office. "You're letting her ride Imp? You've never seen her on a horse and you're letting her ride him, when you won't let me? That so totally sucks, I can't believe it. You're doing it just to punish me, right, because I took him out Saturday—"

"I thought," his dad said, in that voice which

could slice through walls, "I would give the two of you a lesson together. She's bringing her own horse, and you could've ridden the stallion."

With his own shrug, his dad turned back into the office and shut the door. Andrew stood still for a second, paralyzed by the major mistake he'd just made.

Then he picked up a tower of plastic feed buckets waiting to be washed, balanced the stack in one hand over his shoulder and pitched it as hard as he could down the brick-floored aisle of the barn. As far as he was concerned, the clatter of those buckets said all there was to say.

JACQUIE STAYED in the truck after Erin got out to unload and tack up Mirage. She'd brought a book with her and parked the truck in such a way that she had no view of the riding ring. Her investment in the lesson would be nothing more than the time it took, since Rhys had said he owed Erin for catching Imperator.

When she glanced at the rearview mirror though, she caught a glimpse of Andrew astride Imperator. In the bright afternoon sun, the stallion's black coat shone with the gloss of polished lacquer. And the boy-man on his back might have been a young Rhys Lewellyn, filled with the joy of his communion with the magnificent animal.

She was still blinking tears out of her eyes when she saw Rhys himself stride out of the stable. He said something to Andrew, then looked in the direction of her trailer, where Erin was brushing Mirage in preparation for the lesson.

Even through the mirror, Jacquie identified the instant when Rhys focused on her daughter. *His* daughter. The sudden widening of his eyes, the softening of his lips, revealed a vulnerability she would have preferred not to know about. He said he cared, even without knowing Erin at all. Seeing his face in this moment, she believed him.

But she could not—would not—consider Rhys's needs or desires in this situation. Only Erin mattered.

Jacquie opened the truck door and hopped to the ground, intending to insert herself between Erin and any revelation Rhys might think about making. She approached from one side as he drew near in the opposite direction. Between them, their child remained unaware of her role as territory under dispute.

"Hi, Mr. Lewellyn." Erin grinned at him over the horse's back. "We'll be ready in a few minutes."

Rhys's gaze moved beyond her to connect with Jacquie's. Her defiance must have been written on her face, because his expression hardened immediately. He looked at Erin again.

"The lesson begins at four o'clock. You're late."

"I'm sorry—"

"I don't wait on students." The clipped words were an echo of their first meeting, fourteen years ago. Rhys always made sure his students understood his power over them at the very beginning. "In the future, you'll be ready to ride when I arrive. Do your grooming on your own time, not mine." Turning on his heel, he walked toward the riding ring.

With a friendly slap on Mirage's rump as she went by, Jacquie headed after Rhys. She caught up at the side of the ring as he turned toward her. "Good afternoon, Jacquie."

Hands on her hips, she glared at him. "You didn't have to be so rough on her. She's just a kid."

"She's a kid who wants to ride and win, presumably, in an adult world. Therefore, she has to accept adult responsibilities."

"She's not in control. She can't even drive, for pity's sake. The traffic held us up."

"Then you'll have to leave earlier, won't you?" He had the grace to look away from her face after that unfeeling response. "I gave you the same lecture, remember? You survived."

"That's different. I was older."

"Not much. You were eighteen."

"I—" She pressed her fingertips against her eyes for a second. "This is not New York, where everybody is so uptight and stressed. We're more easygoing down here. There's flexibility."

"Not at my barn, there isn't." Beyond them, Erin had saddled her horse and was putting on the bridle. Rhys lifted an eyebrow. "That color can't be real. Why the hell did you let her dye her hair?"

"I didn't *let* her. She surprised me, after your son got on her nerves. Can you believe it?"

He rolled his eyes. "You should make her change it back."

The thought had crossed Jacquie's mind, but now she was certain she wouldn't. "What Erin does with her hair and what I do about it is none of your business."

"All that aside, she's not going to win by being laid-back about the job."

"Riding is not a job, especially not for a ninth-grader."

"Then why is she here? What's the point?" He gave an openhanded shrug. "Either she wants to win big, which means taking lessons from me, or she wants to play around and do something else with her life. It's a choice she needs to make now, Jacquie. You know that, because you faced the same options. She gives her life to the horses, or she's just wasting my time."

"I'm ready." Erin joined them, leading her horse, and looked him in the eye. "I won't be late again, Mr. Lewellyn. Because I have made my choice. I want to win. Like you did."

Jacquie's heart contracted in her chest. Here she was trying to defend her daughter, and Erin not only bowed to the conquest but placed herself firmly on the side of the enemy.

As a reward, Rhys gave her one of his rare smiles. "Okay, then. Let's get started. Andrew, bring Imp into the ring."

Left with the choice of scuttling back to her truck like a beached crab or observing the lesson, Jacquie straightened her back and prepared to maintain her composure for the rest of the hour. She could be indifferent, even with Rhys Lewellyn nearby. No problem.

The riding ring at Fairfield Farm was a large rectangle of well-packed red clay surrounded by a low white fence, with the standard dressage letters marking particular points around the perimeter. Erin guided Mirage through the opening marked *A* in the center of the narrow end, then along the side at a nice walk. Andrew followed, with Imperator sidling underneath him, not totally convinced of the need to go inside the ring.

Beside her, Rhys tensed as he watched his son and his horse. Jacquie knew he wanted to say something, and approved his effort at restraint. Then again, he'd always been a teacher with insight and instinct.

"How old is Mirage?" he said, instead, catching her off guard.

"Um…seven. He's a seven-year-old gelding, Warm-blood sire and Thoroughbred dam."

He had his eyes fixed on Erin across the ring, ignoring the big horse nearby. "Good carriage, good build. She sits him well."

Jacquie couldn't quell a burst of pride. "She's been riding alone since she was three years old."

Rhys smiled tightly. "As did Andrew. It's interesting that we should think so much alike when it comes to training…our…children."

She bristled at the emphasis on *our,* but Rhys walked away, down the long side of the ring, before she could protest. "Pick up the trot, Erin. I want to see strong, forward movement. Andrew, if you can't get the horse under control, get off."

The gibe was unfair, Jacquie thought. Imperator had shaken out most of his high spirits, and Andrew was making progress in settling him down.

"Has he been worked regularly since the season ended?" she asked, following Rhys. "He seems to have the idea that he doesn't really have to do this if he doesn't want to."

Rhys hesitated. "Not regularly, no."

That would explain the fidgets. "Have you decided to retire him to stud?"

"He's a great horse in his prime. Why would I do that?"

"Then why aren't you riding him?"

Instead of answering her, Rhys addressed his students. "More inside leg, Erin. Sit back more in the trot, Andrew. You're letting him pull you forward."

Jacquie refused to be ignored. "Why aren't you riding Imperator? Is he injured?"

Rhys lifted his shoulders impatiently. "Imp is fine. I fell." Staring at him, she waited for further explanation. "In the Adelaide Horse Trials cross-country." He gave her a sidelong glance. "I gather you hadn't heard."

Now she felt embarrassed by her boycott of anything to do with a rider named Lewellyn. "No, I hadn't heard. Nothing serious, I hope." The polite phrase didn't begin to express the sudden gnash of fear in her chest when she thought about what a fall at a championship course like Adelaide might mean.

"I survived."

His dry response told her nothing. Or everything, if she remembered how much he hated showing any weakness. "Did you break something?"

Again he moved away from her and didn't answer the question. "Pick up your canter. I want to see a smooth transition." Mirage fumbled the change from the trot and ended up with the wrong foot in front. "Wrong lead, Erin. Back to trot, try again. Andrew, that transition had all the finesse of a tractor in the middle of the road. Again." For the next thirty minutes, his focus on the lesson was so intense that Jacquie couldn't have gotten another question in if she'd tried.

But she didn't have to, because Terry O'Neal stepped up beside her. "That girl of yours looks like a winner. Light, strong, determined. As her mother was."

"All we need is a star-quality horse. Mirage is good, but I don't think he can take her all the way. He's not big enough to compete with horses like Imperator." She paused while Rhys expressed his critique of a move Erin had just completed. "I understand Imperator hasn't competed recently. Rhys took a fall in Adelaide?"

"He told you?"

"Not willingly. How badly was he hurt?" Why did she have to know?

"Not as bad as we thought to begin with. He was paralyzed for three days, until the swelling around his spine subsided."

An image of Rhys confined to a hospital bed clouded her vision. Jacquie squeezed her eyes shut. "That must have been terrifying."

"Turned out to be just bruising and torn muscles. The doctors suggested a six-month layoff."

"He hasn't worked since November?"

"Not on the champion, here. He's schooled some of the other horses on the flat."

"Is he doing therapy?" She couldn't seem to let the subject drop. "Some kind of treatment?"

"He's got a whirlpool bath, and he does the exercises the therapist taught him most nights. But work is the best medicine for a man like him. And for the horse."

A welcome diversion. "Imperator wasn't hurt?"

"Skinned his back legs, is all. He jumped right up

and covered half the county while the rest of us were looking after Rhys.''

She smiled, not surprised. As Andrew and Rhys put Imperator through his exercises, the horse's energy was easy to see.

''That's good, Erin.'' Rhys nodded and clapped his hands. ''You had him nicely collected there. Andrew, you're letting the horse get away with being lazy. Use your seat to move him forward but your legs keep him slow. That's better.'' When Imp had completed his collected circuit, Rhys clapped his hands. ''Okay, you two, let's move over to the jumping arena. We'll do some stadium work.''

Terry gave a grunt of surprise and Jacquie looked at him. ''What's wrong?''

''Nothing. He's never let the boy jump this horse, is all. There's a first time for everything, though.''

The jumping ring, with its wooden fences painted in bright colors against white, lay beyond the riding ring. Jacquie followed Terry and arrived in time to hear him ask Rhys, ''Are you sure about this?''

Rhys nodded. ''Crossbars, to begin with. Okay, Erin, take this line in front of me at a slow canter. Easy does it.''

Mirage, who considered jumping his raison d'être, sailed easily over the three fences, each with two poles crossed low in the center, supported two feet off the ground by standards on the outsides.

''Good,'' Rhys said, ''though a little fast. Okay, Andrew.''

Imperator's easy canter brought him quickly to the fences, which he barely seemed to notice. Terry moved into the ring and lifted one board to form a straight line across each of the three jumps, setting the other at a prescribed distance on the ground.

"Again," Rhys said, and the horses flew through the air once again, their young riders in control. The bar on the jumps got raised to two feet, three inches, then two-six and two-nine. Rhys added several other jumps to the course, including a lattice work fence and an oxer—a jump with two parallel boards making the fence wider.

"Imp twisted a little on the oxer," Rhys called after Andrew finished. "Did you feel him? Let's run it again before we raise the height."

Erin took her turn and Mirage did his usual magic. "That's it for today," Rhys called. "Good job." Grinning, Erin rode Mirage off to the trailer to untack.

Andrew began his circle toward the line of jumps. Imperator came forward at a reasonable canter, but at the base of the first jump he stiffened his front legs and slid to a complete stop. The boy fell onto the big horse's neck and slipped a little sideways, but managed to hang on.

"What the hell was that?" He looked at his father. "What did I do?"

Eyes narrowed, Rhys shook his head. "I don't know. Come again."

Again Andrew circled and approached the jump. Imperator thundered on until the last moment, then screeched to a halt.

"You're a bit forward on his shoulders. Sit back more."

The third time, instead of stopping, Imperator cut out to the side, away from the jump. Andrew circled back and, using his heels and his crop, tried to drive the big horse over the bar. Imperator bucked and hopped away, with Andrew clinging like a sandspur to his mane.

Both Terry and Rhys wore grim expressions, suggesting they saw more in this rebellion than simple horse fidgets. Erin came up on Jacquie's other side.

"What happened?"

Jacquie explained while Andrew calmed the horse down and then brought him to the side of the ring. "Well?"

Rhys stood silent for a moment. Then he looked at Terry. Finally his gaze came to Jacquie and he lifted a brow in question. "Would you?"

She opened her eyes wide. "Ride him?"

"You've got the skill and the experience to get him across, if anybody here does."

"But you—"

He shook his head. "My...back...is bothering me today. I'd consider it a favor if you would ride the horse over this jump."

How many times in her life would she get the chance to ride an Olympic champion? Jacquie couldn't find the strength to resist. "Erin, run get your helmet for me."

She walked to where Imperator stood and put a hand under his nose. "What's going on, big guy? These jumps are like rain puddles, right? You don't even think about them." He sniffed at her palm and along her wrist. "That's right. You just got confused for a minute, didn't you?"

Andrew slid to the ground with a thump. "I can't think of anything you could do that I wasn't already doing." His face was tight with hurt pride.

"You're probably right, and he'll probably dump me at the first fence." Buckling on Erin's helmet, Jacquie smiled at him. "I'm just taking advantage of your dad's invitation to ride a spectacular horse. Humor me, okay?"

The boy's face softened. "Yeah, okay." He handed her the reins. "Want me to give you a leg up?"

"I'll do it." Terry walked up beside them. "Ready, Miss Jacquie?"

"Sure." No one had used the term "Miss" for her in years, and it gave her the jitters. She grabbed the reins and the back of the saddle, then bent her left leg. Terry took hold of her at the knee and ankle and tossed her up toward the back of the horse. Imperator stood over seventeen hands at the shoulder—a total of sixty-eight inches, three more than Jacquie was tall. The ground looked a long way away. "Okay, then. A couple of warm-up laps, I think." When she glanced at Rhys, he gave her a nod. With a gulp and a deep breath, she set out on the ride of her life.

Rhys watched closely as Jacquie trotted Imperator around the track along the rail of the arena. The first time he'd seen her ride, he'd been impressed with her control, her balance, her intelligence in working the horse. Nothing had changed. She handled Imp as if they'd worked together for years, reading his signals, imposing her will with finesse and strength. When they shifted to a canter, he nodded.

"That's the way a transition is done," he told Andrew. "Just a lift and a step forward in the new gait."

"She's pretty amazing," his son admitted.

Erin, on Rhys's other side, grinned.

After two rounds of canter, Jacquie circled at the

bottom of the arena and came around to the jumps. Andrew and Terry had lowered the poles back to two-six. Imperator started to balk, but Jacquie urged him over with her legs and voice. Still, he twisted his hind feet to the side, as he had with Andrew over the higher fence.

"He remembers Adelaide," Terry commented. "He was pretty badly scraped up after that bloody jump."

"We can work on the twist." After a second go over the three simple fences, Rhys signaled Terry to raise the height to two-nine. Jacquie's riding got the horse across. Even in the chilly afternoon, with the light dimming, Imp wore a coat of lather on his chest and between his rear legs. White foam dripped from his mouth.

Terry grunted. "This is the most he's been worked since November."

Jacquie rode to a stop in front of them. "Do you want to try three feet?" Her face glowed and her eyes were bright with excitement. "Shouldn't be too tough for a big guy like this." She gave Imp a firm pat on the shoulder. "He's an amazing ride. I've never felt such physical power."

Rhys's thoughts jumped back in time…to the nights he'd spent with Jacquie in the apartment over the stable in New York, and how much power they'd shared between them as they made love. Sometimes he'd felt as if they'd lived through an earthquake.

With his eyes fixed on her face, he saw the same memory take hold in her mind. A flood of color swept through her cheeks, and she turned her eyes to Imp's mane. "So, do you want me to try three feet?"

"Sure," he said, struggling to get his mind back on track. Andrew hopped into the arena to fix the jumps even as Terry growled, "Bad idea, if you ask me. The horse isn't jumping right. One of them's going to be hurt."

In the same second that Rhys realized Terry was right, it was too late. Jacquie had made her circle and was coming up to the jumps at a slow, steady canter. *Maybe it will be okay,* was his last thought as Imperator cut violently to the side at the initial fence. He humped his back and kicked out with his rear legs, then sat back on his haunches and pawed at the air with his front hooves. Just as it looked as if the big horse would end up on the ground on his back with his rider underneath him, Jacquie fell off.

Imperator thudded down to earth again and galloped straight out of the arena. Swearing, Terry and Andrew followed.

Rhys was beside Jacquie almost as soon as she hit the ground. She lay on her side, curled into a ball. Her eyes were shut. He couldn't even see her breathing.

"Dammit, Lennon, are you okay?"

"No...air." The words were a sort of gasp.

He ran his hands gently over her back, her arms. No obvious broken bones. "Can you move?"

Her body jerked, and uncurled a bit. "Maybe." One word, but less strained than before. She moved her arms, managed to prop herself up on an elbow. "Knocked...the air out...of me." Her short laugh sounded rough. "Couldn't breathe for a minute there."

If she could laugh, Rhys figured he could do a more thorough examination. He felt her legs from ankles to thighs, took her head in his hands and tilted it gently from side to side. "What hurts?"

"My pride, mostly." She pushed his hands away and got to her knees, then, with Erin's help, to her feet. "I thought I would be the miracle worker for the great horse." Brushing dirt off her shoulder and side, she frowned. "He's afraid of the fences, Rhys. He tenses up as soon as he sees the poles, and the closer you get, the stiffer he feels."

"I'll worry about the horse later. Come into the house and sit down. You need something to drink and some painkiller."

She shook her head. "I'm okay. Erin and I will just load up and get home."

"Like hell you will." He turned and watched as Terry and Andrew led Imperator into the barn, then looked at Jacquie again. "My horse could've killed you. The least I can do is give you a drink."

Still she hesitated. Maybe she thought he was using the invitation as a ploy to get closer to Erin. The truth wasn't much different, he supposed. "I would like to keep an eye on you for a few minutes to be sure you're sound enough to drive home. And I have a project I'd like your help with."

Her eyes widened, and she glanced at Erin, standing between them. "I really don't think—"

"Come on, Mom." Erin put her arm around Jacquie and urged her toward the house. "You'd make me sit down if I'd fallen like that. You practically dived into the grass."

"I thought he was going over backward. I didn't want to be underneath when he hit the ground."

Rhys walked on her other side. "I can't believe I

suggested you ride him to begin with. A stupid idea, if there ever was one, and I'm sorry.''

She let him open the door into the house. ''Don't worry about it.'' He saw her shoulders lift on a deep breath before she stepped inside. And he saw her wince.

''You are hurt,'' he insisted. ''We should take you to the E.R.''

''No. Just a little stiff and bruised. Nothing that a hot bath and a good night's sleep can't cure.''

Damn if she hadn't done it again. Jacquie in the bathtub was a tantalizing thought. They'd shared showers, in that cramped little place she'd rented above the horse barn, but he'd always promised himself the sight of her immersed to her neck in bubbles, and the pleasure of joining her.

Rhys cleared his throat. ''Come on into the library.'' He led the way this time, stopping to greet Sydney as he crossed the carpet. Her arthritis might be bad, but her nose worked just fine, and she discerned immediately that there were others in the room. One sniff at Jacquie's hand, and she knew exactly who. Her body wagged from ear tips to tail as she recognized an old friend.

Jacquie sat in the nearest chair and brought Sydney between her knees. ''Hey, sweetheart. How are you? An old girl now, huh? You remember me, don't you? Yeah, we had good times, didn't we?''

Erin knelt beside them. ''You knew this dog when you were in New York, Mom? She must be pretty old.''

''Ancient.'' Jacquie chuckled. ''It was fourteen—'' Rhys heard her sharp breath ''—years ago. It's good to see her.'' She took the cola he brought without looking at him. ''Thank you,'' she said to Sydney's adoring face.

''You're welcome.'' As he sat in a chair across the room, the tramp of feet in the hallway announced Terry and Andrew coming from the barn. When Terry looked in, Rhys motioned for him to step inside. ''I want to talk to all of you.''

Andrew stood just within the door frame. He grimaced when he saw Sydney fawning over Jacquie and Erin, but said nothing.

''The horse seems none the worse for wear,'' Terry volunteered. ''Plunged into his dinner bucket just like always.''

''Nice to hear. I hope we can say the same for Jacquie when she gets home.'' He smiled at her, trying to ease the way for what he was about to say.

Her lips twitched, but if she wanted to smile she hid it well. ''I think I'll manage soup and crackers, at least.''

''Well, then.'' Hands flat on his knees, he looked at each one of them in turn. ''I have set some fairly big plans into motion, and I wanted to let you know what's going on.''

All of their faces asked the same question—what did Jacquie and Erin have to do with *his* plans?

''I want to have an open house and schooling day at Fairfield Farms. I'd like to let the general community know this is a place to look for lessons, and I want other riders and trainers in the area to be aware we're here. So I'm setting up a combined training event—we'll have dressage, show jumping and a short cross-country course—and a tour of the barn and house, since I'm told this is considered one of the finest old houses in the area. I'm flying in judges from the Northeast, but I'll need lots of other volunteers for all the work beforehand.''

He looked at Terry, who nodded, and then at Erin and Andrew. ''I'm hoping you two can do a lot of the detail chores—making signs, setting up and taking down, not to mention competing in the events.'' Erin nodded enthusiastically. Andrew, as usual, just shrugged.

Then Rhys looked at the woman in the chair. ''I'm really hoping for your help, Jacquie. You probably know every owner and trainer in the county by their first name. I want to send out invitations, and you can help me make up the list. We'll need a farrier on the site, of course, plus EMTs and a vet. I think I can bring off a good show, but I know having your assistance will make a real difference.''

She stared at him with those wide green eyes for a long minute. Finally, wincing, she got to her feet and walked across to set her glass down on the drinks tray.

''Thank you for Erin's lesson,'' she said quietly, directly to Rhys. ''And for the chance to ride Imperator. I'll never forget him.''

He got to his feet to face her. ''But…?''

Jacquie lifted her chin. ''But there's no way in—'' she glanced at their daughter, standing behind her with a startled expression on her face ''—no way in the world I would consider helping you with your 'project' or allowing Erin to compete.''

''Good night.'' She nodded at Terry and at Andrew. ''Come on Erin, let's get home.''

And just like that, she walked out the door.

CHAPTER SIX

Jacquie had the driver's door to the truck open and one foot inside when Rhys caught up with her. "I need to talk to you," he said, his breath a white plume in the cold night air.

She shook her head. "We do not have anything to talk about. Goodbye, Rhys."

He stood with his hands in the pockets of his jacket, his feet planted apart, and stared at her. "If you want me to keep my mouth shut, I suggest you listen to what I have to say now."

"You're threatening me?"

Erin came up on the other side of the truck after transferring Mirage from one of the stalls in the barn to the trailer. "Mom?"

"Get in, Erin." Jacquie tried to do the same, but Rhys clamped his hand on her arm.

"Erin, your mother and I need to talk in the barn a minute. She'll be back shortly."

To get him to let go of her, if for no other reason, Jacquie conceded. She tossed Erin the keys. "Start the engine, so you'll be warm. This won't take but a couple of minutes."

Once in the barn, she turned to face him. "Okay, you've got two minutes." She looked at her watch, intending to hold him to exactly that.

"Why won't you work with me on this show?"

"Because I see what you're trying to do and I won't cooperate."

"And what is that?"

"You're trying to get Erin over here. You want to have her around so one day it'll slip out that you're her father. You're trying to finesse the promise you made to me that you wouldn't."

"Not very honorable of me."

"Neither was sleeping with me while you were still married."

His mouth tightened, and he jerked his head back as if she'd slapped him. Jacquie knew it wasn't fair, but she couldn't let him win this battle.

"Don't make it sound like I'm some kind of Lothario. I was in love with you, Jacquie."

She ignored the hurt of "was." "Are we finished? I'm not going to let Erin run around over here like it's her second home. I'm not going to tell her the truth about you, and—"

"What does that say about you?"

"I beg your pardon?"

"You won't tell our daughter the truth. What kind of relationship is based on perpetual lies?"

"That's the end. I'm leaving." She tried to stalk past him. Again Rhys grabbed her arm. This time, he backed her up against one of the stall doors and held her there with the size and nearness of his body.

"You can't run away from this, Jacquie. You can't run away from me."

For a moment, she forgot why she wanted to run. Within her reach was the power she'd craved all those years ago, the warmth and textures of a body she could still remember, under her palms, against her skin. The diamond-blue gaze speared her, held her motionless but for the pulse pounding in her throat. As she stared up at him, Rhys lowered his head and put his mouth on hers.

After the first shock, her lips softened against his, and warmed. They might have kissed yesterday, or this morning, the feel and the taste were so familiar. They devoured each other, erasing the empty years. His arms locked around her, lifting her against his body, and she grabbed his shoulders to draw him closer still. Rhys groaned and murmured her name.

Jacquie regained her sanity in that instant. She struggled wildly, hitting at his shoulders and twisting until he let go and staggered backward, swearing. Running down the aisle, she thought she heard him say her name, but she didn't stop, and only slowed down as she approached her side of the truck. Over the sound of her harsh breaths, she could hear Mirage contentedly munching hay.

Erin had fallen asleep waiting, thank God. Blinking back tears, Jacquie drove out through the stone arch of Fairfield Farm, promising herself this would be the last time. Coming here was simply too dangerous. For her daughter...

And for herself.

WHEN HIS TEMPER and his desire had cooled, Rhys returned to the house. He found Terry in the kitchen with warm soup and bread set out for their supper.

"The boy ate fast and said precious little." He reached for the whiskey bottle in the cupboard and poured several fingers into a glass which he handed to Rhys. "I'm guessing you didn't make much progress with Miss Jacquie."

"A masterpiece of understatement." Rhys took a swallow of spirits before sitting down, and another afterward. "What do you think about Imperator?"

Terry took a chair across the table. "This was his first time over fences since November. He's got a right to be skittish."

"She says he's afraid of the jumps." No need to name names.

"Could be. One ride's not enough to be sure, though."

"He needs regular workouts. We'll give him tomorrow off, then try again Thursday."

"You won't put the boy up on him again? He's not experienced enough to hold that horse together."

"I know." Rhys propped his head up with one hand and stirred his soup without any twinge of appetite. "I'll ride him."

Terry snorted and got up to take the bowl away. "And what if he rears on you the way he did this afternoon? What if you fall the way she did? Your back's scarcely healed, as it is."

With his eyes closed and his stomach churning, Rhys endured a mental replay of Jacquie's fall. The soft sand in the jumping arena was a lifesaver. Hard ground hurt so much worse...

His vision seemed to waver, shifting until he saw the fall from the perspective of the rider. He knew how time slowed, seemed to crawl, as the jump approached and you realized you weren't going to make it this time, that you'd chosen the wrong angle, set the horse too fast down the hill. The big logs loomed close, the deep ditch even closer...Imperator took off too flat, they wouldn't clear...the rustle of brush on front legs and then the hard smack of hooves against wood and Rhys was tumbling, twisting, landing draped across that log like a piece of laundry hung to dry...

He squeezed his eyes shut, fighting the sickness that threatened to overtake him. When he looked at Terry again, he found the Irishman staring at him with both surprise and concern.

"I wasn't sure till now," his friend said gently. "This isn't about the pain, is it?"

Rhys didn't answer, which was as good as a confession.

"There's no shame in being nervous after a bad fall. Why didn't you say something?"

Nervous didn't qualify. *Terrified* might work. "I'll get past this. I have to."

Terry laid a hand on his shoulder. "Sure, you will. I'm thinking all you need is time. But the horse has his own troubles to deal with. Who'll ride him out of them?"

Before Rhys could reply, the phone rang. He knew it wouldn't be Jacquie...unless something had happened on the way home. The possibility had him snatching up the phone. "Lewellyn."

"Hadn't heard from you since you left, thought you might have vanished amidst the savages." Owen Lewellyn had little use for the normal etiquette of "hello."

"No, sir, just getting settled in."

"Putting the horse back to work?"

"Of course." Not exactly a lie.

"About time. I've got no patience for an animal that doesn't earn its keep."

Rhys pressed the heel of his hand against one pounding temple. "I'll be running him for the first time in about six weeks, at a schooling day I'm arranging for promotional purposes. The first weekend in March, if you'd like to attend."

"From Olympic champion to a dinky farm schooling day. Quite a comedown for the great Imperator."

"Not at all. This is sophisticated horse country, and Imperator will be the drawing card, the premier attraction. Then he'll be perfectly fit in time for the Top Flight trials at the beginning of April. Nothing dinky about that event."

"Well, you'd better see to it that he wins. He's no good to us if all he does is eat his bloody head off."

"I'm the one paying for his feed."

His father cracked a harsh laugh. "Temporarily. I give you six months before you roll up your tents and come back where you belong. Meantime, get the horse in shape and making money, or else I'll call in my option and sell him to the highest bidder." Without a goodbye, the phone line went dead.

"Andrew gets his wish." Rhys put down the phone and looked at Terry across the width of the kitchen. "He'll start working with Imperator on the jumps Thursday afternoon."

"And yourself?"

Shaking his head, Rhys retreated into the hallway and wearily climbed the stairs. As little as he knew *why* he was afraid did he know what to do about it.

But he owed Imperator his best, even if that meant

training another rider to take his place. And who better than his own son?

He stood for a minute in Andrew's doorway, watching him sleep. The room was unnaturally neat, a remnant from the years with his mother. Tonight, he sprawled across the bed in unconscious abandon, more vulnerable than Rhys had seen him since he was a toddler. Olivia had taken the boy away just after his first birthday, holding him hostage to gain a favorable divorce settlement.

Rhys had finally gotten him back last summer, along with the chance to undo thirteen years of estrangement. What he knew about being a parent could fit in a thimble—his own father being an example of exactly how he did not intend to behave. Yet, all too often, he and Andrew seemed to be treading the familiar path of rebellion and retribution.

Not for a lack of concern, at least on Rhys's part. He'd cared deeply about his son from the moment he knew the baby existed, and had only allowed Andrew to leave with Olivia because it seemed best for such a young child to be with his mother.

Now a boy turning into a man, Andrew was worthy of respect from his peers and from his father. His academic gifts surpassed Rhys's achievements, and his riding ability would soon do the same. Rhys wanted—needed—to work with his son, to develop a partnership they would both value. The beginning of that collaboration was not, so far, very promising.

With a sigh, Rhys turned to his own room. Now there was Erin, complicating the situation even further. And Jacquie—a woman every bit as desirable as

she was fourteen years ago. But much stronger. For-
midable, even.

And completely convinced that she never wanted to
see him again.

"WHY DON'T YOU WANT to help Mr. Lewellyn with
his show?" After waking up for a fast food dinner,
Erin voiced her question in the quiet darkness of the
drive home.

"I've got enough to do, just taking care of what we
already have scheduled." Jacquie drew a sharp breath,
blew it out quickly. "I don't have time for such a big
project."

"You said you won't even let me compete."

That had been a mistake, born of panic. "You've
got plenty of shows on your schedule."

"And you're not taking me back for more lessons."
The calm statements were totally unlike Erin's usual
hyperactive dialogue. She sounded like a weary adult.

Jacquie felt like a rebellious teenager. "I told you
this would be the only one."

"You never said why. But I can see you don't like
Mr. Lewellyn very much. Was he mean, when you
trained with him in New York?"

"Not mean. Strict, the way he was with you this
afternoon." She didn't want to think about Rhys.

Erin wanted to talk about nothing else. "I like him.
I want to ride with him."

Fighting the urge to scream, Jacquie couldn't form
a reply.

"Maybe I could get a ride home with Andrew on
my lesson days, and you wouldn't have to drive into
town."

"So I can load up Mirage all by myself, plus your tack and your clothes, and bring them out here? Would you like me to have him saddled and waiting when you arrive?"

Bitch! she screamed at herself.

Erin didn't say another word, but turned her face to the side window and rode the rest of the way in silence. There was no friendly chatter while they fed the horses, no request for homework help after dinner. Once again, they went to their separate rooms for the night with anger between them.

Rhys had been in North Carolina for barely two weeks and already she and her daughter were more at odds than they had been in the previous fourteen years.

How could she possibly allow him any further into their life?

JACQUIE KNEW she'd been given a sign from above when all three of the clients she had scheduled for the last Thursday in January called before 8:00 a.m. that morning to cancel.

"I get a day off," she said with glee as she drove Erin to school. "A whole day without the clang of an anvil in my ears. Can you believe it?"

"Why don't I get a day off?" Erin stuck out her lower lip in a pretend pout. "I'm tired of the whole school thing."

"You'll get President's Day in just a couple of weeks. And winter break. And spring break. Not to mention the whole summer, when I'll be out in the heat shoeing horses while you laze around in the house."

"But I want today, too. What are you going to do?"

Jacquie couldn't actually envision a day empty of hammers and horseshoe nails. "I'm not sure. What do you suggest?"

"Well, first you buy me some new clothes. And some new shoes. And a couple of new CDs, maybe some more new clothes…oh, and you pick me up so we can go to lunch somewhere. How's that sound?"

"Like you're still asleep and dreaming." Stopping the truck in the drop-off lane, she ruffled her daughter's red hair. "Have a good day."

"Oh, sure." But Erin laughed as she closed the door, and ran to catch up with Cathy Parr. The two girls walked together into the school building, chattering all the way.

"Now what?" Jacquie cast a glance at the Carolina Diner just across the street, already tasting her favorite bacon-and-eggs platter. But the bowl of oatmeal she'd eaten for breakfast would be enough calories for the morning, especially on a day when she wasn't doing any actual work. Maybe the diner for lunch. Abby and Charlie made fantastic cheeseburgers.

By late morning, she had gotten the oil changed in the truck, visited a hair salon for a shampoo and trim, checked out a couple of her favorite dress shops. The jeans, sweatshirt and turtleneck she'd started out the day wearing were replaced by a pair of dark brown wool slacks and a heathery green sweater, along with the new pair of clogs she'd needed to match the outfit.

She was standing on Main Street in downtown New Skye, staring at the rings in the window of Ryan's Jewelry Store, when someone spoke behind her.

"Looks like someone is on a spending spree. Are diamonds next on the list?"

"What makes you think I'm spending?" She didn't glance back at him, but felt Rhys come up to stand at her shoulder.

"I saw you in the parking lot at school this morning. You wore a dark blue sweatshirt, a yellow turtleneck, and you had your hair in a ponytail. A nice look, but you've got to admit you've upgraded considerably in the last three hours."

He'd noticed her amidst all the traffic and teenagers? She turned around. "What are you doing in town today?"

"I had to file some forms with the county offices for the schooling day, and I thought I'd spend a little time getting to know my new hometown. Would you like to be my guide?"

"No" came automatically to her lips, but Jacquie hesitated, aware of a sudden, almost painful desire to let herself enjoy his company. She'd never seen him in January before—they'd only spent the months from June until September together. After their...breakup...she'd tried to imagine what he would look like during the other seasons, but finally she'd realized she couldn't keep wondering and expect to heal her heart.

Now she could see that winter was good to Rhys— he looked young and rested and charming this morning in an ice-blue pullover sweater and dark jeans under a green barn coat, with the mild sun glinting in the shock of hair falling over his forehead. His wide shoulders were relaxed, his eyes laughing, his smile a little cocky.

"I won't bite," he promised with a wink, "if you don't."

Jacquie couldn't repress a smile. "It's a deal."

They walked all around downtown New Skye while she explained the ongoing revitalization plans, the push to bring merchants and restaurants back to what had once been deserted storefronts. The leafless pear trees and empty planters along the newly bricked Main Street seemed to blossom with spring flowers as she described the annual Azalea Festival, the New Skye International Weekend, and the Dickens Christmas celebration which took place every year.

"New Skye is small," she finished up, as they came back to the jeweler's window. "But it's a really nice place to live."

"I can see that." Rhys rubbed his hands together. "But with those clouds moving in, it's cold, too. Is there somewhere nearby we could get some lunch? And a hot drink?"

He saw panic edge into Jacquie's gaze. "Nowhere special," he added. "Just a hot dog and coffee."

"Well, there is the Carolina Diner…"

"Too crowded, don't you think?" She wouldn't want to be seen with him. Glancing around, he noticed Drew's Coffee Shop across the street and down a short distance. "How about Drew's? Doesn't look very busy from here."

Jacquie's shoulders relaxed. "That's a good idea. We won't have to drive."

Rhys could hear her unspoken thought—*And I won't have to explain you to anyone I know.*

Then, as he started to follow her through the door into the coffee shop, she stopped dead on the threshold. He put a hand on her shoulder to steady her after their bump, and followed her line of vision to see what had stopped her in her tracks.

"Jacquie!" A lovely woman with short dark hair and a wide smile was coming toward them. "I haven't see you since the holidays. How are you?" Rhys dropped his hand as the woman took Jacquie in a gentle hug. "Not working today?"

"Kate." After a second's pause, Jacquie returned the embrace. "I'm fine. You look wonderful." She lifted her head to greet the man who joined them. "Hey, Dixon. Good to see you."

Taller than Rhys by a couple of inches, Dixon bent to kiss Jacquie's cheek. "You, too, Madam Farrier. You did a great job on those nags of mine, as usual."

"They make it easy." Flushing, Jacquie turned to Rhys. "I always seem to be introducing you to my friends. This is Dixon Bell and his wife Kate, both of whom graduated in my high-school class. I'd like y'all to meet Rhys Lewellyn. He recently moved to the area with his horses."

"Welcome to New Skye," Kate Bell said. "Come sit down with us and warm up. It's getting colder by the minute out there."

They all settled into small ironwork chairs around an equally small ice-cream–parlor table. In the shuffle to get settled, Jacquie's knee pushed into Rhys's thigh. He held himself still, hoping she wouldn't notice, hoping she wouldn't move away.

A waitress with a crew cut dyed lime-green came to take their order. "You need anything else, Dixon?"

"Thanks, Daphne. I'm good."

She closed her eyes. "I'm sure you are."

Mr. and Mrs. Bell and Jacquie looked at each other and snickered. "She's got it bad for you," Jacquie told Dixon.

"I have never encouraged her," he said, holding up his hand as if to swear.

His wife patted his elbow. "You're her fantasy, sweetheart. It's all right." She looked at Rhys. "What kind of horses do you have, Mr. Lewellyn?"

"Rhys, please."

Her smile was a gift. "I'm Kate."

"Kate." He nodded. "I ride eventing horses. Dressage, cross-country, and stadium jumping."

Jacquie rolled her eyes. "Rhys is being modest. He's been to the Olympics twice, and took home the gold in the last games."

Dixon and Kate sat back in their chairs, their eyes wide. "That's right—Imperator," Kate said. "I remember now. I read an article about the two of you last fall sometime, didn't I?"

"You're not just any horseman, then," Dixon said. "Are you planning to continue your Olympic career from this area?"

They talked horses for a while, because it turned out that Dixon kept a couple of his own at Phoebe Moss's barn, and had spent years as a cowboy himself, a type of riding for which Rhys had great respect. The conversation veered through Jacquie's role as the farrier in keeping horses sound and on to Kate's desire to learn freestyle dressage.

"I think I would enjoy the chance to ride in rhythm with music," she said. "Like performing a ballet."

"Or a waltz, or even the rumba," Rhys agreed. "I've done some freestyle in the past and it can be as pleasurable as dancing to great music with someone you love.'' Under the table, Jacquie's leg jerked, and she pulled her chair back a good six inches, breaking their connection. ''If you'd like to pursue freestyle dressage, I'd be glad to work with you.''

''That would be wonderful.''

Dixon shook his head. ''I can see I've got some fancy, high-priced European horses in my future.''

''You'd better write a few more songs,'' Jacquie told him. ''A couple of number-one hits ought to cover the price of a Dutch Warmblood, I think. Dixon writes songs for a living,'' she explained to Rhys, while Daphne set their plates down on the table. ''In addition to being a cowboy and a roughneck and whatever else he did all those years he was gone.''

''I'm not the only one who ran away,'' he retorted.

''I came back before you did,'' Jacquie pointed out.

''Children, children,'' Kate said gently. ''Eat your lunch or I'll send you to your rooms.''

After a meal filled with laughter on all sides, the four of them braved the freshening wind out on the sidewalk.

''It's a real pleasure to meet you.'' Dixon held out a hand to Rhys. ''I imagine we'll be in touch about dressage lessons and all that. For somebody who never rode before, my wife has taken quite an interest in the equine world.''

''It's a good place to be,'' Rhys said. ''Call me anytime.''

''Will do.''

The Bells went to their car, a blue Volvo parked nearby at the curb, and Rhys followed Jacquie in the opposite direction.

"That wasn't so bad," he said finally, when she didn't say anything at all. "Nothing dire happened."

She walked slowly, head down and hands in her pants pockets. "It's only a matter of time."

"If you simply told your friends, and Erin, the worst would be over."

"Except for the fact that Erin will hate me. My parents will be hurt and ashamed. My friends will be disappointed, and—"

"And they'll all get over it. Even Erin."

Jacquie shook her head. "I don't think so. I don't think Erin would ever forgive me."

Rhys put a hand on her arm and turned her to face him. "For caring about her? For sacrificing everything you wanted to be her mother? For giving her life and love and your unwavering support when there were other, easier options?" He shook his head. "Erin is not stupid. She'll understand, if you'll just give her the chance."

Eyes filling with tears, Jacquie stared at him for a moment. Then she stepped back. "I can't," she said in a broken voice. "I can't risk it."

Then she turned, walking swiftly away from him into the gray afternoon, without a single glance back.

"You have to," Rhys told her quietly, though she was long out of earshot. "Because I can't let either of you go."

ANDREW TAPPED HIS PENCIL on the table, then stopped when he got a dirty look from the librarian. "Shh."

He rolled his eyes. Where was this kid anyway, the one he was supposed to tutor in math? At this rate, they'd barely get their books open and the bell would ring for the next class.

The library door squeaked behind him, and he turned around to see Erin Archer coming in.

No. No way. He was supposed to tutor *her?*

She looked as surprised, and as disgusted, as he felt. "You're the third-period math tutor?"

"Yeah. What's the problem?"

"I don't want to work with you."

He flipped his pencil in the air and caught it. "So fail. It's no skin off my nose."

"My mom won't let me ride in the Top Flight trials if I fail math this semester."

"Well, then..." Andrew kicked the chair beside him out from the table.

"Shh," the librarian said.

Erin slid into the seat and put her books on the table. "How's Imperator?" she whispered. "Is he jumping?"

"I've been riding him over the stadium fences for...what?...two weeks now. That's when you were there, right?" He shrugged. "Imp's doing okay. But nobody has tried him on cross-country."

"You could."

"My dad says no." Though Andrew had tried just about every way he could think of to change his mind.

"How's Imp going to be ready for the schooling day, much less the horse trials at the first of April?"

"No clue."

The librarian came to stand over them. "Mr. Lewellyn. Ms. Archer. Either you will focus on the purpose for which you are here, or you will return to your scheduled classes. No more of this horse talk. Do you understand?''

"Yes, ma'am," they said in unison.

"Somebody's got to get Imperator over the big fences,'' Erin wrote on a piece of notebook paper.

"The only question,'' Andrew wrote back, ''is who?''

WHEN THE PHONE RANG on Monday, Groundhog Day, Jacquie was almost relieved to hear Rhys's voice on the other end of the line.

"Jacquie? How have you been?''

"The same as usual. Why?'' Talking with him had to be an improvement over struggling to keep him out of her thoughts, to forget the hour they had spent together downtown, the laughter they'd shared. And that kiss…

"I forgot to ask last week…if you'd come up with anything more serious than bruises after that fall.''

"Nope. I bounce pretty well.''

He chuckled, a low ripple of sound that did lovely, forbidden things deep inside of her. "That's true. I've watched you fall a dozen times or more, and you always get right back up.''

"A useful trick when you're trying to hold on to the hoof of a two-thousand-pound Clydesdale with an attitude.''

"So I understand.''

"Did you really call to talk about my little gymnastics stunt?''

"Er, no.''

"Well?''

"Terry and I were talking about Imperator. Andrew's been riding him over the stadium jumps, and he's improving, but we need to get him back to the cross-country training. We wondered…would you would agree to ride the horse? Train him for us?''

''Rhys—''

''Imperator is at the peak of his powers as an eventing horse—he's smart, and he knows all the tricks. I need someone who's experienced enough to anticipate the tricks and head him off. Andrew simply doesn't qualify.''

The explanation made sense, but he'd glossed over one very important point. ''Why don't you ride him?''

He hesitated for a moment. ''I…the doctors don't recommend jumping just yet.'' Another pause. ''But Imperator has already fallen behind. If we don't start getting him in shape now, especially if he's lost his confidence at the jumps, the whole season will be a washout.''

''I'm not an Olympic-level rider, Rhys. I can't take him over those cross-country fences.''

''You're riding at the upper levels on your mare. If we can get Imp schooled that far, I'm sure he'll do the rest.''

She clutched at her resentment as an excuse. ''Why should I do you any favors?''

''What about the horse? He's a winner because he loves competing. Right now, I think it's just the idea of jumping that bothers him, since the fall. Once he gets over the mental block, he'll be his old self. And you'll have rehabilitated an Olympic champion.''

Temptation, as far as Jacquie was concerned, came in the shape of a horse. Almost every time she'd been in serious trouble in her life, there was an equine involved. The one time it wasn't horses, it was Rhys, himself.

"You're not fair, hitting me where I'm weak."

"You'll do it?"

"I'll think about it. I don't want you to believe I don't see through this plan of yours, though. You think that once I'm coming out to school your horse, it'll be easy to get me working on this schooling day of yours. And, of course, Erin will just somehow keep ending up with lessons, and competing at the show."

"Would that be so terrible?"

"Yes." She didn't dare elaborate. If she tried to explain her reasons, she might get all mixed up and realize that her reasons were the problem in the first place. "I'll let you know about Friday."

"Good. Give me a call when you decide."

Jacquie was prepared for the call to end at that point, but Rhys continued talking. "Erin is quite good, you know. She and Andrew could be burning up the eventing world in a few years."

"I told you so. I've got a savings account set up for the right horse, though it's not growing as fast as she is. Mirage is a great guy, but she needs a big Thoroughbred to be truly competitive."

"There's a promising three-year-old mare back in New York, one of Imperator's foals by Artiste, who won the Rolex a few years back. She'd be perfect."

"Yet another string, you mean, drawing Erin to you?"

"I think I'll say goodbye while we're not fighting."

"We are fighting, we'll always be fighting. We're on opposite sides, Rhys. Accept it."

"Never," he said firmly and, without another word, cut the connection.

CHAPTER SEVEN

THE FIRE BELL RANG in the middle of English class on the first Thursday in February. With a collective groan, Andrew's fellow students got up from their desks and filed out the door, down the hallways and out into a windy, sunny day. Since he didn't know where they were supposed to go, Andrew followed the crowd. Once they got to their assigned spot on the school lawn, he saw that the person standing at the end of the line next to him was Erin Archer, red hair and all.

Her gaze caught his before either of them could look away. After that, talking was kind of mandatory.

"Cold?" he said, as she hunched in her coat.

"Well, duh. It's like forty-five degrees out here."

"That's not cold. Cold in Upstate New York is fifteen degrees with four feet of snow piled up and more coming down."

"If you liked it so much, you should have stayed there."

"Don't think coming down here was my idea. I would've stayed, if he wasn't bringing Imp down with him."

Erin nodded. "I can see that."

"Only now your mom is riding him. I'll probably never get a chance I don't steal."

"My mom?"

Too late, Andrew heard a warning bell in his brain. No use stopping now. "Yeah, my dad arranged for her to come over tomorrow and start schooling Imperator over the cross-country jumps."

"That's right. I just forgot." Erin paused. "You can't ride the advanced jumps anyway."

"Neither can your mom. I heard my dad tell Terry that she'd be training on preliminary level jumps. I could do that with Imp."

"So could I." She said it almost to herself.

The bell rang, signaling them to return to class, and the lines started moving back toward the school. The cool thing would have been to walk in without saying anything else to Erin. But she looked like she might fall apart, or cry or something.

"Maybe I'll see you around this weekend," he said at the doorway. "If your mom and my dad start getting along, she'll probably agree to bring you out for more lessons, right?"

"Maybe." She sent him a little smile, and a nod. "Maybe."

They went their separate ways, but her pale face stayed on his mind the rest of the day. Even if she did think too much of herself on horseback, he didn't like seeing Erin so down.

Evidently *his* parents weren't the only ones who could really screw up their kid.

ERIN CHARGED out of the school building Thursday afternoon, threw her book bag into the back seat and then slammed herself into the truck. "You weren't going to tell me at all, were you?"

Though she was going to be late for her next shoeing job, Jacquie shifted the engine into Park. She didn't intend to argue with her daughter and try to back out into after-school traffic at the same time. "What are you talking about?"

"You're riding Imperator tomorrow. Training him, with Mr. Lewellyn, on a regular basis. And you won't let me take lessons at all. How is that fair?"

"I didn't know you and Andrew had classes together."

"We don't. I talked to him in a fire drill. What difference does that make? You didn't tell me and you knew it would matter."

Jacquie's stomach clenched tight inside her. "I'm sorry—I only called him late last night to say that I would. I didn't think about it this morning before you went to school." The quick call she'd intended had turned into an extended conversation with Rhys about the world of horses, especially eventing. After such a long time on the fringes, she'd enjoyed seeing the business and the people involved from his perspective at the top of the sport. Rhys understood her drive to compete in a way she'd never shared with another soul, except her daughter.

Who was still complaining. "So if you can train with Mr. Lewellyn, why can't I?"

"I'm not training with him, exactly. He asked me to get Imperator over some cross-country fences. After that fall in November, the horse has lost his confidence and Rhys isn't well enough to ride him."

"I could. Andrew could."

"Not at the level I can. Imperator is a four-star horse—he can't go back to jumping novice fences.

You know that. And neither of you is really ready to jump higher.''

Erin sighed, and some of her fury evaporated. "I don't understand the whole issue between you and Mr. Lewellyn. All I know is the greatest chance of my life is right under my nose and I'm going to miss it because you don't like him.''

Jacquie hid her amusement at this adolescent drama. "Maybe not the greatest chance of your lifetime. You can always train with Rhys when you're living on your own.''

"I'll be too old to get anything out of it.''

"Then I guess you'll just have to sulk.''

"I guess so.'' Erin's smile peeked out. She was always quick to forgive. "Permanently.''

With a sigh of relief at having handled at least one disaster, Jacquie reversed the truck and drove out of the school parking lot. Perhaps she wasn't giving her daughter enough credit. Instead of expecting Erin to behave like a child when confronted with an unpleasant situation, she resolved to look for the beginnings of maturity.

Which did not mean Erin could accept the truth about her father without pain, even anguish. Knowing you'd been deceived was one of the worst feelings in the world—Jacquie recalled too well how Rhys's lack of honesty about his marriage had hurt her. How much more would Erin feel betrayed by what her mother had never told her? How much worse would the split between them be?

And, given Erin's impulsive nature, what would she do when she discovered she'd been lied to all these years?

JACQUIE MET RHYS, Terry and Imperator at the start of the cross-country course at Rourke Park on Friday morning. The day was cold and sunny. Imperator, with his wide dark eyes and pricked ears, looked to be as fresh as the wind.

"Ready?" Rhys wore jeans, and a jacket she remembered from her time with him in New York—soft, dark leather with a wool fleece lining. She'd worn that jacket herself once, during a September weekend when they'd left the Lewellyn stables separately to meet in a picturesque Vermont inn. The scent of the jacket—of *him*—was a memory she hadn't visited in fourteen years but, obviously, hadn't forgotten.

She wasn't happy to be saddled with it now. "I'm here, aren't I?"

He lifted an eyebrow at her rudeness, but then shrugged. "I'll hold the horse while Terry gives you a leg up."

That, at least, was a relief. The last thing she wanted was Rhys touching her. "Right."

Bending her leg back for Terry to grab, she bounced a couple of times and then threw herself up onto the horse's back. Imperator shied a little, but not so much she couldn't get herself seated in the saddle.

She settled her feet in the stirrups and drew the reins together. "Okay, what's the plan?"

Rhys had moved to stand beside her boot, a hand on Imperator's neck. "Warm him up, first. Then we're going to walk the course, try out each jump. Take the easiest line, the lowest part of the fence, at a slow canter. Don't push, but do try to get him across the first time. If he cuts out or stops, we'll work on that fence till we get it." He grinned up at her, his shoulder just brushing the front of her knee. "Any pixie dust you can throw on him in the process will be appreciated."

That smile was another prize she would prefer to forfeit. "Sorry, I'm fresh out." She turned the horse away from him. "He'll have to do this with just what he's got." Trotting along the lane, she breathed deeply and tried to focus her thoughts on the job ahead. This morning was solely for Imperator. The entanglements of mere humans should not interfere.

As he watched Jacquie warm up the horse, Rhys felt his grin freeze and then crumble like dry snow. Her resistance thwarted any overture he tried to make.

Too bad, he thought, as he and Terry walked to the first fence. *This time, you can't run away. And I won't take no for an answer.*

After about twenty minutes, the rhythmic thud of hooves on the ground heralded the approach of Imperator and his rider toward the first fence—two straight logs, one on top of the other, with a slight drop behind and trees on either side, so a horse had no hope of running around the jump. Either go over, or don't go at all.

"She's still got a good eye," Terry commented. "Straight line, just the right distance."

Rhys nodded. "He could take this one in his sleep."

But Imperator sat back on his haunches, dug in his front hooves and screeched to halt within an inch of the jump.

Jacquie dropped back into the saddle, shaking her head. Turning the horse around, she headed back the way they'd just come, then tried again at a slightly faster pace. She flicked her crop as they reached the jump, but Imperator halted again. Jacquie sat back and looked at Rhys. "Well?"

With three more tries they got Imp to the point of trotting up to the jump, slowing to look over, and then hopping across the logs.

"We'll take it," Rhys said. "Let's go on." A course that should have taken twenty slow minutes to ride cost them three hours. Some fences they simply could not get the horse over, but he managed to cross a majority of the simplest obstacles.

"Not too bad," Terry commented as he took off the saddle. "Considering how bad that fall was, he's makin' a big effort."

"He is, indeed." Jacquie stood by Imperator's head, rubbing his neck. "I could feel the struggle in him when we couldn't get over a fence. He was as disappointed as the rest of us."

Rhys exchanged Imp's bridle for a halter. "Twice a week like this, plus daily work in the ring, and in a month I think we'll have him back to his old self."

Jacquie's startled eyes met his. "Twice a week?"

"You know once won't be enough. He needs the reinforcement."

Jacquie sighed. "I suppose that's true. Monday and Friday mornings?"

"Sounds good." He made the remark as casually as he could, and hid his smile. At least two days a week, now, to get past her barriers. As they stood by the trailer while Terry loaded the horse, Rhys decided to push his luck. "Andrew's going to be painting poles this weekend, getting ready for our schooling day. Do you think Erin would like to join him?"

She jammed her fists on her hips. "Will you stop? This isn't going to happen and I don't know why you keep pushing for it."

"I'm ready," Terry called, climbing behind the steering wheel of their truck.

"Go ahead." Rhys waved him on. "I'll be back about two." When he looked at Jacquie, he met her suspicious stare. "No, I wasn't making assumptions about you, or planning to hijack you. I'm meeting someone for lunch."

"Oh." Was it his imagination she didn't like that idea?

With perfect timing, a gold Mercedes sedan slid to a stop behind Jacquie's black truck. The blond woman who exited the driver's seat was a walking advertisement for old money, from her 24-Karat jewelry, all the way down to the fur collar on her cashmere jacket.

"Rhys Lewellyn, I can't believe I have to track you down out here in the middle of nowhere." She put her arms around his neck and pressed her cheek against his. "You are the hardest man in the country to get a date with."

"Galen. Good to see you." He returned her hug, aware of Jacquie standing next to him with her eyebrows drawn together.

Stepping back, Galen turned to Jacquie and extended a hand. "Hello, there. Jacquie Archer, right? Rhys told me you'd be out riding that big stallion of his this morning. I'm Galen Oakley and I desperately need a farrier I can depend on."

"This is the friend I mentioned," Rhys added, "who suggested I give North Carolina a try."

Jacquie went from stiff to stunned to stammering in

the space of a minute. "It's g-good to meet you. Rhys mentioned that I was a farrier?"

"He listened to me rant about my latest shoeing fiasco the other night on the phone. It's bad enough that this idiot farrier misses three out of every four appointments we set, but when he starts messing up my horses' feet, I draw the line. Anyway, Rhys said he knew a farrier in town who would suit me perfectly—which is hard to believe since I've been coming down here for a good ten years now, since Daddy died and left the horses to me, and I only convinced Rhys to move here, what…a month ago? But he suggested I come along this morning and we could all go to lunch and talk about what you can do for me."

Jacquie backed up a step. "I'm really not dressed for lunch…I just got off the horse—"

Galen waved away the objection. "You look wonderful, all fresh and energetic. We'll go to the Steeplechase Grille—everybody goes there in riding clothes. You'll fit right in. Do you want to follow us in your truck?"

Rhys would've preferred to have Jacquie in the Mercedes, with no chance of escape. He'd have to trust that the incentive of a new account—a big, important new account—would keep her in line.

"Sure," she said finally. "Lead the way."

JACQUIE FOLLOWED the Mercedes at a safe distance, on the road and in her mind. She refused to be angry or—God forbid—jealous. Or even nosy. Rhys had done her a favor, that was all. He had a friend who needed farrier services and had arranged for them to meet. Period.

Of course, this "friend" looked like a movie star—Grace Kelly, to be exact. Blond, blue eyed and elegantly tall, Galen Oakley also happened to be one of the wealthiest horse owners in North Carolina. According to local gossip, she kept an eighteenth-century house and stable in the horse country of New York State, a penthouse apartment in Manhattan, plus Oakley Plantation near New Skye, where she wintered her fifty or so horses. A farrier could make a halfway decent living off Galen's farm alone.

And she seems to be genuinely nice on top of everything else, Jacquie thought. *Damn her.*

In the parking lot of the restaurant, she took a minute to comb out her "helmet head" hair. Braiding would take too long, so she left it loose, tucked behind her ears. That, and replacing her safety vest with the dark green corduroy barn jacket she'd worn for warmth this morning, were the best she could do at dressing up her boots, breeches and turtleneck shirt. If the Steeplechase Grille wanted horsey atmosphere, she would give it to them.

Rhys and Galen stood just inside the door. "There's a fifteen-minute wait for a table," Rhys said. "We thought we'd step into the bar."

They gathered around a tall, small table with no chairs. Rhys went to get drinks, and Jacquie took a business card out of her wallet. "Here's the phone number and post office box for Ladysmith Farrier Service. That's me. I trained at the University of Oklahoma and have certifications in advanced farrier work. I've been operating in this area for about twelve years now, and I can provide you references."

Galen waved her hand. "Rhys's word is all I need. He says you're the best."

Jacquie looked at Rhys as he set their glasses on the table. "Really? Based on a couple of shoes?"

He jiggled the ice in his whiskey. "I've asked around. I get nothing but rave reviews on your work."

Her temper flared like a bottle rocket. *He'd asked around? He didn't trust her?*

Galen sipped her martini. "I'll have my trainer call you next week, Jacquie, and set up an appointment for the work we need. Now that's settled, I think we should talk about this schooling day coming up. Rhys asked me to help you with the plans."

At that moment, the hostess called them to their table. Galen went ahead but Jacquie hung back, gripped Rhys's arm and turned him to face her.

"Were you always this unscrupulous, or is it a talent you've developed in the last decade?"

He had the grace to look uneasy. "Galen knows a lot of the owners around here. She can give me a list of people to invite."

"That does not explain why you involved me."

"Because you know other people, and between the two of you we can pretty much cover the horse community."

"I told you I would not be a part of this."

"Don't you think it's time you changed your mind?"

She stared up at him, speechless.

"We're blocking the way," Rhys said, taking her arm. "And Galen is wondering where we are."

Jacquie didn't resist as he eased her into the dining room. Crossing the floor, she returned smiles and nods from customers she knew until, all too soon, they'd arrived at Galen's table.

"Sit down, both of you. Jacquie, you must be starved after riding in the cold wind all morning. They have a wonderful tomato-spinach bisque here. Do you like tomato bisque?" She kept up a running commentary on the menu, heedless of the fact that neither Jacquie nor Rhys replied. After a while, Jacquie glanced across the table to see that Rhys, too, was having trouble hiding a smile.

"That's better," Galen declared, watching both of them. "The two of you stalked over here as if you were preparing to duel to the death. I figured if I made a fool of myself, you'd loosen up. Now we can order, and then we'll talk."

Somehow, in the process of eating lunch—including the excellent bisque—Jacquie found herself participating in the planning session for the schooling event. As an advisor only, she rationalized. Galen talked a lot, but she listened, as well, and incorporated several of Jacquie's suggestions into the overall scheme.

"And you'll be on-site as farrier, of course, in case we need one."

She was being steamrollered. And Rhys was sitting over there grinning, damn him. "I don't—"

Galen spoke over Jacquie's protest. "Who would you recommend as the veterinarian for our show?"

"Did I hear somebody ask for a vet?" The new voice came from behind Jacquie. When she turned in her chair, she found Buck Travis, her preferred animal doctor, standing behind her. "How did two such good-looking women end up in the same restaurant, let alone at the same table?''

''Buck, how are you?'' Galen gave him her hand with royal flair. ''You know Jacquie already? And this is Rhys Lewellyn. I'm sure the name is familiar.''

''Imperator. Of course.'' Buck shook Rhys's hand and then bent to kiss Jacquie on the cheek. ''How are you, sweetheart?''

His chestnut hair needed a trim and his hazel eyes looked tired, but his expression was warm, a little sexy. Jacquie suddenly wondered why she'd turned him down the last few times he'd asked her out.

Before she could answer his question, Galen said, ''Can you sit down with us?''

Buck shook his head. ''I'd love to, but I've got a call right this minute—a lame horse needing my attention.'' He laughed and shrugged. ''When isn't there a lame horse needing attention? Anyway, Mr. Lewellyn, good to meet you. Ladies, it was a pleasure.'' With a nod, he left them, taking his cell phone out of his pocket to answer a call as he crossed the room.

Galen looked at Rhys. ''I'll return the favor of your farrier referral and tell you that when you need a vet, you couldn't do better than Buck Travis. I've seen him work wonders on everything from prolonged labor to chronic abscesses. He cured a case of founder in my favorite mare I truly feared was hopeless. I thought we would have to put her down, but Buck saved her. I rode her yesterday afternoon.''

''Sounds like a miracle man, indeed. I'll put him on my list. I have had a few other recommendations.''

''Call Buck first,'' Jacquie told him. ''I've seen his work all over the county. He really is the best.''

Rhys stared at her a minute, his face blank. "Whatever you say. Are we finished with our meal?"

Outside the restaurant, Galen looked at her watch. "Oh, good grief, I'm late for my hair appointment. You can get a ride home with Jacquie, can't you, Rhys? Your place is in exactly the opposite direction from my salon."

In answer to Rhys's enquiring glance, Jacquie could only nod. "We can do that. It's on my way back to town."

Galen nodded. "Lovely. I'll get you that list of addresses this week, Rhys. And I'll start talking with caterers for the party, plus the concessions. You'll see—we'll pull this together in great style. Bye!" Almost before the sound of her words had died in the air, the gleaming Mercedes pulled out of the parking lot.

Jacquie tilted her head toward her mud-spattered truck. "This way."

They rode in silence for several miles. "Is this Buck Travis a local boy?" Rhys asked finally. "You've known him since childhood and all that?"

"No, I think he grew up in California. He was with the army, stationed over in Fayetteville at Fort Bragg. When he got out, he decided to set up practice here."

"You work with him often?"

"He's the one I call if I find a problem that needs veterinary care. And I call him for my own horses."

"You see him socially?"

It was on the tip of her tongue to answer no, but she caught herself in time. "Yes." Not a lie—at other people's parties, she and Buck often spent time talking.

Rhys's fingers drummed on the arm rest. "He kissed your cheek."

She smiled at the final proof of his jealousy. "I didn't get my hand in his face fast enough, like Galen."

With a chuckle, Rhys relaxed. "I quit."

"Good idea. Have you known Galen long?"

"We grew up together, as a matter of fact. Went to the same schools in New York."

"Private schools."

He gave her a surprised glance. "Yes. Why?"

Jacquie shrugged. "I guess I forget sometimes how rich you really are. But Galen reminded me."

"You don't have to be wealthy to go to private school."

"Of course not."

"And because my father has a lot of money doesn't mean I do. I make a living with my riding and teaching, like other people."

"You have a pretty solid backing, though. And easy access to excellent horses."

"I'm earning my way the same as you are. Or Buck Travis."

This time, she didn't think before she spoke. "Maybe we're all fooled by your aristocratic good looks."

He was quiet for a minute. "That's the first nice thing you've said to me since I arrived in North Carolina."

"Well...don't get used to it."

"I wouldn't presume. But I like it when there's not so much friction between us." He paused a beat.

"Then again, friction can be a very good thing, in the right circumstances."

The timbre of his voice hinted at the circumstances he referred to. Jacquie glanced at his face, then quickly away. The truck swerved toward the shoulder of the road as she fought to recover her poise. She couldn't speak over the lump in her throat, which was probably just as well. Who knew what trouble she would get into if she opened her mouth again?

When she finally stopped the truck beside Rhys's barn, she expected him to get out right away. But he seemed in no hurry to leave. "Have you reconsidered allowing Erin to help paint the fences this weekend?

She hit the heel of her hand against the steering wheel. "Do you ever give up?"

"Do you really want me to?"

A treacherous part of her answered no. Suddenly she felt completely worn out by the struggle, tempted almost beyond her strength by the urge to give in and let Rhys have his way.

He must have seen her weaken, because he leaned closer and put a hand over hers. "I told you I wouldn't say anything to Erin, and I meant it. So what would be the harm in letting her come over for some fun and some work? She and Andrew can get a lesson in the morning, then spend the afternoon painting."

"And let me guess—I come to take Erin home and you suggest we stay for supper."

"Not a bad idea. Will you?"

Jacquie leaned her head back against the seat and closed her eyes. What would she do on Saturday night, otherwise? What had she done all these long, lonely years? Dinner with Erin, TV or maybe a movie.

Phoebe joined them sometimes, but she would be a married woman soon. Anyway, the truth about Erin seemed to stand between her and all of her friends, even her family. She was so careful watching what she said—or even implied—to other people these days that half the time she couldn't think of anything to say at all.

Rhys knew the truth, and he hadn't given up, hadn't drawn back. She could be with him and not worry about telling lies. He might be the only adult she could be herself with these days. She desperately needed that freedom.

"Okay. We'll be here Saturday."

"You're painting, too?"

Maybe she'd misunderstood. "If you don't mind."

He reassured her with a squeeze of her hand. "I'd have made the suggestion myself, but I was sure I'd get my nose bitten off."

"No. Not this time."

"Okay." He got out of the truck and came around to the driver's side, where she rolled down her window. "How about a kiss to seal the bargain?"

She frowned at him. "Don't push your luck."

"Oh, Jacquie." He slapped his hand on the edge of the door and stepped back. "Surely you remember— a winner always pushes his luck."

A PHONE CALL in the middle of Friday night changed their Saturday plans. Heart pounding, Jacquie fumbled the phone to her ear. "Mom? What's wrong?"

"Not a thing, honey. We just wanted to tell you that Sandy has left for the hospital. The baby's on its way."

She fell back against the pillows. "Right on time, too. That's terrific."

"Yes. So your dad and I are going down to wait. Jimmy will be in with Sandy, of course."

"I'll wake Erin—"

"You don't need to do that. It'll be hours yet, no doubt, before the baby's born. We'll call and let you know."

"Well, okay. Give Jimmy and Sandy my love."

"Sure will. Love you."

Jacquie let the phone rest on her chest. A new baby in the family would be wonderful. Her mom and dad were born to be grandparents. They'd been Erin's slaves since their first glimpse of her, and their hearts would expand for each and every grandchild.

But what if they knew the truth? The skeptic inside her brain never failed to take advantage of a moment of weakness. *Would they feel the same about an illegitimate child? And what would they think about the lies, the evasions…about you?*

With those thoughts for company, she didn't get back to sleep until almost 6:00 a.m.

Her mother called again at eight. "It's a boy! Mother and son are doing just great."

"I'm so glad. And what did they decide to name him? Last I heard, it was Thomas or Garrett."

Her mother laughed. "They named him after his granddaddies—Edward Bruce Lennon. Both of those old men are strutting around here like peacocks, with their chests puffed out."

"When can we come see?"

"Anytime—Sandy will be here until tomorrow

morning, and she's rooming in, so the baby's right there. None of the rest of us can tear ourselves away.''

''We'll get dressed and be there before lunch,'' Jacquie promised, and hung up as Erin shuffled sleepily into the kitchen. ''Who was that?''

''You've got a new cousin—Aunt Sandy's baby was born early this morning. Edward Bruce. I don't know what they're going to call him.''

''That's so cool.'' Erin rubbed her eyes with one hand and reached for a cereal box with the other. ''I can't wait to see him.''

''Me, too. I thought we'd get the chores done, get cleaned up and go straight to the hospital.''

Her daughter jerked around, eyes suddenly wide. ''But I'm supposed to go to Fairfield Farm this morning, to help Mr. Lewellyn paint the jumps.''

Jacquie carefully avoided any kind of extreme reaction. ''We'll have to cancel, I'm afraid.''

''But I don't want to cancel. Once I'm there, he might let me ride—even give me a lesson.''

''Now we have something more important to do.''

''We can see the baby tomorrow.'' Her tone approached a whine—so much for maturity.

''No, we're going this morning.'' She turned toward the mutinous face across the kitchen. ''We're talking about your family, Erin. Nothing's more important than family.''

Her stomach twisted as that internal skeptic took the upper hand again. *Family? You mean, as in father?*

''Great. Just great.'' Jaw set, eyes flashing, Erin shoved the cereal box back onto the shelf and stomped out of the room. ''I wish I'd been born without a family,'' she yelled, punctuating her thought with the slam of the bedroom door.

Jacquie's laugh came perilously close to a sob.

CHAPTER EIGHT

ON FRIDAY THE THIRTEENTH, Rhys and Terry stood by the jumping ring as Andrew took Imperator around the course.

"He's better," the Irishman said. "But not right."

"No." Rhys shook his head. "There's a lack of confidence and an unpredictability that worries me. With Andrew, and with Jacquie."

"We've got three weeks before the schooling day. You could be riding him by then."

"Could be." An admission of defeat, and they both knew it.

"Who, then?"

Andrew brought the horse to a stop in front of them before Rhys could answer. "That was a good round, right? He's feeling better all the time."

"It was a good round." Rhys put up a hand to rub Imperator's cheek. "You've done well by him, son. He's responding to you more every day."

Under the helmet brim, Andrew's eyes were bright. "Let me try him cross-country, then. I'll start on the easy jumps, and I know he'll do it for me. Please, Dad? It's time."

Rhys was tempted—Jacquie had made progress with Imp, and the horse might, indeed, jump for An-

drew. He had it in his power to earn his son's grati-
tude—his love?—with one word.

As long as he didn't mind risking the boy's life, or
his physical well-being. In an instant, Rhys was back
in the hospital bed, lying flat on his back, unable to
move his legs or even relieve himself without help.
Despite the brisk wind and the bright sunshine, he felt
as if he were suffocating.

"No." He shook his head. "I don't think you're
ready for the solid jumps yet."

Andrew stared at him with his mouth open for a
few seconds. "When?" he demanded. "What do I
have to do to prove I can take this horse anywhere he
wants to go?"

Rhys rubbed his hand over his face. "More experience. More horses. More time."

"Right." Andrew slid down from the horse's back
and stepped close. There was only a head's difference
in their heights, now. "Or am I just supposed to wait
until you get your nerve back? Is that it? You don't
want me showing you up, so you're not going to give
me the chance to ride him at all. Afraid you'll be
replaced, Dad?"

"Watch your tongue." Terry put a hand on Andrew's shoulder. "Treat your dad with the respect he
deserves."

"Respect?" Andrew snorted. "He didn't want me
to begin with, got rid of me—and his wife—as soon
as he could, then ignored me for years until she gave
him no choice but to take me back. And now he's
covering his own ass by making sure I don't get the
chance to succeed. What's to respect?"

Rhys stood without moving as Andrew turned on
his heel and led Imperator back to the stable. Terry

shook his head. "Forget that temper tantrum. You're right, and we both know it. The boy isn't ready to take those jumps, no matter what he thinks. He'll get over this."

"Maybe." He hunched his shoulders, tried to work some of the stiffness out of his neck. "Or maybe he's right. Maybe I just don't want to admit I'm finished."

"You're not finished." Terry grabbed his shoulder and squeezed, hard. "You've got years of competition ahead of you, dozens of medals yet to win."

"But, Terry…" Rhys found that he could actually smile. "First, I have to be able to ride the bloody horse."

THE PAINTING DAY HAD BEEN rescheduled for Saturday, the fourteenth—Valentine's Day. Though Andrew started the morning out with a sullen attitude, Rhys was interested to see that Erin eventually badgered him into a better mood. By noon the two kids were flipping paint at each other and trading good natured insults.

Jacquie, too, took time to warm up. She began working on a pole all by herself, concentrating on getting a smooth line between red and white bars. Then Erin brought her green brush over to paint the center line, teasing her mother about adding a few green dots to the pristine white. Before too long, Jacquie had joined all of them and was trading jokes with the kids, as well as occasional shy smiles with Rhys, himself.

He made every effort to avoid scaring her off. No suggestive comments, no pointed looks, no casual brush of skin against skin. Jacquie needed to feel safe with him, needed to know that he would guard their daughter as carefully as she would, herself. They got through the day, he thought, without a single mistake.

And his reward was Jacquie's offer to help with dinner while Erin, Andrew and Terry finished up in the barn.

"What are we cooking?" she asked as they came through the back door into the long, stone-floored hallway of the house.

He motioned her to go ahead of him into the gathering room. "No cooking involved. Terry's been tending a pot of Irish stew since morning. We'll put some bread in to warm, toss dressing on the salad, and that's the job." At the drinks tray, he poured them both a glass of ice, tonic and lime.

"You three seem remarkably self-sufficient. I thought bachelors ate frozen dinners or ordered pizza." She took the drink he offered and sat down on the end of the couch.

"Terry hates pizza. And he's always been a good cook. I think he might have worked in restaurants before he came to horses."

"You *think*?"

"He's the proverbial gruff Irishman—doesn't talk about himself except under duress." Rhys dropped down into the armchair across from the fireplace. He didn't want her to feel crowded or rushed.

"As opposed to the proverbial blarney-talkers who won't stop?"

He raised his glass to toast her insight. "Exactly."

Seconds stretched into minutes of comfortable silence. "I love this room," Jacquie said softly. "It's grand, yet easy to relax in."

"I wish I could take credit, but we leased the place furnished, down to the bed linens." He looked around and nodded. "You're right, though. This is the perfect place—and the perfect company—in which to end the day." Late-afternoon sun poured through the diamond-paned windows onto warm brown leather sofas and rich wood paneling, while firelight flickered over brass lamps and crystal decanters, bringing life to the golds and reds of the oriental carpet underfoot.

The woman on the couch fit the setting, in her sweater of deep green, with her hair a rosy gold and her skin pale pearl touched with a flush of pink from their day outside. He couldn't keep his eyes off her and, after a few minutes, she realized it. Her flush deepened and her eyes widened. But for once she didn't look away. Rhys allowed the idea of touching her, kissing her, into his mind, and saw his desire reflected in her face.

"You aren't pouncing," she told him in a breathless voice.

His private battle of will had paid off. He smiled slightly. "Are you disappointed?"

Jacquie held his eyes for another moment, then looked away and got to her feet. "We should get dinner ready."

She was grateful to find that the kitchen, though pleasant, wasn't nearly as conducive to intimacy as the gathering room. That moment by the fire had been way too tantalizing.

Yet she couldn't recover the sense of ease she'd felt most of the day in Rhys's company. As they moved around the big kitchen, there seemed to be so many occasions when they brushed shoulders, their hands touched, or his fingers rested at her waist as he reached for a shelf over her head. A kiss by the fire might have defused the tension. Instead she found herself more and more…well, *excited* was the only word. A very dangerous word.

Terry and the kids trooped in as she set the last plate on the table.

"I'm starved," Erin announced. "And it smells fantastic in here."

Rhys brought a steaming bowl of stew from the stove. "Let's eat." They all sat down and Rhys folded in his hands in front of his plate. "We usually say grace, if you don't mind."

"Not at all." Jacquie clasped Erin's hand, and Andrew's on her left. Terry and Rhys joined the circle and they all bowed their heads.

"Like the goodness of the five loaves and two fishes, which God divided among the five thousand men, may the blessing of the King who so divided be upon our share of this common meal." Rhys concluded with a soft, "Amen."

"That's the same prayer we use at home." Erin spoke up as soon as they'd lifted their heads. "Did you learn that blessing when you were in New York, Mom? What was it like, training so far from home? Did you stay in an apartment by yourself? Was there a…what's it called?…a dormitory for the students?"

Her thoughts jumbled, her brain stumbling, Jacquie handed the stew to Andrew and saw that he was interested in the questions Erin had asked. "Um…"

"We usually take on three or four students at a time," Rhys said smoothly. "There are two apartments over the barn and another in the basement level of the main house. Terry's house is separate and has an extra room for a male student or two, if the other three are full."

Only one of the barn apartments had been occupied

that summer. Jacquie tried to block the memory. "Training at Lewellyn Stables was pretty much like a regular day at our farm—feed the horses, turn them out, muck the stalls, clean the barn, groom, tack, ride, unsaddle, groom, tack, ride a different horse. Rhys gave a lesson once a day and either he or Terry supervised the other workouts so all the horses got the proper training. At night you fed, watered, cleaned up, ate dinner and collapsed into bed. We were up every day at six and worked until sundown. Weekends, too, sometimes." She shook her head. "Just remembering makes me tired."

And after dark, there were all the lovely hours in that small, utilitarian apartment, to talk with Rhys, to dream, to make love…

Andrew leaned forward. "Mrs. Archer, how did you decide to train at Lewellyn Stables in the first place? It's a long way from here to New York."

That was an easier answer. "Your dad had earned a silver and a bronze at the eighty-eight Olympics, so his name was all over the eventing magazines that year. I read an article featuring Lewellyn which mentioned that they took students to train, and my goal became to graduate high school and then move to New York to train with Rhys Lewellyn. When other kids were applying to colleges, I wrote a letter with a review of my wins—"

"Which were quite impressive." Rhys helped himself to more stew. "She'd ridden some excellent horses for people I knew in Virginia and Maryland, and scored impressively. Terry agreed just from the letter that she was certainly worth our time."

Andrew turned his gaze to Jacquie again. "But you

didn't stay very long after all, did you? What happened?''

After a moment of frozen silence, Rhys chuckled. "You may have noticed that Mrs. Archer and I don't exactly agree on everything. I was pretty full of myself back then—"

"He's been cured, of course," Terry commented.

"And she was a very argumentative student. We fought one too many times over some minor lesson detail and I suggested she leave."

"Actually," Jacquie said, "we argued and I told him I wouldn't stay to train with him for a blanket chest full of Olympic medals."

"What are the Olympics like, Mr. Lewellyn?" Erin had barely touched her dinner—she was leaning on the table, her eyes bright with excitement. "The horse you took the first time was Conundrum, right? Did you know, going with Imperator, that you had a better chance to win? You looked so cool, on the podium with your gold medal. How could you be calm? I'm going to be dancing on air, I think."

Andrew snorted. "'Going to be'?"

Rhys grinned. "That's the attitude you need to win." He tried answering Erin's questions, and all the ones that followed, with far more patience than Jacquie would have expected—or would have demonstrated herself. His eyes were soft, his smile easy as he talked to their daughter, explaining the life he lived.

And Erin soaked up every word. If she allowed it, Jacquie realized, these two kindred spirits would bond deeply and irrevocably. Was she ready for that?

She got to her feet, ignoring startled looks from Rhys and Erin. "I think it's time to clean up. We've got horses to feed at home."

In the process of putting away leftovers, Erin discovered carrots in the refrigerator. "Can I take them out to the horses before we leave?"

"You can't feed Imperator by hand," Andrew said. "Stallions bite too easily."

Erin gave him a superior look. "Duh. Like I don't know that already?"

"Yeah, well, how am I supposed to know you know what you're doing? Do you have stallions to take care of?"

"As a matter of fact, we do. Sterling has won his share of ribbons, too. He's Mirage's sire."

They continued to bicker as they went down the hall toward the outside door. Terry shook his head, bid Jacquie a short good-night, and stomped up the stairway to the second floor.

With the kitchen neat again, Jacquie drifted into the gathering room and stood by the sofa, looking everywhere but at the man by the fireplace.

"It's been a lovely day," she told the collection of stirrup cups on the mantel. "Thank you so much for dinner."

"I appreciate your help. And Erin's. Barring rain, I plan to get more painting done next weekend. Can she join us?" They stood in the hallway now, forced by the walls to stand close together. The only light came from the gentle lamps in the gathering room.

"I—I'll check my calendar and let you know." Jacquie couldn't take a breath without drawing in his scent…warm, spicy, stirring. She was as captivated by this man as her daughter. "We're meeting Monday, right? With Imperator?"

"Right." Rhys closed the distance between them with a single step. The shadows of the hallway wrapped them in privacy. "Jacquie, when we were alone together earlier, you thought I was going to kiss you."

"I…why would I think that?"

"Because I was thinking that." He put his hands lightly on her shoulders. A shiver ran down her spine.

"But you didn't."

"No." He slid his hands down her arms, over her elbows and to her wrists. She felt the calluses on his palms, the strength in his fingers. "I'm going to now."

"Rhys…" This shouldn't happen. But she couldn't stop it.

"Don't mind too much." Drawing her hands up, he placed them behind his neck. Her body curved against him.

"No." Then, as he bent his head, she pulled back slightly. "Are you sure about Galen?"

"I pulled her pigtails when we were kids. We competed against each other in shows—she fell a month before the Olympics and lamed her horse, otherwise she would have been there instead of me. Don't," Rhys said, grazing his lips across her cheek as he sought her mouth, "worry about Galen."

Soft, smooth, sweet. Clean. When had he last kissed a woman who didn't wear lipstick, didn't taste of the stuff? Jacquie tasted fresh, like wind and sunshine. He ran his hands down her back, brought her closer, and she bent to him like a blade of spring grass. From the curve of her lips, he realized she was smiling.

The pleasure, the joy of it, made him crazy. He wrapped his arms around her waist and lifted her off her feet. She held on to his shoulders, her fingers curled in his shirt, and gave back every measure of passion—with kisses, with sighs, with the tremors he could feel running through her body.

"I've needed you so much." He could hardly breathe to speak. "Where the hell have you been?"

As if commanded by his voice, the door at the end of the hallway opened with a rattle of glass. Shocked, shaken, Rhys stepped in front of Jacquie to confront the intruder—his son.

After a long pause, Andrew said, "Erin's waiting in their truck."

"Her mother was just coming. Did you lock up the barn?"

"I figured you would want to, as usual."

"Why don't you do it tonight? Just make sure all the stall latches are on and turn out all the lights."

Andrew stood motionless for a minute of silent struggle. "Sure."

When he'd left, Rhys turned to Jacquie. "Are you okay?"

She slapped her thigh with her hand. "Oh, of course. I was just caught necking with you by your fourteen-year-old son." Her voice broke. "But I should have known better—you are nothing but disaster for me, whenever I get involved." She stepped around him to walk toward the door.

Rhys caught up and put a hand on her shoulder to turn her to face him. "This is not a disaster."

"Yes, it is. He's already asking dangerous questions. He told Erin I was riding Imperator before I told her myself, so I think it's a good bet he'll keep her informed of whatever he thinks she doesn't know. All he has to do is look at his birthday, and hers, and maybe ask when I left New York. He's a bright kid and he'll figure it out. Then he'll tell Erin."

Rhys couldn't disagree. "I could tell him the truth—"

Jacquie held up a hand. "No. No one else knows until Erin does."

The possibility that she was considering giving Erin the truth held him speechless for a moment. "Okay, then. Can you at least agree to let me give Erin lessons between now and the schooling day? She deserves them, don't you think?"

Her shoulders lifted in a sigh. "I—I…okay."

"Thanks." He wouldn't push for more. Tonight. "I'll walk you outside."

"Please, don't. Just let me leave."

He dropped his hand to his side. "Whatever you want."

She stared up at him through the darkness. "I don't know what I want anymore."

Which was, Rhys reflected as he watched her cross the stable yard to her truck, an improvement over her initial response to his arrival—"stay away from us" had become "I don't know" in a matter of weeks.

As he was pouring a drink to celebrate that achievement, Andrew returned to the house. He paused in the doorway of the gathering room. "'Night," he said, and turned back into the dark hallway.

"Andrew? Can I talk to you a minute?"

The boy paused, then came a short distance into the room. "I suppose you want to explain—justify—why I caught you making out with her."

"Justify, no. The why is none of your business. Where *is,* though, and I apologize for not choosing a more private place."

Andrew hunched his shoulders. "It's no big deal. Kids do it all the time at school."

"Does the principal know about that?"

"Probably. You two were...together...in New York when she was there, weren't you?"

Jacquie would expect him to evade, or lie. Rhys didn't want to do either. Nor did he want to hurt her. "I was married to your mother."

"Yeah, but she told me she left for a while before I was born, and the guy she was with didn't want kids so she came back."

"She told you that?" *The bitch.*

"It was one of her 'poor pitiful me' periods. Between boyfriends, in other words."

"Recently?"

"I was about ten."

"Damn, Andrew." He ran a hand over his face, rubbed his eyes. "I'm sorry I let her take you. I honestly thought she would care for you better than I could."

"Hey, no problem. I like knowing where I stand."

Hearing the bitterness, Rhys knew he couldn't lie to his son, or evade the truth. "Your mother left me in February. Jacquie arrived in June. And, yes, we fell in love and were together while she stayed at the stable."

Andrew nodded. "Thanks. Can I go now?"

"Good night."

Climbing the stairs, Andrew reflected that the old man must still have some life in him, at least as far as women were concerned. That scene had been a shocker, for sure. R-rated, at least.

Even weirder was the possibility that the resemblance between Erin and himself was more than just coincidence. The timing looked suspicious—his birthday, and Imperator's, was in September, just after his mom went back to his dad. Erin had said she wouldn't turn fourteen until May, after the Top Flight Horse Trials…fourteen years and nine months, more or less, from the time Miss Jacquie left New York.

Andrew dropped facedown on his bed, still in his clothes.

He had a sister. Or half, at least. Damn if he'd ever wanted one, or knew what to do about it. Erin didn't seem to know the facts, and nobody was telling. He'd better keep his mouth shut, for the time being.

Stirring up trouble with Erin would be the quickest way to get himself banned from riding Imp. And no girl—even a sister—was worth that.

WITH MIRAGE SAFELY INSIDE the horse trailer, Erin went back into the barn. Imperator stood with his head over the door to his stall, watching her with his big, kind eyes.

"You're not going to bite me, whatever Andrew says. I know you better than that." She rubbed her knuckles over his cheek, under his forelock, then stroked her fingers beneath his chin. "You're a gentleman all the way through.

"But what's the trouble with the jumps, Imp? How come you're not going over? Too high? Too fast…or too slow? You know you're a winner. What can we do to help?"

Imperator shook his head and pulled out of her reach, going to stand with his head in the corner and his tail toward Erin.

"Okay. We'll drop the subject for now. I'll be back, though." The stallion looked at her over his shoulder. Erin smiled. "Yeah. That's a promise."

JACQUIE COULD ONLY HOPE her blush had faded by the time she opened the truck door and turned on the light. Even after the heat in her cheeks cooled, she didn't think she would recover from those kisses in the dark hallway any time soon.

"Hey, Mom, look!" Sitting in the other seat, Erin held one long-stemmed rose in each hand. "The pink one was on my side and the yellow one on yours. Aren't they beautiful?"

Speechless, Jacquie climbed into her seat and took the yellow rose from her daughter. A card dangled from the yellow ribbon tied around the stem. "Have you looked at your card?"

Erin nodded. "It's from Mr. Lewellyn. 'Happy Valentine's Day to a brave and gentle lady.' Is that not just the most romantic thing you ever heard?"

Jacquie smiled wryly. "He does have the touch, doesn't he?" She was afraid to open her card in front of Erin, in case he'd said something she couldn't reveal to her daughter.

"Come on, Mom, what does yours say?"

Biting her lower lip, she opened the small envelope and read the deceptively simple message. "I seem to remember you liked yellow best. I hope that's still the case. As ever, Rhys."

She was relieved to be able to let Erin see the card and yet...had she hoped for something more? Was the card—the kisses—just an opportunity to revisit an old lust, or evidence of a deeper emotion? She'd trusted Rhys Lewellyn fourteen years ago, and had been damaged almost beyond repair. How could she possibly trust him now, with so much more than just her own heart at risk?

And after the disastrous consequences of her first mistake, how could she possibly trust herself?

ON SUNDAY, SANDY and Jimmy brought their baby to lunch. "He's grown already," Jacquie declared as she met them at her parents' front door. "We just saw him a week ago."

"Seems like he nurses twelve times a day." Sandy sighed. "I've never been this tired in my whole life."

"I remember that stage." Jacquie slipped her nephew out of his mother's arms. "Let me hold him while he's thinking about something besides food. You go relax in the den with Daddy and Jimmy." She sat down in the rocker in the living room, where the sweet rhythm of baby-rocking brought a smile to her face. "I love holding babies," she told Erin as she knelt beside the chair.

"He's sweet," she said, stroking a finger down his cheek. "Teddy's a cute name."

Jacquie smiled. "I wonder if he'll look like his dad—kinda big and burly, with all that brown hair."

"Sounds like a teddy bear. I guess I look mostly like my dad, don't I?" Erin glanced around the room at the pictures of their family on the walls. "Nobody here has black hair or blue eyes."

Baby Teddy stirred and fussed a little in Jacquie's suddenly stiff hold. "That's pretty much right. You've got my chin. And I don't think you'll be tall, like he was."

"You know, I never did get to see a picture of Mark," Alicia said from the couch across the room. "I didn't want to bother you at first, and then I guess I just kind of forgot."

"I...don't have pictures." Jacquie felt her heart

pound against her breastbone. "There just wasn't time before he…died."

"Not even photos from before you met?" Her sister could be unpleasantly persistent.

"Sorry."

Alicia shook her head. "It's like he didn't even exist, you know?"

Erin jerked around to stare at her aunt, then scrambled to her feet and left the room.

Teddy, chose that moment to start working toward a full-fledged tantrum on Jacquie's shoulder.

Becky Lennon came to take charge of her grandson. "What a terrible thing to say in front of Erin. Alicia Charlotte, you ought to be ashamed of yourself."

"I didn't mean to hurt her. I would think Erin feels the same way sometimes."

Sandy came in from the hallway. "Did I hear Teddy? Is he okay?"

"He's fine," Becky assured her daughter-in-law.

But Jacquie wasn't so confident about Erin. She found her daughter in the upstairs bedroom she and Alicia had shared. "Hey, kid. What are you doing?"

"Nothing."

"Thinking?"

"Nothing."

"Okay." Jacquie went to the dressing table and fiddled with the brush and comb set there. "Are you thinking about what Alicia said?"

"Maybe." After a minute, Erin flipped around to lie on her stomach facing the mirror. "Why don't we have pictures?"

"I told you. We just didn't have much time."

"But you don't even have pictures from your wedding. Or honeymoon."

"I—" There was no explanation that would make sense, except the truth. And the truth was the one thing she couldn't say. "I'm sorry. It just didn't seem important at the time." Jacquie sat on the bed and put an arm across Erin's back. "But I have lots of pictures of you. Doesn't that count?"

Erin rolled over to look into her face. "I guess," she said. But her eyes were wary and worried, and Jacquie knew with certainty that her reprieve was coming to an end.

ON THE MONDAY BEFORE the Fairfield Schooling Day, Jacquie took Imperator for his last heavy workout before the event. She pulled up beside Rhys after her first run through the course.

"Completely inconsistent," she told him. "He'll balk at fences he cleared last week and decide to fly across ones I haven't gotten him over before. He almost lost me at the water—took two strides in and decided he didn't want his feet wet, so he wheeled around and headed back out and up the hill."

"Did you get him through after that?"

"At a walk." She rubbed a gloved hand over Imp's shoulder. "He doesn't seem to know what he wants anymore. Are you sure he didn't fall on his head?"

"No, that was definitely me. Have another go."

Twenty minutes later, she came back equally frustrated. "We trotted through the water this time. And he did dump me at the ditch and lattice fence. I had to find a stump to mount from just to get back in the saddle."

Rhys put a hand on her thigh. "Are you hurt?"

The horse sidled away from him. Jacquie shook her head. "No. I bounce, remember?" With a quick twist, she brought her leg over the saddle and slid to the ground. Then she led Imp back to him and held out the reins. "Why don't you try a round with him? It very well could be that he and I simply don't have the rapport to get through this. We've made a lot of progress. But I think he needs his real partner to bring him all the way back."

Rhys stared at her hand holding the glossy black leather strips of the reins, and felt as if he'd been hosed off from the shoulders down with ice water. He managed to shake his head. "I...don't think so."

"I doubt he'll improve further until you work with him again."

"Dammit, don't push me." He turned and walked away from her, his legs moving like tree trunks underneath him.

Jacquie followed, leading the horse. "You'd better give me a good reason not to push. I understand you were injured, and maybe it still hurts. But the horse matters most right now. I'm not asking for world-record timing, and you don't have to take the advanced fences. Imp needs you to bring him home."

"I can't."

"I beg your pardon?"

"I can't...take him over the jumps."

She grabbed his arm and stopped both him and the horse. "You're saying you're afraid?"

"No, I'm not saying it." He knew he was behaving like a pouting child. But that didn't change the way his gut twisted at the idea of heading for even the simplest crossbar fence.

One side of Jacquie's mouth twitched into a half smile. "I understand. But that's the situation? Both you *and* Imp lost your confidence in that fall?"

"That's about the size of things."

"You ride dressage, so it's not the horse. Or the height."

"Right."

"Stadium fences and cross-country?"

"I haven't faced either one."

"Yet you've coached all of us."

"With, you'll have noticed, both feet firmly on the ground."

"Okay, then. Get on."

He turned to look her in the eye. "No."

"Rhys, you're letting your brain rule your gut."

"It's my gut threatening to revolt at the thought."

"You're not a coward."

"I wasn't, fourteen years ago. Things change, Jacquie."

"Not this. Please, just get in the saddle. I can't throw you on top of the horse. I can't make you do anything."

"Actually, I believe you could have anything from me that you wanted." After a long moment, he took the reins from her hand and rounded to Imp's left side. "Hold still; old man. I'm not as young as I used to be." Imp was kind enough to stand in one place and Rhys pulled himself into the saddle. They walked a few circles, settling in with each other again. Then Rhys looked at Jacquie. "So?"

She nodded down the leaf-covered lane ahead of them. "This way." They walked to the starting gate of the Rourke Park cross-country course. Open ground stretched in front of them for about two hundred yards, ending at a simple two-log fence. Simple, except for the fact that the logs were twelve feet long and four feet high. Rhys swallowed against nausea.

"Trot over there," Jacquie instructed. "Nothing fancy. For a big guy like this, it's just a hop. So let him hop. He's been over twice today so far—he shouldn't have any worries."

Imperator trotted smoothly enough away from the starting gate. The ground was covered with brown winter grass, but was solid underneath—good footing. They approached the fence with Imp's ears pricked forward and Rhys's hands sweating inside his gloves. He didn't think for the horse at all, let Imp choose his own spot for taking off. At the last second, Rhys closed his eyes.

The horse reached the log, straightened his forelegs, and stopped dead. Rhys hit the bridge of his nose against a strongly arched neck, and fell back into the saddle.

They turned and trotted nicely back to Jacquie.

She was waiting with her arms crossed. "Again."

Rhys rolled his eyes, turned the horse and tried again. He kept his eyes open this time, and he didn't get his nose bumped.

"You'll have to canter," Jacquie said when he went back. "Imp can't have too much time to think about this. Take the crop and urge him through the jump."

The blood rushed from Rhys's head, and he thought about leaving the saddle helmet first. "Jacquie, this doesn't work."

"It does and it will. Be your own student, Rhys. Kick your own butt over the fence."

"Interesting image." He took the crop she held out. "I'm hating you right now."

"Let me count the number of times I hated you that summer."

"I'd rather count the number of times you loved

me.'' With the thought, he circled Imperator in a trot, picked up the canter and headed once again for the fence.

The feel came back as Rhys settled into Imp's rhythm. He could see the spot from which they should take off, knew to look beyond the fence to where they would head next.

But what he saw was the fence itself, the huge wooden logs so similar to the one he'd fallen on last fall. He could almost hear the crack of his back as he landed. His hands and his knees loosened.

Rhys hit the grass in front of the fence face first.

Imperator made the jump clean and clear, and kept on going.

CHAPTER NINE

"OMIGOD...omigod...omigod...omigod..." Racing to the fence where Rhys had fallen, Jacquie whispered a prayer in time with the pounding of her boots on the hard ground. "Don't be hurt. Please don't let him be hurt."

He lay on his side, as still as the logs beside him. Jacquie dropped to her knees. "Rhys?" She put a hand gently on his shoulder. A shudder went through his body. "Rhys?"

After silent and agonizing seconds, he dragged in a long, harsh breath. "Damn, that hurt." He rolled to his back, groaning. "Oh, hell. Bloody, bloody hell."

"Are you okay? Does everything work?"

"As much as it ever did. But...damn." He drew his knees up and crossed his arms over his chest to curl forward, then dropped flat again with a moan. "Where's the horse?"

"He ran on. If you're sure you're okay, I'll go get him." She started to rise, but Rhys grabbed her wrist.

"Let's try this, first." Swearing, he levered himself up on one elbow, flattened his lips against his teeth and gave two sharp, loud whistles.

Jacquie winced. "Ouch."

"Sorry. But Imp usually comes when I—see, there he is."

The stallion came cantering back through the trees, to all appearances carefree. Jacquie got to her feet, climbed over the log fence and waited for him to come near. "Good boy, Imp. Whoa. Whoa." She grabbed at the reins with a sigh of relief. "Let's get you in the trailer, big guy."

"Don't mind me," Rhys said from the other side of the jump. "I'm going to lie here and collect my thoughts."

Once Jacquie and the horse were out of sight, he started the struggle that would get him to his feet. He was soaked in sweat by the time he straightened up. *You're certainly nobody's hero,* he told himself, *if you can't take a beginner fence without breaking down. Maybe Andrew's right.*

He limped back to where they'd parked, and propped himself against the side of the truck bed.

Jacquie came out of the horse trailer looking anxious. "Are you sure you're okay?"

"A little stiff. I've had worse falls." He hunched a shoulder and winced. "Obviously."

"I'm sorry I forced you into jumping. I—"

"Don't apologize. It's nobody's fault but my own."

"You shouldn't blame yourself, either." Her green gaze was fierce on his behalf.

But sympathy was not called for. "I didn't see anyone else on the horse."

"We're all nervous after a hard fall."

Rhys smiled, with bitterness. "This wasn't nerves. This was…failure."

"Failure is not trying at all."

"For some people, maybe."

"You're different?"

"Yes, as a matter of fact." He glanced at her and quickly looked away. "When you perform at the top levels, 'just trying' doesn't meet anyone's expectations."

"Especially yours."

"Especially mine." His head ached and each separate bone in his spine throbbed independently. "But thanks for the effort."

Jacquie stood close beside him, her hand on his shoulder, and he could feel her worry, her longing to make things right. Even after he'd screwed up her life in the most basic of ways, she could offer him her generous concern.

But, God help him, he needed more. He turned his head to look into her eyes, searching for a spark to kindle the passion between them. Since his very first glimpse of Jacquie Archer, he'd never seen her without wanting her.

And there it was, the answer to his desire, in the intensity of her honest eyes. A wise man would have hesitated, even turned away. Rhys curled an arm around Jacquie's waist, pulled her against him and took her mouth with his.

Jacquie was stunned by the desperation in Rhys's kiss, in his arms holding her tightly to him. He seemed to be seeking, pleading for…what? She offered everything she could, answering the press and slide of his mouth with her own.

They broke apart for breath, and a moment later Imperator slammed the side of the trailer with his rear hooves.

"He doesn't like trailers," Rhys said in a rough voice, and Jacquie chuckled. "I should get him home." But for another minute they stood as they were, with her head tucked under his chin, his heart beating hard against her ear, and the wonderful warmth of his body surrounding her.

Then he stepped back, though his hands lingered on her shoulders until the last instant. "And I'm sure you have your own work to take care of."

Jacquie brushed her hair out of her face, trying to descend back to solid ground. "Um…yes. I do have a farm visit to make before I pick Erin up at school."

Rhys backed up until he stood beside the driver's door. "Will she be there for her lesson tomorrow? There are still a few jumps to paint."

She was too bemused to do more than agree. "We'll be there."

His smile was everything she remembered from that summer so long ago. "Excellent. I'll see you then."

TUESDAY AFTERNOON, Erin and Andrew took their last lesson before the schooling day in a cold mist that managed to soak them through without actually forming drops of rain. Andrew rode Ricochet, the horse he would compete on while Jacquie exhibited Imperator. They'd decided not to enter the great horse as a ribbon contender, since his Olympic status meant he could only legitimately run against horses of the same caliber. That way, if he refused the jumps, he wouldn't actually *lose*.

Rhys worked the kids without mercy, focusing on the dressage movements they would perform in the flat ring. By the time he dismissed them, the horses were sweating, even in the chill, and both the riders were pouting.

"Be sure to jump Mirage tomorrow, Erin," Rhys called as she left the ring. "Briefly, just to keep him limber."

For once, she didn't have a smile for her instructor. "Yes, sir."

He watched her ride to the barn with a raised eyebrow, then looked at Jacquie. "Offended, is she?"

"You weren't exactly Mr. Congeniality."

"Yes, that's true. I don't intend to be, or to train a runner-up."

Jacquie sighed and turned away to walk toward her truck and trailer. "I'm too tired to argue with you tonight. We'll see you Friday afternoon."

"Jacquie—" Rhys started after her, but they both stopped in front of the barn to watch a Mercedes SUV pull through the gate, towing a massive trailer behind. Terry and the kids came to stand beside them.

She heard Rhys swear. "I meant to tell you—"

The Mercedes glided to a stop and Galen hopped out. "Good to see you, Jacquie! Lovely weather we're having, isn't it? But the sun will be back by Friday. Rhys, I've brought my horses, my computer and printer, and enough clothes to see me through the weekend. Let's get the horses settled, then I'll set up the computer and we can get to work for real."

Terry snorted and shook his head. "C'mon, you two. Give me a hand here. Only the good Lord knows how many animals she's got in that bus." Erin and Andrew followed him eagerly to the trailer, leaving Jacquie looking at Rhys.

"Galen's staying with you?"

"She thought it would be easier than driving back

and forth for these last few days. There's a lot of work to do before Friday.''

"Smart thinking." Jacquie turned on her heel and headed for the truck again.

He caught her arm and stopped her. "That's all there is to it, Jacquie.''

"What you do is none of my business." Turning her head toward the barn, she refused to look at him, even when he pulled her around to face him.

"You know better than that.''

She chopped at the air with her free hand. "I know nothing, Rhys. You played me for a fool once before. Why should this time be different?''

"Mom?" Behind her, Erin stood watching them, a puzzled look on her face and the lead rope attached to a big Thoroughbred in her hand. "Is everything okay?''

Jacquie tugged her arm free. "Sure, honey. Of course. What do you need?''

"Mirage is loaded. Do you want to go now, or can I help get these horses settled?''

"I think we need to go home.''

"Okay." Erin's round eyes conveyed confusion and worry, as did the fact that she didn't argue or protest.

Jacquie saw her prediction starting to come true— her daughter was already suffering because they'd gotten involved with Rhys Lewellyn.

"I planned to invite you and Erin to stay over, as well," he said as Erin led the horse away. "A house party, of sorts. It's a big place. And I—we—could certainly use your help.''

Shaking her head, Jacquie again started toward her

truck. "I have animals at home. And I'm not a woman of leisure—I have to work."

Rhys stepped back. "Whatever you say. I'll see you Friday?"

"Only if I can't avoid you," Jacquie grumbled, and slammed the truck door between them.

GALEN CALLED Thursday morning. "You've got to come over here and help me with this mess."

Jacquie took firm hold of her willpower. "Why doesn't Rhys help you?"

"Every time the man touches my machine, it locks up. Plus, he has about a million other details to work on—setting up stands and jumps, getting the barn ready. I know you have a Web site, so you must be fairly comfortable with a computer."

"Well, yes, but—"

"And kids these days have to do computers in school."

"So get Andrew to help you."

"Ahem." Galen paused for a moment. "Andrew decided to take the stallion for exercise yesterday afternoon while his father and I were out."

"And...?" Jacquie blocked the idea of Rhys and Galen "out" together from her mind.

"We returned just as Andrew rode in. Needless to say, there was an explosion, followed by grounding and sulking and all the usual Sturm und Drang. So Andrew is not computer cooperative at this point."

"Is he riding this weekend?"

"Rhys says not. No one will be riding, though, if we don't get all these registration forms and schedules organized. Then there's the housework—most of the ground floor rooms haven't been used in years. I can't supervise cleaners, caterers, the florist and the lawn service *and* sit at the computer. Please, I really do need your help.''

''Can you e-mail me the files?''

''Honey, I can't. My system works with cable and Rhys, the dinosaur, only has telephones. You're gonna have to come here.''

Jacquie could feel herself sliding down the slippery slope. ''Galen, I don't want to come to Rhys's house.''

''Look, I know there's something between you, and you're struggling. But if you and Erin come, stay tonight and the weekend, you'll be chaperoned the whole time. Two kids, Terry and me—we'll be sure you don't get into a…what did they call it?…a compromising situation.''

Just being within sight of Rhys was a compromising situation. She'd sworn just Tuesday that she'd never get close to him again.

And yet Mirage would benefit from an extra night in a new stall. Erin could get a good night's sleep before she rode on Saturday. And surely, *surely*, Jacquie could stay out of Rhys's way…. She found herself agreeing. ''Okay. Let me make sure my neighbor can keep an eye on the other horses.'' Hurry would come with them. Rhys had never minded an extra dog or two hanging around.

Galen gave an audible sigh. ''Thanks so much. This will work out beautifully, you'll see.''

Jacquie had her doubts about that. She and Erin arrived just before dinner, to find Terry and Rhys leaving the stable. Terry stared at them for a moment, his brows lowered over his eyes, then stomped into the house shaking his head.

Rhys came over as they got out of the truck. "Hi, Erin. We've got Mirage's stall ready for him—number ten."

"Thanks." Quite recovered from her sulk after Tuesday's lesson, Erin gave him her usual bright smile. "My mom said I could stay home from school tomorrow, Mr. Lewellyn, so anything you need done before the show, I can help with."

"I'm glad to hear that. We'll have plenty of work for you in the morning." He turned to Jacquie as Erin went to unload her horse. "Even with the weird red hair, she really is a terrific kid—enthusiastic, helpful, respectful."

"I think so."

"Whereas my son…" His voice trailed off and he blew out a long breath.

"Has to challenge you," Jacquie told him. "I watched my brother do the same thing with my dad. It's part of growing up."

He smiled wryly. "I'd like it if he didn't kill himself or the horse in the process." With a quick shake of his head, he seemed to throw off the problem. "Anyway, I'm really glad you agreed to come. Galen's tearing her hair out."

"I don't believe you. She wouldn't destroy that beautiful cut." Jacquie started to get her overnight bag out of the back seat, but then decided she couldn't bear to have Rhys there while she carried in her clothes *to spend the night*.

"You're right, she wouldn't." Rhys laughed. "But she's banned me from my own hearth until she gets these papers done. Your arrival will be a blessing to us both.''

Seeing that sexy grin, feeling herself warm and soften in response, Jacquie couldn't repress a sigh. ''I wouldn't go that far. But I'll do what I can.''

To her surprise, the awkwardness she expected from the situation didn't materialize. Andrew took dinner in his room, removing one stress. Erin and Galen between them kept a conversation going nonstop at the table, allowing the rest of them to keep their thoughts private. Rhys and Terry disappeared into the barn after the meal, while Jacquie went to work with Galen in the gathering room, creating and printing all the different forms necessary to make the show run smoothly. Hurry and Sydney engaged in a mutual sniffing session, decided they could tolerate each other, and retired to their warms spots in front of the fire.

Jacquie was still working long after Erin fell asleep on the rug in front of the fire and was sent up to one of the guest bedrooms, and even after Galen had finally surrendered to exhaustion. The last log had burned down and all the lights in the room were still on as she sought out the remaining errors in their documents.

The outside door opened and the men tramped down the hall. She heard Terry's muttered ''g'night'' and his footsteps on the stairs.

Rhys stuck his head around the doorjamb. ''Is it safe to come in now?''

Yawning, she pushed back from the table, slouched in her chair, and closed her eyes. ''Galen's upstairs. I've caught the last of the mistakes, I think, but if not, we have at least an adequate, if not perfect, schedule to work with.''

''At two in the morning, the night before the show, I'll definitely settle for adequate.''

She heard a log land in the fire grate, and the rustle of coals being stirred into life. ''I wish I'd known. We passed adequate about midnight. We could have been in bed all this time.''

Rhys chuckled. ''That is a shame.''

Jacquie kept her eyes shut, trying to pretend—to Rhys, to herself—that she took his comment at face value. This was exactly the situation Galen had promised she could avoid. The wise course would be to get up and go to her room, right this minute.

''I'm glad you don't have to go home tonight.'' His voice was low, and did nothing to restore her good sense. ''I can offer you a glass of brandy with a clear conscience.''

She heard him approach, and opened her eyes as he stood in front of her. ''You need to relax. Come.'' He took her hand, pulled her out of the desk chair and led her to the oversize armchair near the fireplace. ''Sit. Put your feet up.''

Speechless, she did as she was told. Rhys went to the drinks tray and came back with a glass in each hand, holding one out to her as he sat down on the ottoman beside her legs.

''Grand Marnier,'' he said with a smile. ''You liked it, that summer.''

A sip revealed she still did. ''You have a good memory. I haven't yet thanked you for the rose.''

''I was just glad the next morning not to find it on

the ground where you'd parked, petals shredded and stomped into the dirt.''

"I wouldn't do that. Erin loved hers, too.''

Head cocked in her direction, he toasted her with his drink. "You're welcome.''

They sat silent for a while as the new log caught fire and the flames began to dance. Jacquie let herself be lulled by the liqueur, by the warmth, by Rhys himself. She was so very tired of fighting what she felt.

Finally she stirred and took the last sip, setting her snifter on the table at her shoulder. "What else do you remember from that summer?''

He braced his elbows on his knees, rolling his glass between his palms. "Mmm...the weather was hotter than usual. We invited you and the other students to use the pool once your chores were done after dinner. I looked out the window that first night and saw you standing on the side, splashing the water with just one foot. You wore a black one-piece suit. Very dull.''

"My parents wouldn't allow two-piece suits, let alone bikinis.''

"And I thought you were the loveliest, most desirable woman I'd ever seen.''

The breath left her lungs in a rush.

"Later in the summer, you bought yourself a typical bikini. Some kind of blue, wasn't it?''

"Aqua.''

He nodded. "But I liked the black suit. I liked knowing that I was the only man to see all of you.''

A quiver started deep inside of her, moving through her body in ever-widening waves. *Get out of here,* Jacquie ordered herself. *This instant.* She swung her legs off the side of the ottoman away from Rhys, and scooted forward in preparation for getting up.

Rhys turned to face her at that moment, so close she could see the shards of darker color in his blue eyes. He set his glass on the floor, then brought his hand to her shoulder. "You're leaving?" His fingers trailed down her arm.

She could feel his touch through the soft wool of her sweater. "I think I'd better."

"A good-night kiss, first?"

"Rhys—"

But then the magic started, and her chance of escape was lost. He had such a wonderful mouth, firm and smooth, inventive and tender. The orange liqueur spiced each kiss, but the true intoxication came from Rhys alone. When he moved into her, put his arms around her, pressed her back to stretch beneath him in the big chair, she didn't resist. Didn't want to. He was heavy in the way she'd craved for so many years, filled her arms as no one had since the last time they'd loved. The kisses went on and on and she lost herself in the wonder of his hands claiming her, pushing her sweater aside, moving over the skin of her belly and ribs. They both moaned when his palm closed over her breast.

"Jacquie." Just her name, in his rough groan, was enough to bring her to fever pitch. She arched against him, drew him closer, slipped her knees outside his hips so they moved together in the beautiful rhythm of passion. Her fingers, clumsy and trembling, went to work on his belt buckle. Why in the world were they still clothed?

He buried his face in the curve of her neck, nibbling

on the delicate cord there. Then his mouth was over her ear, his warm breath teasing, titillating. "You're on birth control?" he whispered between kisses.

She barely heard him. "What?" Then the words penetrated her bemused brain. With them came sanity. "Stop. Please, stop."

Rhys stiffened as he understood the desperate push at his shoulders. "Ah, Jacquie. Don't tell me…"

"Get off. Get. Off."

He wasn't sure he could. His body was almost beyond his control, throbbing, pounding with the need she'd aroused in him. His hips seemed to move of their own will, pressing against her softness. And once again she yielded.

But once was all. She lay lifeless under him now, staring into his face with nothing but hurt and anger in her eyes, where only moments ago had glowed the desire he'd never forgotten.

His hands fisted, and with a curse he pushed himself up, over, away, to sit with his back to Jacquie. He felt like a randy teenager. Probably looked like one, as well, sitting here sulking.

Jacquie sat with her back to him, breathing hard. After a few moments, Rhys realized she was crying.

He turned to put his arm around her shoulders. "Don't, Jacquie. Please don't. It'll be okay. I'll leave you alone…"

"Doesn't matter," she said into the hands that covered her face. "You've ruined me again, just like the first time."

"No, no, no. Nothing's happened." He took her right hand and she allowed it, but didn't respond with any kind of pressure.

"You've undermined my entire life. Stolen my daughter, kept me away from my work and my own animals. Damn you, Rhys. Now you've made me ache all over again. I don't know if I can stop."

Her sobs broke his heart. "I'll stay away from you. After this weekend—"

She pushed at his shoulder with enough strength to make his back twist. "The damage is done, don't you see? I survived all these years by forgetting you, forgetting everything about us as soon as I could. But when you touch me like this, when you hold me and kiss me...how can I forget? It's all coming back, now. What am I going to do?"

On her feet again, Jacquie fled the room before he could muster the will to stop her. Her footsteps pounded up the stairs to the second floor, and Rhys heard the bedroom door shut firmly. Was it his imagination, or did he hear the turn of the lock?

And was he imagining things, or had all of his hopes for the future just shattered like a crystal glass thrown into the fireplace?

CHAPTER TEN

THE FRIDAY EVENING PARTY for the Fairfield Schooling Day proved to be a smashing success. The judges Rhys had invited from around the country had arrived that morning and were relaxing with drinks and excellent food while they enjoyed impressing all the locals with their credentials. Riders and trainers had come to meet the great Rhys Lewellyn and to talk horses, bringing along their mothers and spouses and friends for a glimpse of the house itself. Galen had opened up the big drawing rooms Rhys never used and made sure they were cleaned and polished, so everyone got their eyeful of elegance.

Jacquie drifted through the crowd, smiling at the people she knew who spoke to her, barely hearing what they said. She'd been in a daze all day, thanks to a night without sleep, which also explained why she hadn't slipped her foot away when Pete the Percheron had put his dinner-plate-sized hoof down on her instep that afternoon. The dressy shoes she'd brought along cut right across the bruise. But at least the pain let her know she was still alive.

Andrew had refused to attend the party, since he wasn't allowed to ride. But Erin had jumped at the opportunity to enter the world of adults, wearing a sophisticated black dress Galen had found for her on a quick shopping spree that morning, and makeup Galen had talked her into trying. With her red hair and her eyes darkened with mascara, Jacquie thought her daughter looked like a stranger.

Or, simply, like her father. At the thought, she glanced across the room and met Rhys's gaze. His eyes darkened, and she felt her face flush as the memory of last night consumed her thoughts. She'd spent the hours when she should've been sleeping regretting that she had let things go so far...and wishing she hadn't forced him to stop.

"Hello, beautiful." Buck Travis appeared beside her. "I've been trying to find you." He tilted his head. "Are you okay?"

Breaking contact with Rhys, Jacquie smiled and turned to face the veterinarian. "A little tired, is all. Are you ready for the big event?"

"You mean, am I ready to stand around all day waiting for a horse to get hurt, while I talk to nice people and eat and drink and generally enjoy myself? Sure. I only wish all my workdays could be so easy."

"Here's hoping that's all you have to do."

"Erin's riding, isn't she?"

"Yes, and Mirage is in good shape. I think she'll do well."

"And will we get to see the great Imperator do his job?"

"I'm afraid so."

"Afraid?"

She shrugged. "I'm the one riding him."

"Not Lewellyn?"

"N-no. He was injured last fall at Adelaide and is still recovering."

"Too bad. I would like to see him ride."

Jacquie sighed. "Me, too."

"So where's the producer of this great party?" Buck pivoted to search the room. "I wanted to tell Galen she'd done a good job."

"Probably somewhere organizing someone's life for them."

He looked at her with his brows raised. "Whoa. That sounds...catty."

"Sorry." Her cheeks heated up. "I'm not in a good mood. Got stepped on today."

"What's Galen been organizing for you?"

"Never mind."

Buck stared at her for a minute. "Okay, I won't torture you for a confession. She can be pretty managing. But it's usually in somebody's best interest. Her motives are good."

Something about his voice, a certain softness, cued Jacquie in. "You're...interested...in Galen?"

He looked down into his wineglass. "Saint Jude is my household saint."

"I don't understand."

"The patron of lost causes." Buck smiled, a little sadly.

Jacquie put a hand on his arm. "Buck, why did you stop asking me out?"

After a long moment, he said, "I realized I didn't have a chance. You weren't free to care about somebody else."

She didn't know what to say.

"I guess some loves are just meant to last a lifetime, even if the one you love isn't there anymore. Your husband must have been quite a man."

In the bustle of the party, Jacquie suddenly felt as if she were standing in a bubble of cold silence. She hadn't thought about her "husband" in weeks. She'd forgotten she was supposed to be a widow.

"Hey, Mom, hey, Dr. T." Sparing her the necessity of an answer, Erin and her friend Cathy joined them. "Is this just the most awesome party, or what?"

"Awesome," Jacquie agreed. The conversation rambled back to tomorrow's event, allowing her to listen rather than talk and, eventually, to ease away altogether. Buck winked at her as she left—he was obviously having fun flirting with the young girls.

Jacquie just wanted the evening over. Her head swam with the noise, the warm air, the smells of wine and food. Someone had lit a cigarette, and the smoke hung in the still air of the house.

Almost without thinking, she slipped into the back hall, shutting the door between herself and the party. She pulled her barn coat off the wall rack, wrapped it tightly around her against the cold night and headed for the stable.

Many of the guests had been out earlier to tour the horse facilities, and some of the lights had been left on. The warmth here was fresh, scented with hay and manure and horse. Nice smells, ones she never grew tired of. Around her, horses munched contentedly, shuffled in their bedding, snorted and snuffled and snored. With a sigh, Jacquie sat down on a stack of hay bales set against the outside wall of Imperator's stall. She scooted backward until the bale supported her aching foot off the ground, then closed her eyes. Peace. At last.

Rhys found her there, fast asleep, after midnight.

"Jacquie?" She didn't stir—a measure of her exhaustion. He knew how she felt—he hadn't slept last night, himself.

Kneeling beside the hay bale, he put a hand on her shoulder and shook her gently. "Jacquie? Wake up, sweetheart. You need to come inside."

Finally her eyelashes fluttered, lifted. She looked at him in confusion. "Rhys? What's wrong?"

He couldn't hide his smile. "You're sleeping in the barn, woman, when there's a perfectly good bed waiting for you."

She started to smile back at him. "Didn't mean to." And then full consciousness returned, and the smile died. "Sorry."

"I...we were worried about you, that's all. Erin couldn't find you when the party ended. I finally thought to look out here." He got to his feet and held out his hand. "Come on, let's go into the house."

Jacquie hesitated, then put her hand in his and allowed him to pull her to her feet. She took one step forward, gasped, and would have fallen if he hadn't been close enough to get an arm around her and hold her up.

"What is it? What's wrong?"

She pressed her head against his shoulder. "M-my f-foot."

"Asleep?"

"Don't I wish. I got stepped on today by a Percheron I was shoeing."

"Is it broken?"

"No, just bruised." She shifted her weight and gasped again. "But it hurts. A lot."

"Right." He bent and put his free arm under her

knees, lifting her high against his chest. "Here we go."

"Put me down. Rhys, you'll hurt your back." She beat a fist against his shoulder. "I can walk, dammit. Put me down!"

He ignored her frustration and the ache in his back as he carried her to the house. Erin opened the door when he got there, and Galen and Terry were waiting in the hallway. Amid much worry and fussing, he carried Jacquie upstairs to the blue guest room and set her on the bed. Then he straightened up, rubbing the shoulder she'd assaulted.

"Remind me never to get into a fistfight with you."

She stared at him in fury, unrepentant. "That was not necessary."

Rhys shrugged. "It's done. Let's take a look at that foot." Grudgingly she pulled off her shoe. He hissed air through his teeth when he saw the black-and-purple stain covering her small foot from toes to ankle. "Are you sure it's not broken?" Jacquie hesitated, and he knew the truth. "You aren't sure."

"I don't think so. I walked fine afterward. But then the swelling started, and the bruising."

Galen appeared at the door. "Here's ice and extra pillows."

Without protesting any further, Jacquie leaned back and let Galen take care of the foot. "Thanks. That feels much better."

Erin sat on the other side of the bed. "Wow, Mom. How are you going to get your boots on to ride to-morrow? Your foot is about twice its regular size."

Jacquie looked at Rhys, then away. "I'm sure it will be better by morning."

"Right," Rhys said. They both knew the chances of her being able to ride were slim. "So let's all go to bed and get some rest." The chances of that were almost as slim, at least as far as he was concerned. "We've got a big day tomorrow. Erin, you'll help your mom?"

His daughter, so grown-up in her dress and makeup, nodded earnestly.

The situation was too much for him, all at once. He managed to say good-night politely and left them— his love and their child—to shut himself safely behind the door of his own empty bedroom. Everyone he cared about…his *family,* dammit…was here tonight.

But what should have brought joy had, instead, created heartache. His love for Jacquie made her miserable—that much was clear from her words last night. As much as he wanted her, needed her, he would not torture her any further. Even if he had to leave this house, abandon the small, friendly town he'd begun to look on as home.

And his daughter. The image of Erin, just down the hall, stayed with him through the dark night. She was everything he would have asked for—spirited, independent, ambitious and determined. Yet there was a gentleness inside this lovely girl that he recognized, the same concern and kindness he'd been drawn to in Jacquie. He wanted the chance to talk with Erin, discover her thoughts about…well, about everything. He wanted to train her to the highest levels and then show her off in Europe as one of the best in a new generation of riders. She and Andrew would take the horse world by storm.

Rhys realized he could dream up a whole lifetime

centered around Jacquie and Erin and Andrew, a life-time of laughter and excitement and love. But dreams belonged to the sleeper, and he was all too wide awake. Awake and certain that he'd never get the op-portunities he craved. His role in Erin's life would be brief, and only as a friend, at best. He'd had so little of her.

And now he would have to give her up altogether.

"WHAT?" Andrew struggled out of bed in the dark-ness to answer the rap on his door. *"What?"*

The great Lewellyn stood there, dressed for the day and looking as if he hadn't slept in weeks. "It's al-most dawn and you're riding Imperator today. Get dressed and get outside."

He turned away and would have left, but Andrew caught his sleeve. "Why? What's happened?"

"Jacquie's hurt her foot and it's too sore, too swol-len, to get her boot on or to ride safely. The crowd wants to see Imperator, and you're the only rider we've got. You'll be riding Ricochet, too." He sucked in a deep breath and blew it out again, then his mouth curved in a tired smile. "Today, your wish comes true. Get to work."

Andrew let go and turned back into his room, scared and excited and amazed beyond belief. The old man had changed his mind—Hallelujah! Sure, he'd done it for the horse, not Andrew, but who cared? At least he hadn't offered the chance to Erin.

He stopped with his shirt buttoned halfway as a question occurred to him. Had his dad asked Erin first, and she'd refused?

Then he shook his head and finished the buttons.

Erin would have snatched at the invitation with both hands. Andrew pulled on his breeches, satisfied that he had been his dad's first choice. Finally he would get to show what he could do with Imp, on the flat and over the jumps. Cross-country, too.

Man, what a great day this would be!

FROM BEING A RIDER, Jacquie found herself demoted to a mere spectator, unable to do more than hobble around with a cane and assure Galen that everything was perfect. She caught glimpses of Rhys as he strode through the event, keeping the schedule running smoothly, keeping the judges happy, greeting guests, all while managing to coach Erin and Andrew as they prepared their mounts to compete.

Fifty horses had been entered to perform dressage tests, show jumping, and the short cross-country course. All three trials were occurring simultaneously, which called for a large number of volunteers. Phoebe Moss had been one of the first, and was stationed at the dressage ring, keeping the riders organized.

"What did you do?" she said immediately upon seeing Jacquie's limp. Jacquie explained about the Percheron. "Those horses are huge—I know that must hurt. Why don't you sit here for a while?" Rhys had insisted that all the volunteers have a chair they could use when there was time.

"I think I will, thanks." Jacquie sank gratefully into the folding chair. "How's it going?"

"Good. Everybody's here, everybody's right on time. Erin will ride in twenty minutes."

"Jacquie Archer!" Her mother's voice carried over

the crowd noises. "Goodness gracious, girl, what have you done now?"

She looked over to see Becky and Ed Lennon standing a few feet away, staring at her with dismayed expressions. How many times had this happened in her life?

"Hi, Mom." She waved. "Hey, Daddy. I got stepped on, that's all. Just a bruise."

Her dad put a hand on her shoulder. "Bad enough for a cane?"

"My friends insisted." She shrugged. "Y'all are here right on time. Erin should ride in the next few minutes. You remember Phoebe Moss?"

"Our mayor's future wife?" Becky Lennon gave Phoebe a hug. "I should say so. How are the wedding plans coming along?"

The tension eased, and they chatted until Erin arrived at the gate of the dressage ring to sign in.

"Good luck," Jacquie told her. "Mirage looks terrific."

"He's in a good mood," Erin said. "I think this is our day."

The rider before her left the ring and Erin entered, trotting Mirage around outside the white fence until the bell rang, signaling her to go in. Just as she entered the ring, Rhys stepped up beside Jacquie.

"She should do well," he said without looking at her.

"Thank you for helping her." Jacquie remembered the protocol from her own training days. "Can I pay you a schooling fee?"

He whipped his head around to stare at her with a mixture of hurt and anger and injured pride. "No, thank you.'' Turning on his heel, he went to stand on the opposite side of the ring.

Phoebe took his place. ''I haven't had a chance to say hello to Rhys today. Every time I see him, he's got about forty people around him, asking questions.''

''That's Rhys Lewellyn?'' Her mother turned and watched Rhys for a long moment, or so it seemed to Jacquie.

''Let's be quiet,'' Jacquie said. ''Her test is beginning.''

Erin's exercise went very well. Mirage moved through his figures gracefully, with his neck arched nicely in front of Erin's quiet hands. At the canter, at the trot, at the walk, he performed as well as he ever had in his life. As Erin completed her test, Andrew rode up on Imperator.

''She was good,'' Andrew commented. ''High score, I bet.''

''Thanks. What are you doing next?''

''Imperator's demonstration dressage.''

Jacquie bit back a curse. How had that happened? She'd tried to be sure the kids were in different places throughout the day, to avoid having comparisons made. ''You were scheduled later, right?''

''Dad decided we should go before lunch.'' As he spoke, Rhys's voice over the loudspeaker announced Imperator's first demonstration. The crowd began to flow in their direction.

Crushing her program in her hand, Jacquie fought the urge to strangle Rhys and his son. ''Well, good luck to you, too.''

''Thanks.'' He patted Imperator's neck with a gloved hand. ''This guy knows his stuff.''

Erin rode out of the white ring and Andrew moved forward to take her place. For a moment, the two of them were side by side on their mounts. In dark riding coats, breeches and boots and helmets, absolutely the only difference between the two was the horses they rode.

Beside Jacquie, Phoebe gasped softly. "That's amazing."

Jacquie looked for her mother, and met Becky Lennon's considering expression. There could be no doubt that she'd noticed the resemblance between the kids. While she watched, her mother glanced at Rhys again. *And so it begins.*

As the crowd gathered around the ring to watch the great horse at dressage, Jacquie spotted a friend of hers standing nearby. Shuffling and limping, she made her way through the crowd to stand beside him. "Rob? How's it going?"

The tall, blond man in a baseball cap turned his head. "Hey, there, Jacquie. I should've known I'd find you here." He noticed the cane and his smile disappeared. "What'd you do now?" They'd been good friends since kindergarten—Rob had seen or heard about most of her accidents and injuries over the years. There was only one part of her life she hadn't shared with him.

"Had my foot in the wrong place." A heart-shaped face peeked out from behind Rob, and Jacquie smiled. "Hi, Ginny. We're twins today, aren't we?" She held up her cane.

The girl moved forward on her set of aluminum crutches. "Sort of. I've got two." Rob's seven-year-old daughter, Virginia, had been born with cerebral palsy.

"With all these people pushing, I'd rather have two, too. Are you enjoying the horses?"

Ginny's eyes took on a fanatic glow that Jacquie recognized all too well. "They're so big. And so beautiful!" Looking at Imperator, just beginning his performance, she sighed. "I want to do that."

Jacquie watched with her. Imperator was incredible in dressage—balanced, precise, fluid and strong. Andrew handled him well although, with her experience, she could see the slight mistakes that Rhys would not have made.

"You can do that," she told Ginny, leaning down to speak quietly in the girl's ear. "All you need is a horse and some lessons."

Ginny stared at her with big, brown eyes. "Really? Really? I could ride? That horse?"

Oops. "Maybe not at first. We'd start you on someone smaller. But, eventually, you could even ride Imperator."

"Daddy?" She tugged on her dad's jacket. "Daddy, I want riding lessons."

"You got 'em, sweetheart." Rob looked at Jacquie. "What have you done to me now, Ms. Archer? I have the feeling I'm in a boatload of trouble."

She put her hand on his arm. "Just bring her out to my place. Erin and I will make sure she's safe and she'll have a blast."

He nodded. "That's what counts. I'll call you. Soon."

"Good." She turned back to catch the end of Imperator's show. The applause was thunderous, and Imperator bowed his head toward the audience, accepting the accolade as his due.

But if the spectators had seen Imperator's greatness, they had also noticed the uncanny resemblance between Erin and Andrew. Most riders looked alike in their riding togs—discipline and uniformity were the point. Such similar faces, carriage and movement as the two kids displayed, though, was evident to interested eyes.

The comments came to her during the day from friends and strangers alike. "I saw Imperator's dressage test," Buck Travis said as they watched Erin prepare for her cross-country run. "Magnificent horse. But for a minute I thought it was Erin riding him."

"She would love to," was Jacquie's weak return. Rhys stood beside Erin, giving last-minute instructions on the cross-country course. The likeness between them was clear to her, and she groaned silently. This had been a mistake from the very beginning.

The volunteer starter at the cross-country course was Dixon Bell. He was, of course, too busy to talk, but Kate came over to stand with Jacquie. They hugged and then turned to watch as Erin and Mirage entered the starting gate.

Two women Jacquie didn't know walked up beside them, programs for the show in hand. "That's the Lewellyn boy, right?" one said. "But that gray horse is not Imperator. Maybe the boy's riding two different horses."

"Maybe…" The companion consulted her program. "No, wait. Says here that Erin Archer is number one-oh-three, riding Mirage. So that's not Andrew Lewellyn."

"Sure looks like him."

"Everybody looks the same in all that gear."

"I suppose so."

Jacquie closed her eyes and gave thanks for the reprieve.

With her bum foot, she couldn't run along to see Erin at every jump on the mile-long course, so she simply had to wait, more than a little anxious, to get a report at the end. Her parents had walked farther along the course to watch some of the interior jumps, but Kate waited with Jacquie, talking about people they knew in town, which helped calm her nerves. Finally Mirage galloped up the hill and took the last jump—a zigzag fence with bushes before and behind—in perfect form.

At the finish line, Erin hopped down and pulled off her helmet. Again her face glowed with happiness. "What a great ride! He was so awesome, Mom. The best he's ever been." She put her arms around the horse's neck and gave him a hug.

Rhys joined them. "Excellent run, Erin. I'm proud of you." And he was—his eyes were warm, almost tender. Then he looked at Kate. "It's good to see you again. Are you enjoying the day?"

"It's wonderful, of course. I'm only sorry we couldn't come to the party last night. We had a family birthday to celebrate. My husband's grandmother turned eighty-five yesterday."

"Definitely the better celebration," Rhys agreed, grinning. He turned to Erin. "So, scamp, all you've got left is the show jumping. I'm sure you'll run through with no problems."

"I hope so." Erin, ever impulsive, threw her arms

around Rhys's neck and hugged him just as she'd hugged the horse. "Oh, Mr. Lewellyn, thank you so much. This has just been the best day of my life!"

After a frozen moment, Rhys put his hands gently on Erin's back. His eyes closed, and then he turned his head away. "Thank you, sweetheart. Working with you has been…great for me, too."

Blinking back the sting of tears, Jacquie looked toward Kate, only to find her friend staring at man and girl with an arrested expression on her face.

"Damn," Jacquie muttered under her breath. "Damn him." The pair separated, but the damage was done.

"And damn me."

ERIN'S SHOW JUMPING went well, though she came in second behind Andrew on Ricochet. But Ricochet's cross-country time wasn't as good as Mirage's, so their dressage scores would determine the winner. Andrew finished his dressage round on Ricochet, then rushed to prepare for Imp's cross-country run, the final event of the day before the awards were announced.

The entire crowd lined the course, wanting to see the big horse run. Rhys had no idea how the next fifteen minutes would turn out. Imperator could sail across the easy fences and impress them all. Or he could balk at every single jump and give birth to the speculation that his career had ended.

"Do what you can," he told Andrew as he checked the girth and the stirrup leathers one last time. "Don't drive him hard, give him time to see the jump before he gets there. Be sure to take the easiest line."

Andrew tightened his helmet strap. "I've got it, Dad. You said all this ten minutes ago."

"I'll wait for you at the finish." He looked up into his son's face and saw the likeness to Erin. "Good luck, son."

The boy's grin was just like his own. "Thanks. This has been one incredible day."

He trotted Imperator to the starting block and backed in, as required. Rhys watched the horse, saw by the prick of his ears that Imp recognized what was coming. His attitude changed, right at that moment, taking on an edge of nerves quite unlike his confidence earlier in the day. Eyes wide, tail flicking, the stallion waited for his cue. Andrew pressed his heels against the horse's sides, and Imperator exploded onto the course.

The first jump was in clear view. Andrew followed Rhys's directions, approaching the triangular pile of logs at a slow canter. Rhys held his breath. Imp shook his head from side to side as they got near, and would have pulled Andrew from the saddle if the boy hadn't had such an excellent seat. At the last second, Imp decided to do what he was asked. He took the jump, awkwardly but cleanly.

Polite applause rose from the crowd. "I looked for more finesse," a man beside Rhys commented. "Maybe it's the rider. Lewellyn's son, I think. Could be he doesn't have his father's talent." Rhys clenched his hands into fists but refrained from punching the guy out.

The second jump, a lattice structure painted in red and black with stop signs on either side, was visible in the distance. A groan went up as Imperator refused the fence. Andrew circled, brought him back. If he refused again, the ride would be over. But Imperator, great performer that he was, made a supreme effort and got himself and Andrew over the lattice. They vanished into a stand of trees, leaving Rhys to follow the course in his mind, with periodic reports from each fence on the two-way radio. He stared at his watch, calculating where the pair should be at any given moment. As the sweep hand ticked off seconds, Jacquie came up beside him.

"He should finish soon, right?"

"Thirty more seconds would be a winning time."

But the thirty seconds passed without a reappearance of Imperator and Andrew.

Rhys gave up on the watch. "Something's happened."

Jacquie put a warm hand on his arm. "Imperator probably refused and Andrew's struggling to get him over."

"Probably." His worry escalated with every extra second.

He took the radio off his belt. "This is Lewellyn," he said into the speaker. "Somebody tell me what's going on."

"Fence six," a voice came back. "Imperator refused and the boy is still trying to get him over."

"Tell Andrew to bring the horse in," Rhys ordered. "We'll calculate the scores and award the ribbons."

He turned to Jacquie. "Well, so much for a month of training rides. Imperator still won't take the fences.

"I've got a million-dollar horse that can't— won't—perform. What do I do now?"

CHAPTER ELEVEN

ANDREW WALKED Imperator all the way back to the barn, avoiding the crowd by taking the path through the woods. By the time he reached the stable, everyone had gathered around the jumping arena for the awards ceremony.

The announcement came through loud and clear, even inside the stall. "The blue ribbon for first place in the Fairfield Schooling Day Preliminary Class goes to…Miss Erin Archer and Mirage!"

There was no missing the pleasure in his dad's voice. He really liked seeing the girl win. And what would the great Lewellyn have to say about Imperator's refusals? None of the ribbons Andrew had won over the years—and there were a lot of them—compensated for his failure with Imp.

With the saddle and bridle put away, the horse brushed, watered and fed, Andrew slipped out of the barn and into the house. In the hallway, he nearly ran into a woman who stood by the door to the gathering room."

"Sorry," he murmured, going past.

"I was just touring the rooms," she said. "That's all."

"Sure. No problem." He started again for the stairs.

She came after him. "You're Andrew, aren't you? Mr. Lewellyn's son?"

"Yes, ma'am."

"I'm Mrs. Lennon. Erin Archer's grandmother."

"Hi." He could see that Mrs. Archer did look like her mother. Not Erin, of course.

"You rode that big horse really well today." Her eyes hadn't left his face. He felt like an insect being studied under the microscope.

"Uh, thanks."

"I'm sorry he wouldn't take the fence for you. That must be so disappointing."

The gentleness in her voice, the kindness in her soft face, put a lump in his throat. "Yes, ma'am." His grandmothers were both a very different type of person.

"Well, I'd best get back to my family." She touched his arm for just a second. "It's nice to meet you, Andrew."

He couldn't find his voice, but he lifted a hand to say goodbye. The hallway seemed darker, somehow, after Mrs. Lennon went outside.

ERIN'S WIN WAS duly celebrated with champagne for all the volunteers, once the horses were stabled and the crowds dispersed. Cathy Parr had taken fourth place in one of the lower level classes. Both girls were nearly incoherent with pride and excitement.

"This was a really successful event," Rhys told them all, raising his glass in a toast. "I can't thank each of you enough for your efforts. You'll always have a welcome at Fairfield Farm, whenever you come by."

As darkness fell, the volunteers, too, went home. Leaning on her borrowed cane, Jacquie said goodbye to Phoebe and Dixon and Kate at the door. "I do appreciate y'all coming out."

"We wouldn't have missed seeing Erin win her ribbon," Dixon said. "And now Kate knows exactly what she's aiming for." He hugged his blushing wife around the waist. "I'm kinda tempted, myself. Those cross-country jumps are spectacular to watch!"

Last to leave was Buck Travis. "What a great day." He took her free hand in both his own. "I'm really proud of Erin—and of you, as her trainer. You're doing a great job."

"Well, you know we were glad to have you here."

"My pleasure." He leaned in and kissed her cheek. "Do you need a ride home, with that foot?"

"It's my left. I'm fine for driving."

"Okay, then." He dropped her hand and turned away, hesitated, and looked at her again. "Would you like to have dinner sometime? Soon?"

Jacquie opened her mouth, though she had no idea what her answer would be. Footsteps approached from the hall behind her, and she looked over her shoulder into Rhys's stiff face.

"Thank you for your help," he said to Buck, extending an arm to shake the vet's hand. "I'm glad we had nothing much for you to do."

"Me, too." Buck looked from Jacquie's face to Rhys's and back again. "I'll see the two of you around, I'm sure. Good night." This time he walked away without looking back, and Jacquie understood that she'd lost her last chance with a good man.

Maybe Galen would be smarter, fare better.

Rhys shut the door with a snap. "You shouldn't be standing—come in and sit down."

"No. Erin and I are going home." Hardly a gracious answer, but she couldn't manage anything better.

He stood still for a moment. "If that's what you want. I hope you know how grateful I am for everything the two of you have done."

She couldn't think of the right answer for that, either. "I'm glad the show went well. I'm sure you'll get a lot of good publicity. I noticed several reporters wandering around."

"Yes, and what they'll report is Imperator's loss of confidence. There will be some interesting fallout, I'm sure."

"At least you know Andrew can keep him under control. You won't need me to ride him now."

"I suppose not," Rhys said slowly.

Jacquie swallowed hard, then nodded. "Well, then. I'll say goodbye."

"Good...bye." He appeared to be struggling with the meaning of the word. Finally he lifted his hand and brushed his fingers lightly over her cheek, from temple to chin. "Right. Goodbye."

He opened the door again and stepped outside so she could pass easily. Erin had finished loading Mirage in the trailer and was waiting by the truck.

Jacquie limped away without looking back. She stumbled into the driver's seat, started the engine and pulled forward into the night.

There should be music playing, she thought, *or at least a voice-over, with some wise words to say about the end of an interlude*. But the silence seemed to speak for itself, and she didn't spoil it.

Halfway home, Erin sat up with a gasp. "Oh, no."

"Oh, no, what?"

"I left my ribbon! I hung it outside Mirage's stall—there were so many people walking through and I wanted them to know he was the winner. And I forgot to pull it off before we left."

"You can call and ask Andrew to bring it to school for you Monday."

"If he doesn't rip it to shreds, first."

"He wouldn't do that."

"I'm not so sure."

"We'll drive by on the way home from church tomorrow. You can get the ribbon then."

Afterward, she would put the memories of these weeks into the hole she'd made once before in her mental basement, then brick up the opening so tight she couldn't remember more than the delight of Erin's win. And that would be the end of her relationship with Rhys Lewellyn.

Again.

THE PHONE RANG Sunday morning before Rhys had done more than squint at the rain outside his window and groan. After finding Andrew asleep in his room, he'd slept at last, himself, for the first time in three days. Waking up really hadn't been on his to-do list for this morning. At least not until after 7:00 a.m.

Terry's knock sounded on the door. "It's your dad."

Rhys groaned again. "Thanks." This would not be a good start for his day. He swung his legs off the bed, rubbed his face, then picked up the phone. "'Morning, Dad.''

"'Morning, my ass.'' Owen Lewellyn had always been a plainspoken man. "What's this I hear?''

"I have no idea what you've heard. How's Mom?''

"Well, as always. But from what I'm told, Imperator is practically on his last legs.''

"Someone doesn't know what they're talking about. Imperator is healthy and strong.''

"And refusing.''

"I...see. You got a report on the schooling event yesterday.''

"I heard our horse wouldn't perform, yes. And Andrew lost on Ricochet to an unknown of questionable breeding. A girl, for God's sake. How could our horse be beaten by a girl?''

"Horses are an equal opportunity sport, you'll remember. Women and men compete together.'' *And the girl was my daughter. That makes her as good as any boy, including my son.*

His dad had a foul word for that idea. "What's the problem with Imperator?''

"He's lost some confidence over the cross-country fences. We're getting him back in shape.''

"You're saying he's afraid?'' Another curse. "The two of you are a pair, I'll give you that.''

"As I told you, we're working with him. He'll be back to his old self in short order.''

"Well, he'd better be. Sheikh Al Fahed has made me an extremely handsome offer for Imperator. One-point-five million, he's willing to pay. The horse will be worth more, of course, in stud fees. *If* he's a winner. You tell me you can't get the beast back into shape and winning again, I'll sell him and get my money out of him that way.''

Rhys sucked in a harsh breath. "You can't sell the horse.''

"Yes, I can. Imperator is stable property, and I am the majority shareholder. So either the stallion succeeds, or he's gone. I expect you to enter the Top Flight trials, and I expect you to win.'' He disconnected without another word.

Drawing his arm back, Rhys started to throw the cordless phone against the wall. But at the last moment he simply fell back on the bed, instead, and let the phone drop to the floor.

There were only two ways to enter Imperator in the Top Flight Horse Trials. Since he'd been to the Olympics, Imp was only allowed to compete, for the record, at the very highest level. That meant using a rider who could take him over the most difficult advanced fences. Not Andrew, nor Erin, nor even Jacquie possessed that kind of experience. Rhys would either have to hire a rider…

Or ride, himself.

He was still mulling over the issue as he sat in the barn office after lunch, staring at the entry form for the Top Flight event. Hiring a rider would be admitting defeat. Letting go of Imp was simply inconceivable. If there was another answer to the problem, he couldn't see it.

"Your old man stuck it to you, didn't he?'' Terry stood in the doorway, a cleaning cloth in one hand and Imperator's bridle in the other. "What're you gonna do?''

Rhys flipped the registration form across the desk. "Why don't you tell me?"

Terry shook his head. "I know what's best, but I've no way of making it happen."

"And just what is best?"

"You, riding the horse in the trials. You've got a month to work out the kinks. The weather's warming up, we can train every day."

"It's already warm in Florida. We wouldn't have to chance the weather."

"What's Florida got to do with this?"

"I was thinking of moving on down there. The Baileys' place is still for lease—I called them this morning. We could be there in a week."

"Why would you be thinking about moving to Florida? We've got everything we need right here."

He hadn't come up with an explanation that would satisfy Terry, let alone Andrew, without exposing Jacquie. "I'm not comfortable here, is all."

"What you mean is, you can't work things out with Miss Jacquie, you're miserable about it, and you want to move on instead of solving the problem."

"Something like that."

"Well, let me tell you, boyo, you've got a wrong-headed notion if ever there was one." Terry looked up from the bridle and caught Rhys's eye. "I left a family once, a woman and a little girl. Thought I could do without, or maybe I'd make it big and go back rich to take care of them. I don't remember anymore just what my reasons were. I did go back, eventually, only to find they'd vanished. I searched high and low—as you did—but there was no finding them. I could have grandchildren today, and what do I know? Nothing. Nothing at all.''

Terry knew about Erin. ''You're saying—''

''I'm saying you've found your daughter and you're a fool if you up and leave the chance to know her, let her know you. Erin is a sweet and loving girl. She needs her dad. Whether or not you and Miss Jacquie work things out, you've got a right to be a good parent to your own flesh and blood.''

The gasp they heard was small, but it seemed to shake the whole barn. Rhys jerked around to stare at the doorway, where a slight, sturdy figure stood silhouetted against the gray afternoon light. He got to his feet, reached out.

''Erin…''

She backed up a step, and another. And then, before he could reach her, she turned and ran out into the rain.

JACQUIE WATCHED in the rearview mirror as Erin dashed into Rhys's barn and then back to the truck.

''Got it?''

With her face to the window, Erin held up the award which had sent her to bed last night so joyful. The blue ribbon trembled between her fingers.

''Are you cold?'' Jacquie reached out to turn up the heater. ''I said you should wear your coat. Moms always know best.''

When Erin didn't respond, she glanced over. The ribbon had fallen into her lap, and she was still staring out the window, with her fingers pressed against her lips.

''Did something happen? Was Andrew in the

barn?'' He was the only person Jacquie could think of who might have upset Erin this much.

When she didn't get an answer, she put a hand on Erin's leg. "Honey, are you okay?"

Her daughter moved away from her touch. Fear settled in Jacquie's stomach, began to grow. She didn't push further, but clenched her teeth and concentrated on getting home. Fast.

Inside the house, Hurry greeted them as if they'd been gone for weeks, instead of a couple of hours. Jacquie stooped to pet the dog. Erin walked through the kitchen toward her bedroom.

"Wait, Erin." Jacquie followed her into the living room. "I think you need to tell me what happened in the barn. You're obviously unhappy about it."

The girl stopped and, after a moment, turned. She looked like a stranger again today. The effect had nothing to do with makeup and a new dress, but with the expression in her eyes.

"Erin—"

"You lied to me." Her voice was that of an adult. "My whole life, you lied to me."

The fear flowed into Jacquie's chest, began to rise up to her throat. *What happened?*

"I heard them talking." For a second her face softened with wonder, only to quickly harden again into a frozen mask. "Rhys Lewellyn is my father." Not a question.

Oh, God, help me. "Yes."

Erin nodded and pivoted on her heel, headed again to her room.

Jacquie stayed where she was. "Would you like me to explain?"

At the door of her room, Erin paused. "I think I get the picture. You slept with him and got pregnant. He didn't want me, didn't want to marry you, so you left and went to Oklahoma so nobody here would be ashamed of you. Ashamed of me. Mark Archer must have been a nice guy, to marry you when you were already expecting a baby."

So the last blow was hers to deliver after all. "There was no Mark Archer. I invented him…to make things look better."

"Got it. Thanks." She went into her room and carefully closed the door. Jacquie heard the lock click.

Her legs collapsed underneath her. She sat down hard on the floor. Hurry came to cuddle in her lap and Jacquie buried her face in the dog's soft coat.

The phone rang several times as she remained where she'd fallen, unable to summon the strength to move. Shadows claimed the room as the afternoon passed, and she realized the horses needed to be fed. She'd neglected them enough this week as it was, without making them wait in the cold rain to eat. Ignoring the blinking light on the answering machine, Jacquie went out to take care of her animals.

When she returned to the house, Erin's door was still closed. Hurry sniffed at the bottom and whined, but didn't get an answer. In the kitchen, Jacquie prepared the dog's food, always aware of that red message signal, knowing who the caller must be. She wasn't ready to talk with Rhys yet.

When the phone rang again, she almost let it go unanswered. At the last moment, though, she picked up. "Hello?"

"Jacquie." Rhys sounded shaken, completely unlike himself. "Have you talked to Erin?"

"More or less."

"Terry and I were in the office. We didn't know she'd come into the barn."

"She'd forgotten her ribbon."

"Is she okay?"

She gave a harsh laugh. "What do you think?"

"I want to talk to her."

Her temper surged. "Just move in, Rhys, take over. Don't mind me—I'm only the person who's been here for her the last fourteen years."

"That is not what I meant."

"Of course it is. You're ready to be her daddy now. How kind of you. Well, thanks but no thanks. Practice your fathering skills on your own teenager. We're fine without you."

She hung up on him and buried her face in her hands. The phone rang again, and again, but she didn't answer.

ANDREW CAME INTO the gathering room as his dad hung up the phone. The look on his face telegraphed major bad news.

"What's wrong?"

"Sit down."

He glanced at Terry, who jerked his head to back up the command. "Okay, then." Slouched in the corner of the sofa, he looked at his dad again. "What did I do wrong now?"

"Nothing. I need to tell you…some pretty painful truths." His chuckle sounded like the clank of a rusty chain. ''A good example of 'do what I say, not what I do.'''

''I'm all ears.'' He'd been wondering when the shit would hit the fan.

''Erin Archer is...'' He seemed afraid to say the words.

So Andrew did. ''My half sister?''

His dad stared at him, his eyebrows low over his eyes. ''You know?''

''I guessed.''

The great Lewellyn dropped into the armchair by the fireplace. ''How?''

''We look the same. And she's a lot like you. Rides like you.'' Andrew shrugged. ''The dates fit. That explanation made more sense than pure coincidence giving all of us black hair and the same blue eyes.''

''You didn't say anything.''

''It's been a little crazy since I figured it out.''

''Yes.'' After a while, his dad looked over. ''Erin knows now. Her mother...'' He lifted a hand, as if the words wouldn't come.

''She didn't tell Erin, I got that much.''

''And the man she said was Erin's father didn't exist.''

''Oh, man. That's really bad. Has Erin gone ballistic?''

''Would you?''

Andrew considered. ''Yeah.'' Given the same situation, he knew his own choice would be to run. Escape from the miserable situation, get as far away as possible. He'd tried it with his mom, which was one reason he'd ended up with his dad.

Was his *sister* like him in that way, too?

When the phone rang a few minutes later, his dad snatched up the receiver. "Jacquie? Yes?" His face turned white. "When? How? Have you called the police? What can we do?"

He'd never seen the great Lewellyn so out of control. Helpless, angry, desperate—all at once. Just watching made Andrew nervous. Things weren't supposed to be like this.

"I want to help...she is my daughter, as well..." Mrs. Archer's voice could be heard, though not her words. But the gist of the message came through. His dad's shoulders slumped. "If that's what you want. Yes, I promise. Please call me when you've found her." Without a goodbye, he hung up.

Then he looked from Andrew to Terry, and back to Andrew. "Erin's run away." His voice shook. "Her mother has no idea where she might have gone."

Andrew thought about it for a minute. "You don't suppose," he said uneasily, "she would come here?"

SHE'D CALLED RHYS first, in a blind panic after finding Erin's room empty, the window open, a few clothes and her overnight bag gone. Her daughter had sneaked out of the house rather than face her. All Jacquie's worst nightmares were coming true.

Hysteria stood at her shoulder, but she had no time for falling apart. She did have faith that Erin wouldn't just strike out for somewhere unknown. Surely she had gone to someone else, someone safe. The question was simply...who?

Her mother answered on the first ring. "Hi, Jacquie. Thanks for calling back. I was beginning to wonder if you'd got my message."

"Message? I didn't see it."

"We need to talk, the sooner the better. I met—"

"Sorry, but this is an emergency. Have you seen Erin this afternoon?" She blurted the question without any sort of finesse. "Has she shown up at your door?"

"Of course not." After a pause, she asked, "Don't you know where she is?"

"Um…no. She left her room through the window. I haven't seen her since about two, and didn't know she was gone until a few minutes ago."

"Five hours? What in the world happened?"

She would have to explain. But not now. "We had a disagreement, but not worth this kind of stunt." Another lie. Would they never end?

Her mother's voice sharpened. "Surely she wouldn't set out in the rain and cold to come this far."

"Just call me if she gets there, okay?"

"Maybe your daddy should drive out to look for Erin along the road. He's standing right here, ready to go."

Jacquie closed her eyes. The help would be welcome. But she couldn't depend on her parents to solve her problems. "N-not yet, okay? I'll get back to you."

"I'll be waiting by the phone. And we still need to talk."

"Sure." She cut the connection and put her head in her hands. Soon everyone would know the truth. Her mistakes and misjudgments, her lies, would be out in the open. All of her friends and family would look at her with dismay…Kate, Abby, Phoebe—

"Phoebe." Jacquie punched the autodial number on her phone. "Phoebe, it's Jacquie. Erin's with you, isn't she?"

"Yes." Her own relief was echoed in her friend's voice. "I would've called you, but she threatened to leave if I did. I've been sitting here praying for the phone to ring so I didn't have to break my promise."

"Thank God." The tears that had refused to flow dripped down Jacquie's cheeks. "Oh, thank God. Is she all right?"

"Physically, at least. She fell asleep on the couch about an hour ago. What in the world happened? Why did she run away?"

Another lie might have served well enough. But Jacquie had run out of lies. "Phoebe, I have to tell you…about Erin. She found out this afternoon that— that Rhys…" The words were unbelievably hard to say.

After a long pause, Phoebe said them for her. "Rhys is Erin's father?"

"Yes."

"That's been the real problem, hasn't it? Does he know?"

"I told him, just after he arrived in January."

Another long silence. "So you left New York, met Mark Archer in Oklahoma and married him. Did he know…?"

Jacquie drew a deep breath. "There was no Mark Archer. I made him up. My fake husband."

Phoebe gasped. "You aren't—weren't married?"

"No."

"All this time, I thought…"

"That's what I wanted everybody to think. So I lied. Even to you."

"Oh." The taint of deception hung in the dead air on the phone line. Phoebe didn't make a sound. Jacquie wanted to excuse, to explain. But there didn't seem to be anything left to say.

Except, "I'm sorry."

"I know." Already, Phoebe's voice had taken on a reserve that was entirely new in their relationship.

"I'm not sure I can ever make this right again—with Erin, or with you. But I'm so grateful you were there, and that she's safe. I'll be right over—"

"No." Phoebe's soft voice was stiff, unyielding. "I think you should leave her be, at least for tonight."

"But—"

"Erin's distraught, Jacquie. Devastated, if you want the whole truth. She told me absolutely nothing, but I can see it all in her face. She needs time to think without being pressured."

"I would not pressure her."

"Just your presence, at this point, is pressure. I'll take good care of her, I promise. I'll get her to school, and bring her home with me. My sincere advice is to give her a respite."

A respite? From me? In that moment, Jacquie distinctly felt her heart break. Not with a wrenching pain, but with a soft, despairing sigh.

But she knew good advice when she heard it. "Maybe you're right. I'll leave Erin alone with you—for a day or so, anyway. Let me know what's going on, please?"

"I will. Why don't you try to get some rest now? I'll talk to you tomorrow when I get to work."

Now that she knew Erin was safe, she couldn't control the fear. "Wait—we could meet for breakfast at the diner, as usual. And I could talk to Erin then."

"Too soon, Jacquie. Too soon." Phoebe sighed.

"Good night." She cut off before another word could be said.

Jacquie let the phone fall to her lap. She would have to call Rhys and her parents, to let them know Erin was safe.

But she sat still for a moment in her empty house, listening to her own pounding pulse. She'd never realized, until tonight, how loud silence could be.

CHAPTER TWELVE

CALLING HER PARENTS again proved to be unnecessary. Becky Lennon showed up at Jacquie's door only fifteen minutes after they'd talked.

"Erin's okay," Jacquie said immediately. "She went to Phoebe's house, just down the road."

"Thank God." Her mother sat in the rocking chair by the fireplace. "So many terrible things happen. I could imagine…" She shook her head. "Let's just be thankful. Phone your daddy to let him know."

Jacquie made coffee while she talked with her father and brought in two mugs when she came back to the living room. "He said he'll wait up for you."

Her mother smiled. "He always wants to know I'm in the house before he can sleep." She took a sip of coffee. "When is Erin coming home?"

"I'm not sure. Phoebe suggested giving her some space to sort things out."

"What things?"

"Mom, I…" The second time wasn't any easier. "I haven't been honest with you about…Erin."

"Let me save you some trouble, here. Soon as I saw Rhys Lewellyn yesterday, I knew what must have happened. Erin's his baby, isn't she?"

Feeling her face heat up, Jacquie nodded.

"I met Andrew, too, and he and Erin are alike as two peas in a pod."

"I know."

"And they're about the same age, so I presume…" Her mother set her mug on the coffee table and clasped her hands together. "I presume you were…together…while he was still married." Her countenance faltered, and she looked at the picture of Erin on the mantel.

Jacquie swallowed hard. "I thought, at first, he was divorced. Before we…slept together, I asked him and he said his wife had left him for another man. He'd filed, but the divorce wasn't final yet. Then his wife came back, pregnant."

"Our church doesn't recognize divorce, Jacquie."

"I know."

"So he decided to stay with her, even though you were expecting his baby?"

"I didn't tell him."

"Oh." After a long pause, Becky said, "You made up Mark Archer, didn't you?"

That insight surprised her. "How did you know?"

"I never saw a single picture of him, even when the baby was newly born. What kind of woman wouldn't keep a picture of her dead husband in the house? And since you aren't that kind of woman, I had to believe he wasn't real."

"You've known that all these years?" Guilt and relief washed through her. "Why didn't you say something?"

"I tried not to think about it too much. I figured maybe this was just something else I didn't understand, like you going all the way to New York to begin with, going to Oklahoma afterward. So many things you did never made sense to me."

"I'm sorry."

Her mother moved to sit beside her on the couch. "I don't say I was always right and you were always wrong, honey. I'm just saying we're so different, sometimes I don't know what to think about you. I'd never heard of a girl shoeing horses, until you told me that was what you planned. And now here you are, a successful businesswoman, admired and needed by the people you work for."

"You wanted me to be a nurse."

"Because I wanted to be a nurse when I was young."

"Why didn't you?"

Becky joined her hand with Jacquie's. "I fell in love with a handsome young farmer. Instead of going to school, I started cooking and cleaning and having babies. It's a good life, and I wouldn't change it if I could."

"I'd change everything about my life right now, just to get Erin home and make her happy."

"I know you would. She ran away because she found out that Mr. Lewellyn is her daddy?"

"I think she ran away because she realized I'd lied to her for her whole life."

"Why did you not tell her the truth? Why didn't you tell us? Were we so...so hard?"

Jacquie got to her feet and walked to the window. "No. I knew I wasn't what you wanted, but—"

"Such hogwash. You were always yourself. What else would we want in a daughter?"

"Alicia." Jacquie sighed. "A neat, organized, smart, pretty girl."

"We had one of those. We needed a tomboy for balance."

"How could I have come home like that—pregnant, with no husband or any hope of one? I couldn't embarrass you and Daddy like that. I couldn't embarrass the family. Or myself."

"Poor child." Her mother crossed the room and put her arms around Jacquie. "You were too hard on yourself. We would have survived a little embarrassment. And you wouldn't be in such a terrible situation now. Does Mr. Lewellyn know about Erin?"

"I told him, when he first arrived in January. I thought I could keep them apart, keep people from finding out."

"Oh, honey, I could've told you that wouldn't fly. A secret's bound to get out, especially in a town this size."

"So what do I do now?"

"I think you wait a little while. See how Erin feels. Let God do a little work on the situation. You've already tried to handle too much on your own."

Jacquie put her head down on her mother's shoulder. "I should have told you from the first, shouldn't I?"

"I'm certain of that. Moms always know best."

RHYS TOOK ANDREW TO SCHOOL Monday morning, a silent drive except for a few comments about the weather, which was still rainy, and Imperator. "Jacquie suggested you ride him," he told his son. "I think that's our best bet for getting him in shape."

"But I screwed up on Saturday. I figured you'd..." He hesitated.

"I would do what?"

"Be mad, at least."

"You did your best. The horse has a problem we have to solve. Which is why you and Terry will work on the cross-country jumps."

"You're not going to jump him again?"

"I...don't know." Hard to admit, impossible to ignore. "But if we want to keep him, he has to win at the Top Flight trials."

"Who would ride him, since I'm not old enough?"

"We'll worry about that later."

"But—"

"Enough." The word echoed in the space around them, and Rhys winced. "Sorry. I've got enough to think about right now. We'll talk about riders another time."

Andrew shrugged one shoulder. "Whatever."

Great parenting. He'd effectively shut his son down, at a time when they needed to work together. Rhys was beginning to think he should stick to horses and leave human interactions to those more qualified. Then again, he wasn't doing so well with horses these days, either.

From school, he drove straight to Jacquie's farm. He'd never been there, but with the address—Bower Lane—he had no trouble finding the place. Her little clapboard cottage sat right beside the road, its blue metal roof slick with rain. The barn and paddocks stood behind, all painted a clean white like the house. Three good-looking bay horses grazed in the pasture beyond the barn, while Mirage and a gray stallion stood together in one of the paddocks, stoic under the drizzle.

Jacquie's truck was parked close to the barn, underneath an overhang that kept the truck bed out of the rain. As he braked his own truck nearby, she stepped out of the wide barn door, carrying several boxes of nails in each hand. When she saw him, she stopped and simply stood, waiting.

He cleared his throat as he reached her. "How are you?"

Her expression didn't change. "What are you doing here?"

"Checking on you."

"A waste of time, Rhys." She stepped by him and put the nail boxes on the tailgate of the truck, then turned back into the barn. "I'll be okay."

He followed her down the aisle of the neat and tidy space. He recalled that her apartment had always been a little messy that summer, with clothes left out and dishes in the sink never quite caught up. She'd spent most of her waking time with the horses, or with him. In the years since, she'd obviously learned to take care of her property.

But she wasn't taking care of herself. "You're still limping. Have you had that foot x-rayed?"

She stood in a stall-turned-storage-room, sorting prefabricated horseshoes into a wooden box. "No. It's getting better."

Rhys decided he would take her word for that. "Have you slept since Sunday? Eaten anything at all?"

Jacquie sighed. "I don't remember."

"Do you have work this morning?"

"Would I be here at nine o'clock if I had a job to do? No." She rubbed at her temple, and he knew she had a headache.

He waited for her to finish sorting her shoes. Then he stepped in and picked up the box, wincing as the weight pulled at his back. "Do you want this in the truck?"

After gaping at him for a couple of seconds, she pressed her lips together. "Yes, thanks."

He set the shoe box in the truck bed, moved the nails into the chrome tool chest underneath the rear window, then raised the tailgate and shut it. Jacquie came out as he turned around.

"What are you doing? I want to go through my stuff, clean out the junk and reorganize."

"Not this morning." Rhys walked around behind her, put his hands on her shoulders and propelled her into the rain. "You're going to get something to eat."

She leaned back, trying to stop their forward progress with her heels dug into the soft ground. "I'm not going anywhere."

He kept pushing, forcing her to walk. At the truck, he opened the passenger door. "Get in."

Jacquie looked at him with tears in her eyes. "Please, Rhys. I can't go anywhere."

"You don't have to hide, Jacquie. You don't have to punish yourself like this."

With her head hanging, she got in the truck, only to sit hunched in her seat, leaning against the door, as if she could pretend she wasn't there at all. The drive into town was even more silent than the earlier one with Andrew. But as they got to the outskirts of New Skye, Jacquie sat up and began to finger her hair.

"I'm a mess," she complained. "I barely brushed my hair this morning."

"There's a comb in the console," he said. "Be my guest."

She cast him an irritated glance, but took him up on the offer. By the time he stopped the truck, she looked as neat and in control as usual.

"Better?" she asked, with a phony smile.

Rhys nodded. "You still look exhausted, and immensely sad." Her smile faded. "But always beautiful."

A flush stained her cheeks; she turned her face toward the window and the building outside. "The Carolina Diner? Why did you come here?"

"I like it. Friendly people, good food."

"Couldn't we just get some fast food? Take-out?"

"No. I want a real breakfast. You need one." With a hand on her arm, he gave her no choice but to go with him to the front door, sidestepping puddles in the gravel parking lot on the way. The diner was crowded, most of its tables and green vinyl booths already filled. As Rhys let the door swing shut behind him, he saw Charlie Brannon, the owner, gesturing for them to come forward and pointing to a free booth at the same time. Rhys led Jacquie in that direction.

Charlie brought menus as they sat down. "Hey, Miss Jacquie. Rhys, good to see you. What can I get you two to drink?"

"Coffee?" Rhys looked at Jacquie, who nodded.

"Be right back." Charlie slapped the table with his big hand and limped away.

Rhys looked at Jacquie. "He ran into a land mine in Vietnam, he told me."

She nodded. "He came home, started up the Carolina Diner with his wife, and has been here ever since. All the kids from the high school come for snacks after the game or burgers before the movie, that kind of thing. Charlie makes a terrific banana split."

"Maybe you should have one for breakfast."

Her lips curved in a weak smile. "I'll settle for bacon and eggs." Then her focus settled on someone across the room, shifting to follow their movements.

He turned and saw Abby, simultaneously clearing a table and pouring coffee. "She's really busy this morning."

"Yes, she is."

Charlie brought their coffee out, took their orders and returned shortly with heaping plates of food. Abby still hadn't come near their table.

"She's avoiding me," Jacquie said, stirring her eggs without eating them. "She found out, and she won't talk to me because I lied."

He'd heard the whispers at the schooling day, and knew the rumors had spread. He'd gotten a couple of impertinent phone calls himself. "Give her some time. We'll be old news in a matter of days."

"Not to Erin. Not to my friends." She glanced across the room and lifted her hand to wave at a guy paying his bill at the register. "Hi, Rob."

Very tall and lean, the man walked slowly toward their table. "Hey, Jacquie." His smile looked a little forced. "How are you? Still walking with a cane?"

"Nope, I ditched the cane. Did you have a chance to meet Rhys Lewellyn at the horse show? Rhys, this is a good friend of mine, Rob Warren. We grew up together. Rob's a locksmith, so if you ever get shut out of your house, he's the one to call.''

Rhys stood up to shake hands, but thought Warren's response was a little weak. ''I'm glad to meet a locksmith. Did you enjoy the show?''

''Oh, sure.'' He stepped back. ''I was happy to see Erin win.''

''Don't forget to call me about Ginny's lessons,'' Jacquie said. ''I'm looking forward to that.''

''Um…sure.'' Warren's expression was wary. ''I'll see what I can do. Gotta get to work. Y'all have a good day.''

Jacquie didn't bother to point out Rob's distant attitude to Rhys. He would have seen it for himself. They sat without saying anything for a long time, their food cooling, untouched.

''There's nothing I can do for you with Erin,'' she said finally, bluntly. Might as well get everything out on the table. ''She won't even talk to me. She made Phoebe promise not to call to tell me where she was.''

Rhys looked up from his coffee, one eyebrow lifted in question. ''Jacquie, I didn't come expecting you to do something for me.''

She was too tired to think anymore. She propped her chin in her hand. ''Then why am I here?''

He folded his arms on the table and leaned a little forward. ''Do you really have to ask?''

At that moment, the puzzle of her life got shaken up and put together in a brand-new way. The answer to her question was there in Rhys's face, in his sharp blue eyes—love and worry and tenderness, desire and a fierce concern. The fulfillment of every dream she'd ever had.

Jacquie turned her head away. "I can't," she whispered.

There was a moment of silence, while the pieces of the world shifted back again.

Rhys took a deep breath and sat back against the booth. "Someone needs to talk to Erin, try to explain."

"Phoebe says she doesn't need more pressure right now."

"But she can't stay with Phoebe indefinitely."

"I understand that. Erin will calm down when she gets over the shock." She did not need his criticism. "This was exactly what I didn't want to happen— some kind of accidental revelation."

His face stiffened. "Well, then, you should have told her the truth yourself, shouldn't you?"

Her defiance crumbled as quickly as it had formed. "Yes. I should have told her the truth."

He reached across the table to touch her hand with his fingertips. "Jacquie...I'm sorry. You did what you thought best."

"Did I?" She shook her head. "I'm not sure anymore. Maybe...maybe the person I was really protecting was—" she took a deep shaking breath "—myself."

The bell on the door to the diner jingled again, as it had every few minutes. Escaping from Rhys's intense gaze and her own thoughts, Jacquie glanced at the new arrivals and saw Adam DeVries come in. With Phoebe.

In another moment, the engaged pair stood beside their table, exchanging reserved greetings.

"Can you sit down with us?" Jacquie asked, though she was certain she already knew the answer.

"Thanks," Adam said, "but I've got a c-couple of people joining me for a m-meeting." The bell tinkled again and he glanced at the door. "There they are, now. Phoebe, I'll see you when you're ready?"

"I'll be right there," Phoebe told him. Then she looked at Jacquie. "How are you?"

She shrugged, brushing off the question. "How is Erin?"

"Subdued. She ate breakfast, though, and took lunch to school." Phoebe smiled at them. "I think it's a good sign when teenagers eat."

"Has she said anything at all about—" Rhys looked down at his hands "—the situation?"

"Yes."

Jacquie sat forward, bracing her palms on the tabletop. "What did she tell you? How does she feel? Will she talk to me?"

Phoebe's gray eyes softened. "I wish I could say yes. But Erin only had one thing to say."

"What is that?"

"She wants to see Rhys."

ERIN DIDN'T APPEAR in the school cafeteria Monday for lunch, so Andrew went looking for her. He met Cathy Parr in the hallway near the library. "Have you seen Erin?"

The blonde looked at him suspiciously. "Why?"

"I wanted to talk to her but she didn't come to lunch."

"Oh." Cathy looked up at the ceiling and all around them in the hall, as if she could see something he couldn't. "Sorry. I can't help you." She brushed past him and hurried away, with one quick glance at the library door.

"Right." Andrew stepped quietly inside the double doors and glanced around, without seeing Erin at any of the tables near the front desk. Moving through the shelves of books, he checked the study carrels along the back wall and finally noticed the top of her head in the corner farthest from library traffic. A good place to hide.

He walked quietly, then stopped a little ways off so he wouldn't startle her. "Erin?"

"Go. Away. Now." Her voice sounded thick and rough, like that weird Southern food called grits.

"I wanted to make sure you're okay."

"I'm great. Go away."

"Are you studying your math?"

"No. Go away."

He set his backpack on the floor and sat down on the table of the carrel. "Want to talk?"

She didn't answer.

"You did a good job with Mirage on Saturday."

"Go away."

"You're gonna get through this, you know. Your parents can really mess you up sometimes, but what they do doesn't change who you are. Or who you want to be. You have to figure that out for yourself."

"Easy for you to say."

"Not. I got messed up living with my mom. Then she dumped me on my dad. He only cared about the horses." *And now you.* But he wouldn't give her that much. "I survived."

"Nobody lied to you."

"Worse—my mom told me the truth. Nobody wanted me. They just didn't have the guts to get rid of me before I was born. Your mom could've done worse than just lying."

He slung his backpack on his shoulder and walked out of the library, into the crowded, noisy hall. He'd said what he came to say, done all he could do.

Whether it helped or not was up to Erin.

IN HIS LIFETIME, Rhys had met several members of Britain's royal family, haggled with an Arab sheikh over the price of a horse, and eaten dinner with a U.S. president.

None of those occasions had created the kind of nervousness he now felt as he waited to see his daughter on Tuesday afternoon. He had no idea what to say to this girl who had just learned the truth about their relationship. He hoped the right words would be there when he needed them.

Terry and Andrew had taken Imperator down to the cross-country course to work on the jumps, insuring that Rhys would have uninterrupted time alone with Erin. Now, standing at the window in the gathering room, he watched Phoebe's lime-green Volkswagen bug drive through the Fairfield Farm gate. For a second, he couldn't remember how to breathe.

He reached the outside door at the same time Erin did. "Hi," he said, feeling a little stupid. "Come in."

They went to the gathering room and faced each other across the width of the carpet. The crackle of the fire sounded loud in the silence. Rhys cleared his throat. "Sit down. Can I get you something to drink? Do you want a snack after school?"

"No, thanks." Erin clearly had more self-possession than he had managed so far. She sat on the couch and looked up at him. "You're my biological father."

He winced at the term. "That sounds so…technical. Like a machine on an assembly line."

"What would you call it, instead?"

Rhys sat down at the other end of the sofa. "I was in love with your mother. We were very happy together, and we created a child out of that happiness—you."

"Why didn't you marry her?"

The explanation never got easier. "Before your mother ever came to New York, I had filed for divorce from my wife…Andrew's mother. She'd left me for someone else. But then she came back, without warning." He could still remember his nausea when Olivia walked into his father's house wearing a tight maternity top chosen specifically to emphasize how pregnant she was. "She was carrying my child. I thought the right thing to do was to try again to make our marriage work."

Erin looked down at her fingers, twining in her lap. "Did you know about…me?"

"No." He had to be careful here, or the blame would fall solely on Jacquie's shoulders. "Your mother had planned to tell me, that night after my wife returned. But instead I told her…well, what I'd decided. The next morning, your mother was gone."

"She could have stayed. Fought for you."

"That would have made the situation very difficult for all of us."

"You could have looked for her."

The implied accusation piqued his temper. "You're drawing some false conclusions, Erin. Why would you assume I didn't?"

"You didn't find us."

"Maybe you should credit that to your mother's intelligence and her ability to stay hidden. She disappeared without a trace."

His daughter looked at him, her blue eyes ice-cold with anger. "And she made up a fake husband. A fake dad for me to believe in."

He held up a warning hand. "I can't talk about that with you. I wasn't part of that time in your life."

"But she lied to me!" Erin jerked to her feet and paced across the room to the window. "She let me think there was this man who cared about me, even before I was born."

"All your mother wants," Rhys said softly, "is for you to be safe and happy."

"Well, she really screwed that up." The words were particularly ugly, coming from her. "How can I ever trust her again? She's ruined my life."

Laughing, at this moment, would be exactly the wrong thing to do. "That's a little extreme. Nothing's changed, except in your mind."

"Like all my friends won't find out? The people at the show were whispering, I heard them. 'She looks so much like him. Do you think there's a connection? Is that how she won?' Erin leaned her forehead against one of the windowpanes. "I'll be a bastard," she said softly.

"That's not so terrible these days, sweetheart." Rhys crossed the room to put a hand on her shoulder. "Nobody cares much about legitimacy anymore."

His daughter looked at him over her shoulder. Her lower lip trembled and her eyes shone with unshed tears.

"I do."

HE CALLED JACQUIE once Phoebe had left. "We talked for a couple of hours, then she went out to visit the horses."

"What did she say?" Her voice sounded ragged, as if she'd been weeping.

Recounting the conversation, he tried to soften the blows. "Erin didn't really understand everything that happened. I tried to explain the whys."

"She wouldn't let me tell her my reasons, wouldn't talk to me at all." Jacquie was quiet for a moment. "Does she look okay?"

"Same as usual. She's not suffering physically, don't worry about that. And, somehow or another, we'll get her through the emotional trauma."

"'We.' It's beginning to sound as if we're divorced parents instead of..."

"Lovers?" He heard her take a sharp breath. "Or how about unmarried parents? Erin is worried about being illegitimate. I tried to suggest it doesn't matter much these days."

"She knows better. The news will be all over our church, and everybody will be looking at Erin like an escapee from a freak show."

"That's their problem."

"No, that's my problem. Mine and Erin's. Did she say anything about coming home?"

Now, the bad news. Rhys took a deep breath. "She's still furious with you. I suggested she think about going home, but she resisted mightily. It's going to take some time, that's all.''

"So she's back at Phoebe's house?''

"Er, no.''

After another long pause, Jacquie said, "No? What does that mean?''

"She asked if she could stay here, with me.'' He hesitated, then finished in a rush. "What else could I say, besides yes?''

CHAPTER THIRTEEN

"No. NO WAY." Andrew dropped the predinner sandwich he'd made on the kitchen counter. "She's not staying here."

"Yes, she is." His dad rubbed a hand over his face. "And I expect you to be at least pleasant. Erin is your sister."

"Half sister." He got a dirty look for that. "Why can't she go home?"

"You're aware of the situation. Figure it out."

"Does Mrs. Archer know?"

"Of course."

Andrew chuckled. "Man, she must be pissed."

Eyebrows raised, arms folded over his chest, his dad stared at him. "I'm so glad we're amusing you."

He felt his face get hot. "I'm not...it isn't...I know it's not funny." For something to do, he picked up the sandwich again, though he couldn't imagine eating it now. "How long is she staying?"

"Until...she's ready to leave."

"That could be forever."

Again his dad stared at him. "She's my daughter. If she needs forever, she's got it. Do you understand?"

He understood, all right. He understood that Erin Archer was going to prance around like a princess—

having her little drama, crying and sulking, grabbing everybody's attention. His dad and Terry would be worrying about her and taking care of her and spoiling her. They'd be lucky to have any time left for the horses.

Unless, of course, they decided the princess was good enough to train Imp. Instead of Andrew.

Dropping the sandwich into the trash can, he headed for the barn. The weather was warming up and the days were getting longer, which meant more time spent in the barn after school. In New York, winter was still in charge. For once, he wasn't complaining about the move south.

Until he found Erin standing at the door of Imp's stall. "What are you doing?" The stallion had his head over the lower half of the door, nudging at her shoulder with his nose while she stroked his cheek.

She didn't look at Andrew. "Hanging out."

"He'll bite, if you're not careful."

"I'm careful. And he won't bite me."

"Yeah, right." He wasn't going to leave the barn with her still here, so he might as well finish up his chores. Grabbing a pitchfork, he pushed the wheelbarrow to the door of Abner's stall, right next to Imp. For a while, the only sound in the stable was the thunk of horse dirt hitting the bottom of the barrow.

Then Erin looked in. "Want some help?"

"No." The stalls were his job and he wasn't giving up any part of it.

"Want me to clean the water buckets?"

A job he hated in winter, because he got wet and cold. "No."

"Sweep the aisle?"

"No."

"Do you even know what a big jerk you are?"

"No...I mean..." He glared at her. "Shut up."

She stuck her tongue out at him. "Make me."

"Like I couldn't?" A quick picture of what his dad would do to him if he beat her up flashed through his mind. He shook his head. "You're not worth it."

Her eyes widened, then went all teary. To his surprise, Erin turned away and walked out of the barn without another word. Imp whickered after her, but she didn't look back.

Andrew tried to feel victorious. He'd gotten rid of her. For the time being, at least.

But he'd fought dirty. And a win by cheating wasn't really a win at all.

AFTER A FEW DAYS in her dad's house, Erin had started going to the barn early in the morning to talk with Imperator, the way she'd talked to Mirage where she used to live.

"I miss him," she told Imp as she stroked his big nose. "And I know he's missing me. I'm sure she's feeding him and stuff. But it's hard when your friend goes away.

"I don't know when...if...I'll go back. I bet they'll try to make me, though.

"Then I'll miss you. And wonder if you're figuring out what went wrong at that fence. I wish I could help. I have a feeling only Rhys can do that. The problem was you and him, wasn't it? Then I think the answer has to come from the two of you working together. You'd like that, wouldn't you?"

Imperator rubbed the side of his face against her

leg, then lifted his head and rested his chin on her shoulder.

"I thought so. I'll see what I can do."

BY THE TIME ERIN had been at Rhys's house for a week, Mirage missed her almost as much as her mother did. Though she hadn't changed his food and had ridden him often, the horse was losing weight, acting listless.

Just like Jacquie.

To be safe, she asked Buck to check Mirage for any health problem she might have overlooked. The veterinarian arrived late on Thursday afternoon and performed a thorough exam.

"I'll run some blood tests," he said finally, "but I'm not seeing anything physically wrong." He watched for a minute as Mirage stood with his head low, his eyes half-closed, barely interested in what was going on around him. "He's sure not happy, is he?"

"No, he's not." She sighed and led the gelding back to his stall and his nightly bucket of grain.

"So, where's your girl?" Buck bent over to scratch Hurry's ears as Jacquie came down the aisle. "She's usually standing right here, asking me more questions than I could answer in a year of vet school."

Jacquie stopped dead. She hadn't even thought of what to say about Erin's absence. With her clients, she made the excuse of too much homework. But she didn't have an explanation for Buck.

His eyes were worried as he looked at her. "Jacquie? What's wrong?"

"Erin…" Tears stung her eyes. "Erin's at Fairfield Farm. With her…father."

Buck simply stood there, arms at his sides, his eyes unfocused for the seconds it took him to understand what she'd really said.

Then he crossed the space between them and put his arms around her, pressed her head onto his shoulder. "I'm so sorry, honey. Is there anything I can do?"

She was still crying into Buck's flannel shirt when a cough from the front of the barn signaled that they were not alone.

"Excuse me," Rhys said.

With a sniff, Jacquie stepped out of Buck's hold. "What are you doing here?"

"I came to find out how you're doing." His eyes raked her, and then the veterinarian. "Well, I see."

"Don't be a jackass" was Buck's comment. He turned back to Jacquie. "You call me if you need me." Then he left the barn, brushing past Rhys without another word.

Neither of them spoke until the sound of the vet's truck had faded into silence. Rhys shifted his weight from one foot to the other. "Do you have a problem with one of the horses?"

"Mirage misses his rider, is all." She lifted her chin, tried to brighten up. "How is she? What's going on?" They'd talked every day, and she knew Rhys did his best to convey the details of Erin's life. He couldn't be blamed if his best wasn't any kind of substitute for her daughter's presence.

The day he described as she fed the rest of the

horses and closed up the barn sounded much like the days she and Erin usually shared.

"Andrew still won't allow her to clean Imperator's stall," Rhys reported, as he petted Hurry and enslaved the dog for life by rubbing her stomach. "But he's granted her permission to shovel manure for the rest of the horses."

Jacquie felt an odd urge to smile. "How kind."

"She's been riding Ricochet, practicing for the Top Flight trials, and doing a good job with him. He's sweet tempered, but inexperienced. Ric has been Terry's special project, so he's having a good time with the two of them. He approves of Erin's light hands on the reins, protecting his baby's mouth."

"And Andrew's still jumping Imperator?"

For the first time, Rhys hesitated. "Yes."

She turned to look at him. "Top Flight is two weeks away."

"I'm aware."

"You're not planning to ride?"

He didn't answer, which was an answer in itself.

With her chores finished, Jacquie turned off the barn lights and pulled the sliding doors together, leaving a small opening to bring in fresh air. Rhys walked beside her as she looked at the three mares in the pasture and Sterling, alone in his paddock.

"This is a nice place," he said quietly. "You've done really well for yourself, Jacquie."

She shrugged. "It's not Olympic gold. But we've been happy." Tears threatened, and she shook her head. "Do you want some coffee?"

"Sure."

With his first step into Jacquie's house, Rhys experienced an immediate sense of homecoming. This was the woman he remembered. Unlike the tidy barn, disorder ruled here. Stacks of papers occupied the counter in the kitchen, along with sunglasses, gloves, various key chains, and several leather straps which proved to be parts of a bridle. In the family room, a wrinkled quilt thrown over the couch revealed where Jacquie had spent the night. Books about horses, dogs, wolves, and eventing sat on every available surface. A picture of himself riding Imperator as they took their victory gallop at the Olympics confronted him from the seat of a chair. He winced, closed the magazine and moved it to a table.

"You haven't changed, after all," he told Jacquie as she handed him a mug of steaming coffee.

"What do you mean?" When he gestured around the room, she nodded. "Housework isn't high on our priority list. Maybe I'm rebelling against my mother, the best cook, the best housekeeper there ever was. As a kid, I was always getting yelled at—about my messy room, my dirty clothes, my tangled hair. I swore I'd never do that with my own children."

She sat down on one end of the dark blue couch and Rhys took the other, sinking deep into the soft cushions. Hurry jumped up between them, circled three times, and settled into a curl of black and white pressed against Rhys's thigh.

Jacquie's worried eyes found his. "Maybe my mom had the right idea. Is...Erin...being a slob at your house?"

He shrugged. "I haven't noticed, but then, I haven't looked at her room. The housekeeper hasn't complained. She's just thrilled to have another female around the place.''

"That makes this arrangement sound...permanent." Her coffee mug started to shake, and she put it down on the table beside the couch. "Are you suggesting that Erin won't ever come home?''

Rhys tried to choose his words carefully. "I want—''

She didn't allow him to use them. "Because I'm telling you that's not an option. I'm holding on by my fingernails here—and they're breaking—to give Erin the space she needs, the time to adjust. But I'm not giving her up. Not to you, not to anyone. When all's said and done, my daughter will live with me.''

"*Our* daughter," he said through clenched teeth. He had sworn to himself that he wouldn't lose his temper tonight.

"A week doesn't make you a parent," she shot back sharply, her voice slightly superior in tone.

"Fourteen years doesn't make you an expert. Will you stop trying to fight with me?''

"I don't know what you're talking about.''

The pattern had just become clear to him. "You're doing your damnedest to keep me at a distance, if by no other means than making me mad.''

"Why would I do that?''

"Because you're afraid of what happens when we don't fight.''

She turned away from his face. "That's... ridiculous.''

"Prove it.''

"How?''

"Just sit here with me, quietly. Enjoy the end of a day's work, good coffee, a warm, quiet house." He had wanted to share this with her, a long time ago. He'd thought they would have years and years of evening peace together. Instead, this hour might be his only chance.

She made him wait a long time before she agreed. "We could have a fire," she said finally, "to take the chill off."

"Good idea." He set his mug on the coffee table and slid forward on the deep, wide cushion in order to leave the couch. A vise of pain gripped his back, and he took a quick breath.

Jacquie sat forward. "What's wrong?"

"Nothing. Just a twinge."

"Let me get the logs."

He turned to her. "I'll get the logs, Jacquie. Relax." Kneeling on the hearth, he transferred three of the logs stacked nearby into the grate, added kindling and tinder and struck a match. The flame caught and spread quickly.

"Nice dry wood," he said, and started to get to his feet.

In an instant, he was down on his hands and knees, his whole back in spasm.

"Rhys?" Jacquie came down beside him. "Tell me what to do."

"Pretend this isn't happening." Teeth gritted, he crawled the short distance to the table, put his palms on top and pushed himself upright. From there, using just his legs, he managed to stand up. Stiff, in agony, but fairly straight.

"Now, what?" Jacquie looked up at him. "Do you want to lie down? Should I drive you home?"

"No, and no. Give me a minute, I'll be okay." He reached backward, trying to massage the worst ache with his fingers, but he couldn't get to the right spot. "Gimps 'R Us."

She walked around behind him. "Does massage help? Here?" He felt a tentative pressure near his spine. "Here?"

"A little higher." As a mere mortal—and a man, at that—he simply couldn't find the nobility within him to give this up. "To the right. Ah…there."

Jacquie pressed her palm against Rhys's back, feeling the tightness in the muscles. She could imagine how such tension must hurt.

"I need some resistance," she told him. "Can you brace yourself on the mantel shelf? And this'll work better with your sweater off." She helped him pull the soft gray lamb's wool over his head, leaving him in a long-sleeved T-shirt. "That's good."

Beginning in earnest, she used the fingers of both hands, pressing firmly, moving in circles. She repeated the motion a few inches higher, and then higher again.

Rhys's breath hissed through his teeth, and she jerked her hands away. "No, don't stop." He sounded hoarse. "This is the best thing that's happened to me in a long time."

Pressing, kneading, she worked up and down both sides of his spine. Rhys put his head on his arms, and she could feel him relax as she worked. The fire at their feet crackled and burned, just short of a blaze that would be too warm to stand close to.

Still, she felt heat building inside of her, and her

breath became uneven. Her seeking fingers slipped again and again on the smooth knit of the shirt, until she clucked her tongue in frustration, then reached underneath, gliding her hands over his smooth, firm skin. She heard Rhys's breath again—but not, she thought, in pain.

The contours of his back were amazing, a landscape of sleek curves to be explored by touch…and sight. Impatient with the shirt, Jacquie pushed the cloth up to his shoulders and, a little roughly, over his head. Without a word, he pulled the sleeves off his arms and dropped the shirt out of reach of the fire, returning to lean his arms on the mantel.

He was as beautifully made as she'd remembered in her dreams. Strong, square shoulders, shaped by years of hard physical labor, softened under her hands. She stroked his ribs and felt the roughness of his breathing, the quick beat of his heart. Pressing into him from behind, she laid her cheek against his back, testing the contrast of textures, drinking in his clean scent. At last, almost without thought, she turned her face and touched her lips to those poor, abused muscles.

"Jacquie." Rhys tightened his hands until he thought his knuckles might break. What she did to him…her hands, her face…dear Lord, her mouth… His body had gone tight as a bowstring. *Yes, and the arrow is strung, all right.* He almost chuckled at the thought. Did she understand what she'd done to him? Did she expect him just to walk away after this?

Her arms came around him and stilled, with her palms resting over his breastbone. After a moment, she said, "Is that better?"

Then he did chuckle. "Yes. And no." He turned within her hold and put his arms around her, pulling her tight against his body. "I've got a different set of aches altogether now."

"I think I have the cure."

Stepping away, she took his hand and led him into the darkness of her bedroom. Rhys lay down carefully on the bed, hoping to keep the spasms at bay, unwilling to take his eyes off the silhouette of Jacquie as she undressed. Disappearing clothes revealed her skin white against the black around her, her hair an occasional flicker of gold. He'd left his slacks on, but when the bed dipped she came to him completely naked, a slender porcelain figure fitting into his hands as if made for him alone.

She is, he thought fiercely. *Mine alone.*

Her mouth came to his, soft, coffee-glazed lips playing with his own. He cupped her shoulders with his hands, stroked his palms over her ribs and the velvet skin of her bottom.

"Nothing," he groaned, "nothing has ever felt this good."

"Mmm." She murmured against his jawline, nipped at his ear and chuckled when he gasped. "Tell me more."

He set the words free, then, praising every part of her he could touch, taste, take. Pain forgotten, he rolled to his side, bringing her up against him so that every inch of her lay within his reach. Desire mounted them, drove them on a ride wilder than anything they'd known with a horse. Harsh breaths and soft moans filled the quiet night, while their hands relearned long-forgotten trails of pleasure. At the end, she sobbed out his name and he answered with a growl of satisfaction. Together, they took the final, magnificent fall.

JACQUIE AWOKE without any recollection of having gone to sleep, or even to bed. Memory came slowly, and with it, awe. And then concern, because she lay alone in her bed.

"Rhys?"

"I'm here."

She pushed her hair out of her face and sat up, pulling the sheet over her bare breasts. Her love sat in the chair in her bedroom by the low lamp on the dresser, wrapped in a quilt from the waist down. He held a big book in his hands—one of the albums in which she stored pictures of Erin. His daughter.

"Cute baby." Smiling, he turned the page. "Looks like she kept you moving."

"She ran as soon as she could walk." Wrapping the sheet around her, she went to kneel by his side. "That's her second birthday." She pointed to the picture of Erin with goats in the background. "That was a petting zoo, and when we went inside, she ran after all the pygmy goats and the lambs, saying, 'Baa-baa-baa-baa.' Endlessly. I bet those poor animals have never been so glad to see anyone leave."

Together they leafed through the pages, while Jacquie tried to give back the years he'd missed.

The last page was an eight-by-ten picture of Erin on her first pony, Dusty. "I wish I'd been there," Rhys said quietly.

She could have wept at the ache in his voice. "So do I."

Thinking back, she remembered the first lonely days. "I thought you might try to find me, so I could tell you about the baby, so we could share. But…"

He set the album on the table where she kept the others. "I did look for you. I hired three different private detectives. But you weren't in your hometown, you weren't in New York State, and you didn't show up on employment records anywhere in the country."

"I came back to New Skye, eventually."

On a deep breath, he sank a little deeper into the armchair, putting his face in shadow. "I stopped looking after about a year."

Unwisely, she asked, "Why?"

"What else could I do? The reports were all negative, and it was pretty easy to recognize that you did not want to be found. Plus…"

When he didn't continue, she prodded. "Go on."

"My…Andrew's mother intercepted a bill from one of the P.I.s. Not surprisingly, she threw one of her famous tantrums and threatened to take the baby and leave for good if I didn't stop the search. I'd already failed once at this marriage. I wanted to give it my best effort. And I had a son to consider."

"You had a daughter, too."

"I didn't know that, did I?"

The momentum had changed between them. Caught between hurt and fear, Jacquie didn't know how to regain their balance. "You didn't exactly give me a chance to tell you, that night."

Rhys leaned over and picked up his slacks from the floor. "You could have told me anything you wanted."

Still on her knees, Jacquie turned her gaze to the

window. She couldn't bear to see him getting dressed, preparing to leave her. "I hadn't had much practice in announcing I was pregnant."

"And I'd already heard it once that day. Believe me, I wasn't any better at receiving the news."

"Exactly." Trailing sheets, blanket and bedspread, she followed him into the living room where he bent to pick up his shirt. "I guess your back is better?"

"Yes, thanks. What does 'exactly' mean?"

"You stalked into my apartment and started unloading all this anger and shock on me—how you were trapped, no choices left, nothing to do but go on with the marriage, what a bad time this was for a baby, anyway. Was I supposed to say, 'Oh, by the way, guess who else you knocked up?'"

He stood rigid in the center of the room. "I made love to you every time we were together. I made love to my wife in one last, desperate attempt to save the relationship. I have never 'knocked up' anyone." After a glance at his watch, he pulled on his sweater. If his back hurt, he didn't give any indication. "It's 4:00 in the morning. I ought to be home before Terry gets up, not to mention the kids."

There it was again, the implication that somehow her daughter had become a permanent part of his life. While *she* was not.

The time had come to push the issue. "I want to see Erin."

"I don't know if she's ready to see you."

"Have you asked? Have you talked to her about me?"

His hands went into his pockets, and she heard his keys jingle. "She'll talk when she's ready."

"As a parent, you have a responsibility to make her do what's right and what's best, whether she's ready or not."

"You expect me to tie her to a chair and lock the two of you in the room together?"

"I expect you to convince her that she owes me a chance to explain, out of love and respect."

"I'm not ready to force her into a situation she doesn't want."

"Instead, you want to gain her love...at my expense. You keep her in your big house and let her ride your wonderful horses, with a minimum of chores and probably more spending money than she knows what to do with." Rhys looked at the floor, and she saw his face flush. "Right. I'm sure she's got a great new wardrobe. In the meantime, her horse is starving himself for loneliness and the responsibilities she has in my home are being neglected. That's not fair."

Rhys lifted his head. "You're just one more person whose expectations I can't measure up to." He walked past her into the kitchen, opened the back door, then glanced back. "And though I would like things to be different, all I can say right now is...that's too damn bad."

CHAPTER FOURTEEN

"GOOD NEWS," Terry said as Rhys walked into the kitchen two hours later.

"I could use some." He took down a coffee mug and the bottle of ibuprofen.

"Your dad called. He's coming down for the Top Flight trials. Bringing the sheikh with him to watch Imperator win."

"Excellent." Throwing the pills at the back of his throat, he chased them with a gulp of coffee. "That should make the day a real picnic, since I've decided to scratch the horse. His Highness or whatever can just hand over the check and drive off with the goods."

Terry gripped his arm. "You're scratching the horse? Giving up?"

"Imp has several years of good competition left in him. Why tie him down, leave him standing around with nothing to do but eat his head off, when he could go somewhere else and practice what he loves? There's no one to ride him here."

"I would," Andrew said from the door to the hall.

Rhys shook his head. "You won't be ready to ride him at that level until he's past his prime. I know you love him, but sometimes we have to do what's best for the creatures we love, even at our own expense."

He winced as he heard his own words echo what Jacquie had said earlier. He'd known at the time she was right, but hadn't been able to crawl past his own stubborn, arrogant pride.

"You can use him for stud," Andrew said desperately. "You know he's worth thousands. That's why this Fahed guy wants him."

"True. But before Imperator goes out to stud, he deserves all the success he can win."

Terry clanked his mug down on the table. "Aren't we forgetting the teeny fact that the horse still isn't reliable over the jumps? So far, he's not looking like winning anything, if you ask me."

"He's waiting for his rider." Erin stood just behind Andrew in the hallway. "Until he can jump with you, Mr. Lew—Rhys, he'll never be whole again."

"Yeah, right." Andrew snorted. "Sounds like a fairy tale to me."

Terry shrugged. "I've heard stranger ideas."

Rhys had, as well. "What makes you think so, Erin?"

She eased past Andrew and came into the kitchen. "That's where his failure was, right? He fell and you fell with him. He failed, and hurt you. So I think he wants—needs to take responsibility for keeping both of you safe."

Her words went with Rhys through the day, especially as he watched Imperator caper in his paddock. He could almost imagine the big horse demonstrating his talents, begging for the chance to make things right.

But Imperator was not the only one with mistakes to repair. When the kids got home from school, Rhys sent Andrew and Terry to the barn for afternoon chores, but asked Erin to take a walk with him to the pasture where they'd turned Imperator out for a few hours of play.

Imp lifted his head for a moment as they reached the fence, greeted them with a toss of his head, then returned to nosing the new-grown grass.

Erin propped her elbows on the top board and her chin on her fists. "He's so beautiful. Do you think I'll ever get to ride him?"

"I'll make sure you do."

"What if you sell him?"

"You'll get your ride before he leaves." The prospect of losing Imperator dimmed the day for both of them. Rhys turned his mind to the reason he'd brought her out. "Erin, we have to talk about your mom."

She didn't reply.

He braced his back against the sun-warmed board of the fence. "You were angry, and everybody understands that. But it's time to grow past the anger. She needs you. And you need her. Mirage misses you."

"I like it here." In a lower voice, she added, "But I do miss Mirage."

"I'm glad that I could help you get through a bad time. It's time I took a role in your life." He pulled in a deep breath. "But this…arrangement…was never intended to be permanent. You must go home."

To his surprise, she hid her face in the crook of her elbow and started to sob. He couldn't understand the words amongst the tears. "Erin, sweetheart, what's wrong?"

When he put his hand on her shoulder, his daughter

launched herself against him. Automatically he closed his arms around her shoulders, cradling her like the small child he'd never known. "Come on, Erin. Tell me why you're crying."

"I'm scared," she moaned between sniffs.

"What could you be scared of?"

"My mom." Before he could ask, the words started flowing. "How can she love me anymore? After what I did? How long I've been gone?"

Rhys had never been at such a loss. He'd already proved his incompetence as a parent with Andrew—how could he possibly cope with Erin's fears? What should he say?

"You told me you were able to see Mirage being born, didn't you?" Ridiculous, but all he could think of.

Erin nodded against his ribs.

"And you've been with him since then, training him, taking care of him, watching him grow."

Sniff. "Yes."

"We know horses are not really predictable, though. If they are frightened, or feel threatened, they bolt. Or kick. So, suppose you were riding Mirage and….and…and a kite dropped out of the sky in front of him."

She drew back to look at him. "That's weird."

"It happened to me once, actually, during a dressage test near a city park. So a kite flutters out of the sky and lands at Mirage's feet. Your horse, thinking he's about to be eaten by a monster, bolts as if he's running the Derby, rakes you under some tree branches and finally leaves you on the ground while he gallops back to the stable."

Giggling, she nodded. "Okay."

"Do you stop loving him? Do you stop taking care of him because he was scared and reacted with instinct instead of rational thought? Do you sell him to the next person you see for dog meat?"

"Of course not!" She thumped on his chest with a fist, then stepped back, out of his hold. "That's mean. I'd be mad, but I wouldn't…" After a pause, she looked up at him and smiled. "I get it."

He nodded. "Love doesn't end because the one you love hurts you. Maybe you're a little cautious for a while. But true love always wins out. And your mom loves you very, very much."

They began walking back toward the barn. "So I suppose I should call my mom," Erin said. "Although it'll be…scary."

"You're brave."

"Sometimes." After a moment, she said, "I'll make you a deal."

"What kind of deal?"

"Well…I'll call my mom, if you'll ride Imperator on the jumps."

Rhys stopped walking. "It's not at all the same thing."

"No, my mom is scarier than any horse."

"True," he said, and they both laughed. "Erin, I don't think Imp will magically recover his confidence just because I'm on his back." *And I'm damned sure I won't recover mine.*

"Why not? How can he understand what's happened, except that he made a mistake and you haven't ridden him like that since? Wouldn't you be confused?"

"I suppose I would."

"Then you have to be brave, if I do." She looked up at him out of the corners of her eyes. "I'll watch you take Imperator over the cross-country course, and then I'll call my mom."

Laughing, Rhys ruffled her short hair. "Something like that, scamp. Now, go get your chores done, and we'll put you up on the stallion for a jog."

"All right!"

His heart lifted as she ran screaming across the yard. Suddenly, even hope seemed possible.

THE HOURS BEFORE Erin's arrival were the longest Jacquie had ever known. She found herself cleaning up the house, just to stay busy and avoid going insane. Erin probably wouldn't recognize the place, wouldn't realize the neat yellow bedroom—with its vacuumed blue carpet, freshly made bed covered in a galloping-horse print and sparkling clean windows—was hers.

Searching for a vase in which to put a bunch of daffodils she'd picked on the edge of the woods beyond the pasture, Jacquie could barely fight off yet another round of tears. All these surface details didn't really matter a damn. The facts of her life, and Erin's, hadn't changed. And if her daughter couldn't accept and forgive her mistakes, they would never recover the closeness she'd depended on all these years.

Rhys's truck pulled into the driveway at exactly four o'clock. Andrew and Erin sat in the back seat, but only Erin got out. She came to the front door and knocked. Nearly suffocated by apprehension, Jacquie opened the door to her daughter.

"Hi, sweetheart." As the adult, she ought to be able to handle the situation with calm, right? "Come in."

"Hi." And then, with much more enthusiasm, "Hi, Hurry! How are you, huh?" She bent to hug the shepherd dancing at her feet. In the process of playing and getting reacquainted, Erin came into the house.

When Hurry had calmed down, she straightened up and looked around at the living room. A deep breath lifted her shoulders. "This is…nice."

"Thanks. I've got some tea made, and some gingersnaps."

"I'm not hungry."

"Me, neither." They shared a tentative smile. "This is hard, isn't it?"

Eyes round with nervousness, Erin nodded.

"Let's…sit down." She took her usual seat at one end of the couch and Erin, she was thrilled to see, naturally gravitated to her personal space on the other end. Hurry jumped up between them, curled into her favorite position, and with a satisfied sigh put her head on Erin's thigh.

Jacquie cleared her throat. "How was school today?"

"Okay." She stared at her twisting fingers for a moment. "How's Mirage?"

"He's lost some weight. He misses you."

Her "yeah" was a confession, of sorts. "I rode Imperator yesterday."

"How was he?"

"Awesome. Incredible. Like riding Pegasus. All I had to do was think, and he made the change I wanted." Her expression changed from ecstatic to worried in an instant. "I hope they get to keep him."

"Why wouldn't they?"

"Rhys…Rhys says that if Imp doesn't win at Top Flight, he'll be sold to some sheikh."

That didn't sound like the man she knew. "He would sell the horse?"

"No, he doesn't own Imp. I didn't understand everything, but I think Andrew's grandfather is the one who makes the decision."

She should have thought of that. Rhys wouldn't necessarily own the horse he rode for the stable. And, yes, she could believe Owen Lewellyn would do something so mean. "When did this happen?"

"I think…the morning after the schooling day. Somehow Andrew's grandfather found out that Imp refused the jump and called. Or something like that."

She'd talked with Rhys many times since then, and he hadn't shared something this important, this vital to his concerns, with *her*. Jacquie pushed the hurt down deep, to be ached over later. "Erin, I'm truly sorry you found out about your father the way you did. That was never my intention."

More twisting of the fingers. "You never meant me to know at all."

"I'm not sure. I might have decided to tell you, when you were older."

"You lied to me. My whole life."

"Not just you. I had never told anyone the truth." She took a deep breath. "Until Rhys came."

"I missed him, you know. My dad." Erin got to her feet and went to the window. "I used to imagine he was watching me, taking care of me from heaven. I talked to him, sometimes, told him what was going on. And he's not real. Never was."

Jacquie gripped her own hands together. "I am so sorry. I wanted to protect you. And myself. People can be cruel, without meaning to be."

"Yeah." After a pause, she said, "You didn't even tell Grandma?"

"No one."

"Why? Were you scared of her and Granddaddy?"

"Not exactly. Just…ashamed…of myself for disappointing them. They didn't bring me up to be the girl who had a baby at nineteen without being married."

"Do they know now?"

"Yes."

"And…are they? Disappointed in you?" Her voice sank to a whisper. "In me?"

"Oh, no, Erin. There's no blame in this for you. You're still the darling of their eye." She wanted to take her daughter in her arms, but Erin still seemed very far away. "They don't blame me, either. They just want us to be happy again. Together."

"I like Rhys."

"He's a good man. As soon as I told him about you, he began to care." Jacquie took a risk. "What you said…about your dad watching over you…in a way, you might have been talking to Rhys. You might have been in his mind, without him knowing." Erin looked at her, and she shrugged. "I know, that's weird. But you two are so much alike, maybe… Never mind."

"No, I get it." Another deep breath. "Andrew said that the truth can be worse than lies. His mother told him he wasn't wanted, by anybody."

"That's not the truth. The whole truth, anyway. His

dad was surprised to know there was a baby, but he was always committed to taking care of his son.''

"Did *you* think about…abortion?''

An easy answer. "Not for a single instant.''

Erin's tense stance eased slightly. "Were you sorry?''

Not easy at all. "Let me ask you a question. You've got big plans for yourself—lots of competition, the Olympics, the whole world ahead of you. Suppose you find out tomorrow that all those plans will have to change. Something is going to happen in your life—something wonderful, if unexpected. Nothing will ever be the same for you again. Your money, your time, your energy will all go in a different direction. How do you feel?''

"I'm not sure. I wouldn't want to give up my riding for anything.''

"But in this situation you will have to, at least for a while.''

"I—I would be mad, I think.'' She nodded. "Yeah. And sorry.''

"That's your answer. I wanted Rhys's baby—you—because I loved him. But my dreams of the Olympics, Rolex and all the big events…gone. I was scared, because I had nobody in New York except Rhys, and he wasn't mine anymore. I was guilty, because I'd been with a man I wasn't married to, a man who was still married, himself. Eighteen years of church school had taught me how wrongly I'd behaved.'' She gave a wry smile. "I had very little money, but I couldn't go home to face my family and friends with my 'sin.'''

Erin came back to the couch. "That sounds horrible."

"Yes, it was. Until you were born, and I held you in my arms and saw just how lovely, how sweet, how perfect you were. All the pain went away, all the regret. And I haven't felt sorry since. Until I hurt you."

They sat for a few minutes without talking at all. Erin stroked her hand over Hurry's side, a soft brush of sound in the silence.

"How do we do this?" she said finally.

"What?"

"Do you…want me here?"

"Oh, Erin." She reached out to clasp her daughter's hand. "Of course."

"Can I still see…my dad?"

"I hope so." Though the prospect of being involved in Rhys's life—or rather, on the edge of Rhys's life—terrified her. "I don't see why not."

"Okay." Pulling free, Erin stood up and walked to the door of her bedroom. "Wow. I didn't remember the rug was blue."

Jacquie followed, but stood back a bit in the hallway. "We haven't seen it in a long time, have we?" They both chuckled. "I'll expect your room—the whole house—to stay like this from now on. I'm really liking the neat look."

"Maybe I will go back to Rhys's house. They have somebody who comes in to clean."

"Too late. You're trapped." She stretched her arms from wall to wall, pretending to block the way.

"I will escape." Grinning, Erin put her head down like a football player intent on breaking through the defensive line. As she passed, Jacquie dropped her arms and caught the slim body close.

"Gotcha."

She'd intended to let go immediately. But Erin froze in her arms and then, suddenly, collapsed in tears against her breast.

Jacquie sank to the floor, bringing her daughter with her, holding the sobbing girl in her lap, smoothing her hair, stroking her back, whispering words of comfort and love. Her own tears had dried with the knowledge that Erin was coming home.

As long as they were together, they could work things out.

"THIS COULD TAKE FOREVER," Andrew said, as Erin stepped inside the small white house. "And you know she's gonna stay here. Why can't we just go home and send her clothes?"

"She needs to know she has a choice," Rhys said. He rubbed his tired eyes. The possibility of a good night's sleep seemed like a figment of his imagination these days. "Backing a horse—or a person—into a corner is a sure way to make them fight."

A long-suffering sigh came from behind him. "I'm supposed to ride Imp this afternoon."

"You'll have time."

"Have you decided who will ride him in the Top Flight trials?"

Rhys put his head back against the seat. "I will."

When Andrew didn't say anything, he turned toward the rear of the truck. "Well?"

The boy nodded. "Cool. That's what I wanted you to say."

"We could easily lose. Erin's theory is mostly wishful thinking. I'm not at my best, physically, and—"

"Dad. Whoa. I get the picture."

"I just want to be sure your expectations are realistic. Imperator will most probably be sold whether I ride or not."

"As you're always saying, we'll jump that fence when we get there. Just ride the one coming up."

"Somehow, I'm not enjoying having my own words thrown back at me."

"That's what kids do."

"Terrific." Rhys met Andrew's eyes in the rearview mirror and smiled. "But I suppose it could be worse."

"I can work on that, if you want."

"Don't do me any favors."

The tree shadows had grown long by the time Erin and Jacquie came out of the house. Erin was smiling, tossing a ball for Hurry. She came to the truck ahead of her mother and opened the back door.

"I'm gonna stay," she announced. "I need my book bag now, but I can get my clothes the next time I'm over." A frown took over her face, and she came to stand beside Rhys's open window.

"I—I mean, is that okay? Can I still visit you…and Imp and Mr. O'Neal? Do I get to come back?"

"If that's what you want. I was hoping you would." He held out his hand, palm up, and she put hers into it. "I don't want to lose you again, scamp. We'll see each other. Often."

Her sunny smile returned. "Good."

In the back seat, Andrew groaned. "Don't I have anything to say about this?"

Rhys said, at the same instant as Erin, "No."

"Just asking."

"I'm gonna go see Mirage," she said. "But..."

"I'll call," Rhys promised. "Go on."

As she ran off, Andrew opened his door. "I'm tired of sitting. I'm going to look at this stallion she's always bragging about. Honk when you're ready to go."

Jacquie came closer, though not close enough to touch. "Thank you," she said simply. The stress of the past weeks showed in the shadows under her eyes, the thinness of her cheeks. At least the sadness, the worry, had left her eyes.

"Better?"

"I think so. I have to earn my way back to full trust, I imagine. That's understandable."

"Erin wasn't hard to convince. I think she really wanted to come home."

"She wanted to stay with you, too. A hard choice."

"She's welcome at Fairfield anytime. And..." Touchy subject. "I would like to give her more lessons. On Mirage, and...some of my bigger horses, as well." He decided not to mention Imperator, since that option was likely to disappear.

But she was ahead of him. "I understand Imperator will be sold if he doesn't win at Top Flight."

"My father doesn't want to keep a horse that isn't winning."

"You didn't tell me about this."

"There have been...complications, wouldn't you agree? The horse was the least of them."

"Who'll be riding him in the Top Flight trials?"

He have her a half smile. "Your daughter made me

promise I would. She suggested that facing you was the more frightening of the two challenges."

Jacquie grimaced, but came forward a couple of steps. Within reach.

"So you're going to ride Imperator cross-country. I think that's the right thing to do. And I think you'll be fine."

"I was just telling Andrew—the chances of winning are slim. And that's my father's condition. Win, or the horse will be sold."

"He has a buyer?"

"He says so. One-point-five million."

She whistled. "That's a big sale." Her forehead furrowed as she considered. "What if he got a counteroffer for more money?"

"I suppose he would consider the bottom line and take the better deal."

"So we should offer one-point-six?"

Rhys glanced at the barn. "Are you spinning hay into gold in there? Or do your horses digest grass into cash?"

Her laugh sounded sweet in the late-afternoon warmth. "I wish. But that would give us insurance, right? Just in case the ride doesn't go the way we hope?"

He couldn't begin to understand what she might be thinking. "Yes. I suppose so. Where would we get that kind of cash?"

She put a hand on the edge of the door between them. "You have friends, Rhys. I have friends. And between them all, we might get a lifeline, at least."

He stared at her hand for a moment, saw again the strength and grace contained there. "You keeping saying 'we.''' Before she could draw her hand away, he caught hold and looked into her eyes. ''Why?''

Jacquie started to stammer something foolish, evading his gaze and the truth. But a sudden serenity fell over her. The time for defensiveness and insecurity had passed.

''We share a child, and we both care about her. Those bonds will always tie us together.''

''Only those bonds?''

She wasn't quite prepared for that question. ''I don't know.''

Rhys nodded his head once. ''Right. So you want to put together a consortium to offer for Imperator. Who, exactly, are you planning to ask?''

''I think we should start at the top.'' She grinned. ''Can you give me Galen's phone number?''

LONG AFTER ANDREW and Rhys had left, after her mom had cooked her favorite macaroni and cheese for dinner, with gingersnaps and lemonade as dessert, Erin went back to the barn to be with Mirage.

She stroked her hand along his ribs, which she could see even in the dark, and his hip, where the bone poked up too high. ''You are sooo skinny. Did you think I wouldn't come back to you? Did you really believe I would go away and leave you behind? I couldn't do that. I love you too much!

''I just had to see my life from somewhere else, you know? Perspective, we humans call it. My whole world used to be here—the pastures, the house, the barn. My mom. And then this other world opened up, and I couldn't tell where I belonged anymore. I wasn't even sure this world, the one I trusted for so long, was real.''

With her arms resting on Mirage's back, she put her cheek against his side. ''Took me awhile, but I figured out that I can build my world anywhere I want. So I'm getting ready to create this great big place where I can have everything—you and Imperator and Hurry and Sydney, my mom and my dad and Mr. O'Neal. Even Andrew. We're gonna have an awesome time, Mirage. I can hardly wait.''

Mirage shifted his hips, snuffled in his hay, flicked his tail at a fly. Erin smiled, to him and to herself.

''And no, I don't love that big horse better than you. He's special, but you're special, too, in a different way. You're my best friend.

''Forever.''

CHAPTER FIFTEEN

THE IMPERATOR CONSORTIUM, as Jacquie called it, met on Wednesday night at Charlie's Carolina Diner, with only ten days to go before the Top Flight Horse Trials. Their conference room took up the center of the restaurant—three tables for four set end to end. The refreshment of choice proved to be coffee—or, for Erin and Andrew, milk—and Super Duper Triple Scooper Banana Splits all around.

"My thanks to all of you for coming," Jacquie said from one end of the table. "I know this isn't convenient, and you don't have a compulsion to be here, except that you're all really nice people who want to help out a friend."

"And you said you were buying the banana splits," added Dixon Bell. Kate, sitting beside him, shoved her elbow into his ribs.

"Right." She grinned at him. "Okay. The problem is simple. I would like to be able to make a purchase offer on the stallion Imperator. Most of you have seen him, and I sent you the details of his breeding, his wins, his current stud fees, and his potential. This is an investment opportunity. He's sound, he's got great spirit. The last few months have been rocky, but we think that problem is on the way to being solved. Rhys and Imp rode the cross-country course at Fairfield Farm yesterday without a refusal.''

Beside her, Rhys tilted his head and acknowledged the applause.

Adam DeVries raised his hand. "How much money are we talking about?"

"As far as we are aware, the current offer is a million and a half dollars."

The mayor blinked and glanced at Phoebe, on Jacquie's left. "That's a lot of money."

"I know. If each of us contributed equally, counting engaged or married couples together, we would put in three hundred thousand apiece. But that's not what I'm asking, because…we have a fairy godmother."

At the other end of the table, Galen smiled widely. "Ooh, I like that idea. Do I get a magic wand?"

Jacquie winked at her. "Definitely. Galen is a horsewoman and owner of some renown and she knows exactly what she's doing when she buys an animal. Imperator will be an excellent match for some of her mares. She has agreed to provide the balance of the money for Imp."

"But not all?" Buck Travis asked. "Why would that be?"

"I do have a limit to my resources," Galen said frankly. "And our bargaining position is better if I don't use all my available capital up front. This way, if our competitor tries to bid us up, I've got something to go up with."

Buck stared at her. "An intelligent woman is worth her weight in gold. Will you marry me?"

Jacquie held her breath and the whole table watched as, for probably the first time in her life, Galen Oakley was completely taken aback. Finally she regained her poise. "I'll think about it."

"That's all I could ask." He sat back in his chair with a satisfied smile.

"Well." With a shake of her head, Jacquie refocused. "What we're here for tonight is to discover if you're interested in contributing to the purchase price and how much, and to set down the operating rules for our consortium to everyone's satisfaction. We have legal advice from Attorney Edward Bowdrey, Kate's dad." She nodded at the distinguished gentleman next to Kate. "And Rhys can answer any and all questions on Imperator. We will take offers in a sealed envelope, so your contribution will remain private."

She stacked her papers together. "And here's the bottom line—if any one of you doesn't want to contribute, can't, won't…whatever…there will be no hard feelings. I know I've…made some mistakes, and hurt the people I care about most. I really appreciate that you've come tonight, despite that. This isn't a test. Feel free to accept or decline as you are persuaded."

The meeting ran late into the evening as they wrestled genially about regulations and organization, with several refills of coffee cups by Abby and her dad Charlie. Erin and Andrew were playing Hangman and Battleship at a different table by the time Mr. Bowdrey had drawn up his notes and the envelopes containing the various offers were collected.

As her friends prepared to leave, Jacquie went to stand by one of the diner windows. Lost in her thoughts, staring out into the night, she jumped as a hand fell on her shoulder. Looking around, she found Kate behind her. "I didn't mean to startle you."

"It's okay. I was just thinking." Regretting. Hoping. Wishing for the moon.

Kate smiled and turned to lean back against the window. "I wanted to tell you...don't blame yourself too much for what happened in the past."

"If only it were just the past. I was...deceiving...all of you just a couple of weeks ago."

"We'll get over it." Kate leaned in to kiss her cheek. "Just take care of yourself. And Erin." She glanced across the room. "And Rhys."

That brought her back to her thoughts. Jacquie sighed. "I'm not sure I deserve the chance."

RHYS STOOD BY the diner door to speak with everyone as they left. Not that words were easy for him tonight. The kindness and concern of these people overwhelmed him. He'd never known such generosity of spirit.

Galen caught him in a hug. "This will turn out so beautifully. Your father won't know what hit him."

"I can't tell you—"

"Then don't." She smiled and moved past him. "I'll call you with details in a few days. Buck, are you going to walk me to my car?"

The veterinarian stepped up quickly. "Wouldn't miss the opportunity." He clapped a hand on Rhys's shoulder. "Good luck," he said. "I'll be there to see you and Imperator take the ribbon. Coming, ma'am." he called to Galen, who stood tapping her foot on the sidewalk outside.

Adam came last. "An interesting proposition," the mayor said, shaking Rhys's hand. "I'll try to get out to your place soon to meet this fantastic horse. If not before, I'll come to the—what's the right word? Trial?—to watch him run." As he finished, his fiancée stepped up beside him, having just given Jacquie an enthusiastic—and no doubt healing—hug.

"Drop by anytime. And, Phoebe, thanks so much for taking care of Erin. You really were a lifesaver."

Her smile was serene. "That's right, I haven't given you my bill yet, have I?"

"There's a bill?"

She nodded. "I have a stallion at my place named Samson. He was abused in the stable where he was boarded, and he's gone crazy as a result. I've worked with him for months now, and I can barely look him in the eye before he takes off, practically cartwheeling across the pasture."

"And…?"

"And I want you to help him. Settle him down. Turn him into a horse who enjoys people, can maybe even be ridden."

"Ah." The challenge appealed to him, of course. "We'll work out the details. I'll be glad to do what I can."

"See, I knew you would. Now we're even." To his surprise, she stood on tiptoe to kiss his cheek. "Good night, Rhys."

"Sure."

He turned to the table, where Jacquie sat with the envelopes in her hand, staring into space. Her expression gave nothing away. Abby and Charlie had disappeared into the kitchen to finish washing up.

"Do we have an answer?" Rhys sat down in his

chair on Jacquie's right. "Is there good news? Or bad?"

Her gaze focused and she looked at him. "I don't know what to say. I never expected..." She looked down at the envelopes. "I mean, except for Galen, we're all pretty ordinary people. But between us—"

"Wait a minute." Abby came out from behind the counter to hand over an envelope. "I wanted to give you this."

"You don't have to—" Jacquie began.

"I know that. But Daddy and I wanted to be in on the fun, too. So you just put us on your list." She scurried back to the kitchen where the clatter of dishes got suddenly louder.

Jacquie opened the envelope, and gasped. "Oh, my goodness."

Andrew and Erin came over. "What's wrong?"

She looked at the kids, and then at Rhys. Her eyes shone with joy. "That's done it. Including what Abby just gave me, and Dixon and Galen and all the others...

"We can bid up to *two million dollars* to keep our horse!"

Erin screamed, and threw her arms around Andrew, who pushed her away, and then Rhys, who didn't. As soon as he returned his daughter's hug, he turned to Jacquie.

"Thanks to you," he said softly. He stroked his hand along her cheek. "Only you."

ANDREW'S GRANDFATHER ARRIVED on the Thursday morning before the Top Flight event, in a long black limousine.

"Is this a funeral?" Andrew murmured in Erin's ear as they peered through one of the drawing-room windows, watching the car crawl up the front driveway of the house.

"Well, there is the body I buried out by the barn."

He snorted. "That was a grass snake."

"Who says a snake can't have a funeral?"

The driver opened the rear door and his granddad stood up out of the car. White-haired and tall, with the blue eyes Andrew saw every day in the mirror, Owen Lewellyn looked around him with pursed lips, and Andrew could practically see the cash register in his mind, ringing up the worth of the place.

Following Owen out of the car was a man in a suit and an Arab headdress.

"The sheikh," Andrew said, faking an excited voice.

His dad walked by and cuffed him on the shoulder. "Come. And be polite."

They waited at the front door as the two men climbed the steps. "Welcome, Dad." Father and son shook hands as if they hadn't met before. "And welcome, of course, Mr. Al Fahed." The dark man nodded and bowed.

Once inside, Owen turned to Andrew. "You're growing, I see that. You look just like your father at that age."

What was the polite answer? "Uh…thank you. Sir."

Those cold eyes moved to Erin's face. "What's this?"

His dad went to stand behind Erin with his hands

on her shoulders. "This is my daughter, Dad. Erin Archer."

"Your what?"

"I'll explain in private."

"You'd damned well better. Meantime, Al Fahed and I want to see the horse." The three men went toward the back of the house, disappearing through the door under the staircase.

Erin sank into a heap on the floor, her face hidden by her arms, her shoulders shaking. She didn't move even when Andrew nudged her with his foot. "Come on. Forget him. He's like that to everybody."

She looked up at him, and he saw she was laughing, not crying. "What a character. He's like somebody in a movie or a book, too evil to be real. Was he ever nice to you, when you were a little kid?"

"I didn't see him much after my mom and I left. He's pretty much always been the same."

"Does he even like horses?"

"That's about all he does like. He's really different with them. You'll see."

When they got to the barn, his dad had Imperator on a lead, with Owen and Al Fahed watching. Imp held his head high, and his eyes flashed fire. He enjoyed showing off.

"Let me have him," Owen ordered, and took the rope out of Rhys's hand. "C'mon, Imp," he said, clicking his tongue. "Trot."

They made a strange picture, the white-haired man in a black suit running across the yard with the big black stallion beside him. But their antics also looked like a game they'd played many times before. Owen feinted left and right, and Imp would follow, imitating the movement. Imp stopped hard, and Owen would turn to back him up—not in anger, but in fun. Andrew had never seen anything quite like the relationship of his granddad and that horse.

He'd never before, in his whole life, seen his grand-dad grin.

"Wow," Erin said. "He can't be all bad."

RHYS MET WITH HIS FATHER alone in the gathering room before everyone else came downstairs for dinner.

"So explain this daughter," Owen said, pouring himself a whiskey.

For what he hoped would be the last time in his life, Rhys gave some of the details about that summer. "Jacquie left without notice, if you'll remember. I discovered when I got down here in January that we had a daughter together."

"She must not have thought much of you, if she didn't bother to tell you in—what?—fourteen years."

"That's hardly an issue now. I'm happy to acknowledge Erin as my child and hope to be a decent father to her."

His father snorted. "Whatever that means."

Rhys held his temper. "I would appreciate it if you refrained from venting your wit or your anger on her for the duration of your visit. Jacquie will be at the horse trials, and I'd prefer you not talk to her at all. If you can't say something nice, don't say anything."

"I'll say what I like and be damned to you." Owen's Welsh accent returned when he got mad.

"Then I can and will arrange to have you removed from the grounds."

After a moment, Owen dropped his gaze to his glass and took a long gulp. Terry came in a minute later—though Rhys suspected he'd been listening in the hallway all along—and soon Andrew and Erin and the sheikh appeared, as well. Rhys thanked God that Jacquie had had the good sense to decline his invitation to dinner.

Galen, however, arrived "by accident" just as they went into the dining room. She swept into the house in a cloud of expensive perfume, her mink stole trailing from one shoulder.

"Rhys, I just had to come by to wish you luck tomorrow. You know I'll be there watching." Her surprise, when she saw his guests, looked authentic. "Mr. Lewellyn, what a pleasure to see you, sir. It's been years, but I would have known you anywhere. You haven't changed at all, except for that distinguished white hair."

"You have," his father said. "I remember pigtails and crooked teeth."

She laughed as if he'd given her a compliment. "I'm so glad to have grown up." She turned to Al Fahed. "Have we met?"

In the course of introductions, another place was set and Galen allowed herself to be persuaded to stay for dinner. She dominated the conversation, of course. By the end of the meal, both men were quite charmed by her presence.

"I must run," she said, as they all got to their feet. "I will look for you all at Rourke Park tomorrow afternoon. We can talk more then. It's been a pleasure, gentlemen." She allowed both Owen and the sheikh to kiss her hand. "Good night."

At the door, she whispered to Rhys, "Just keep them mellow. I'll do the rest."

"Oh, sure," Rhys countered. "Give me the hard part."

JACQUIE'S SCHEDULE on Friday, the first day of the Top Flight Horse Trials, became crazy, thanks to an emergency call for shoe repair. She stayed at Rourke Park long enough to watch Erin and Andrew perform their dressage tests at the lower levels, then rushed off to a farm halfway across the county. She returned on Friday afternoon as Terry unloaded Imp from the trailer. "He looks fantastic." She walked around the horse, examining each detail. "Every braid in his mane exactly like the next, tail silky, hooves shined, face and ears all shaved and clean…perfect." Lifting the horse's chin with one hand, she kissed his nose. "Be a good boy today, okay?"

Then she looked at Rhys, so elegantly handsome in his cutaway black jacket, white breeches and gloves, and top hat. "You'll do, as well," she told him.

He tipped his hat. "Thank you, ma'am. I aim not to disgrace the horse."

She stood with Erin, Andrew and Terry as Rhys and Imperator performed their dressage test with control and grace. A sizable crowd gathered to witness the famous stallion's return to top-level competition, and Imp rewarded them with a stellar performance.

"One down," Rhys said as he slid out of the saddle. "Two to go." He looked beyond Jacquie. "Prepare yourself. This next few minutes will be tough."

When she turned, she saw the man in the suit and Arab headdress first, then noticed and recognized his companion. The resemblance between Rhys and his father was pronounced, even though the elder Lewellyn's hair had gone pure silver-white.

But Erin had warned her about Owen's attitude, so she thought she was prepared for the worst.

"I remember you," he said, without further introduction. "You were a graceless, snippy thing that summer. And now I hear you ran off because—"

Rhys gripped his father's arm. "I meant what I said. Another word in that line and you'll be headed back to New York before you can sneeze twice."

Owen removed his arm from his son's hold with an attempt at dignity. "Don't manhandle me. The horse looked good on the flat. Is he ready for the jumps tomorrow?"

That was the question on everyone's mind as they all met at the horse trailer on Saturday morning. The members of the consortium had turned up to wish Rhys good luck in person.

Galen immediately took control of Owen and Al Fahed, strolling arm in arm with them, introducing them to the horse people she knew in the crowd, which was just about everyone.

Phoebe and Adam, Dixon and Kate and her teenage children, along with Erin and Andrew, gathered around Imperator as Terry gave him a final once-over. Rhys, however, had disappeared.

Jacquie found him in the only private space on the course—the horse box of the trailer. She looked in the door to see him leaning against the wall, one foot flat on the bulkhead while he stared at the helmet he was turning between his hands. He wore his dark blue safety vest over a gold knit shirt, tan breeches and tall, shiny black boots.

"Shall I go away?" she asked softly.

He smiled at her. "No, come into the parlor and admire my decorating."

She stepped over several piles of horse droppings. "Early manure styling."

"Imperator is quite a talented designer."

"So I see." She paused, and he went back to staring at the helmet. "How do you feel?"

"Calm. Terrified."

"Of the fences?"

Rhys shook his head. "No. If that comes, it'll be at the fence itself. I just...would hate to let everybody down."

"That will only happen if you don't ride at all. And you're here, so you've already met all our expectations."

"I'm sorry about my father."

"Don't be. He doesn't bother me anymore. I don't need his approval of my life. Neither do you."

"No, I don't, thanks to you and Galen. Just the ability to purchase Imperator sets me free from him."

"She's got him completed enchanted, if that's any comfort. Eating out of her hand. I think he'd *give* her the horse at this point. Al Fahed's a little stiffer, but I expect Galen to have him under control by the end of the day."

Outside, the loudspeaker announced that the first rider would begin the course in twenty minutes.

Rhys straightened up. "We go tenth, so I'd better start warming up." He closed the distance between them. "I really appreciate everything, Jacquie. Your help, your support...and our daughter."

She touched his face. "Good luck," she said softly, and drew him down to her for a gentle, wondering kiss.

When he lifted his head, they both smiled. "After that," Rhys said, "how can I lose?"

THE CROSS-COUNTRY COURSE at Rourke Park wandered over rolling hills and down into the dells between them, across the creek running through the land and in a track around the flat pasture once used for crops. The fences were varied and challenging, including an original tobacco barn requiring horse and rider to go inside and then take a drop jump to get out.

Erin hopped up and down with excitement as they waited for Rhys's start. Andrew had dropped his usual blasé air, and fidgeted just as much as his half sister. The adults tried to control their nerves, but anxiety and anticipation were in the air.

"He's as ready as I can make him," Terry commented to Jacquie. "And I don't know if it's enough."

"He'll do it," she said confidently. "I believe he's going all the way this time." They both knew they weren't talking solely—or even mostly—about Imperator.

Hearing her name called, Jacquie turned toward the entrance to the course and saw her parents coming toward them. "What in the world are y'all doing here?"

"We wanted to see the horse." Her mother hugged

her, brushed the hair back from her face and dusted a speck off her shirt. "And we wanted to see Rhys Lewellyn ride him."

"You're just in time."

The loudspeaker crackled. "That was rider number nine finishing, Bobby O'Connor on Caymus. Our next rider will be the Olympic champion duo, Mr. Rhys Lewellyn and Thoroughbred stallion Imperator!" Even with the crowd spread out over miles of course, the applause sounded strong.

The bell rang for Rhys's start.

From where they'd positioned themselves at the top of a hill, Jacquie and her friends could see the first three fences and the last two. They would miss the rest of the course.

Phoebe came to stand by Jacquie. "Want to hold my hand?"

"Please." On her other side, Erin wove their fingers together.

Imperator came into sight, galloped across level ground, then downhill to the first jump, a double wall on either side of a wide, shallow spot on the creek, requiring the horse to land in the water and take off again immediately. Rhys looked balanced, in control, as Imp approached the jump.

Jacquie held her breath.

Imp slowed at the base of the hill, but she thought it was Rhys holding him back, setting him up for the jump. Quick as lightning, almost before she could see what happened, they were up, over...bounce...up and over.

A cheer rose around her. Phoebe squeezed her hand.

The next fence was called a coup—a triangular box,

long and high, with daffodils planted at the base and bushes at both ends. Imp sailed over. But at the third jump, a zigzag log structure, the horse began to toss his head as he approached. Jacquie moaned and shut her eyes.

"No, Mom, it's all right." Erin shook her hand. "Look, he's okay."

Just as Jacquie opened her eyes, Imperator lifted himself off the ground to land safely on the other side.

"Yes!"

And then the horse disappeared into the trees, and there was silence. No hint as to what was happening, what might be coming up. Jacquie had walked the course yesterday with Terry and Rhys, Erin and Andrew, discussing options, lines of approach—the technicalities the rider needed to take care of for the horse to do its best. Now, everything depended on Rhys's judgment and Imperator's spirit.

The object of the ride was to take all the jumps cleanly, within a certain time frame. Too fast was considered unsafe and penalized. Too slow deducted points from the overall score for the event. Jacquie had deliberately left her watch at home this morning. She did not want to know if Rhys's pace was on, or off.

In the far distance, a cheer sounded, and then another. Spectators had stationed themselves all along the course, so she could only conclude they were applauding Rhys's jumps.

At last, the beat of hooves against the earth announced Imperator's return. Yet another cheer hailed his presence at the bottom of the hill on which they stood. Then there he was, charging up the slope, his coat lathered, his mouth flecked with foam. The expression in his eyes was one of pure joy. Rhys bent over the stallion's neck, urging him to the next fence—a huge chair built of logs and lattice, painted a silver gray. Up, up, up...and over.

One more. One more jump to go.

Rhys looked ahead to the last fence—easy enough, three giant logs with brush ahead and a ditch behind. His watch showed their time a little slow. With a flick of his crop and the press of his heels, he asked Imperator for everything. Easing the reins, he looked ahead to the finish line.

Three strides to the fence, two, one...over, with room to spare. A wild gallop, green grass rushing underneath him, with people screaming on either side. Standing tall in the stirrups, Rhys pumped his arm in the air. He'd done it, by God. *They'd* done it. He and Imperator.

And Jacquie. Erin. Andrew. Terry. All his friends.

Imp was breathing hard, needed a long cooldown. Completely out of breath, Rhys turned the horse and they trotted back to the top of the hill, where everyone waited. They mobbed him as soon as he slid out of the saddle, before he could give Andrew the reins.

The boy fought his way to Rhys's side. "Awesome, Dad. Just totally awesome."

Rhys grinned. "Yeah. Cool him down?"

"Sure." Andrew hesitated a second, then gave Rhys a quick hug. "You're back," he said, taking the reins without meeting his father's eyes.

Then Terry stood beside him, gripping his hand. "Good job, son," he said. "A damn good job." Before Rhys could answer, the Irishman blinked, sniffed and faded away to follow Andrew and the horse.

The crowd pressed in again, shaking his hand, patting his back. Rhys nodded, laughed—God, it felt good to win again. But all the time he searched the crowd. Where was she?

A tap on the shoulder turned him around. And, yes, finally, Jacquie stood before him, her face the best, brightest sight he could have imagined.

"You're back," she said.

"You're damn right I am," Rhys told her. Then he took her in his arms and swept her with him into a wild, triumphant kiss.

IMPERATOR'S RUN was not the fastest over the cross-country course, which left the winner of the event in doubt until Sunday morning and the stadium jumping competition. Again, Rhys and Imp went tenth, and though several of the horses ahead of them rode clear rounds, with no poles knocked off the fences, Imperator, in his flawless style, turned in the best time by several seconds to win the Advanced Class of the Top Flight Horse Trials.

The crowd, the judges, the volunteers for the event and all of the competitors applauded as man and stallion rode their solo victory lap, the blue ribbon on Imp's bridle flying like a banner in the wind.

Once back at Fairfield Farms, the celebration began in earnest. Cases of champagne appeared by magic—Galen's work, no doubt. Rhys hadn't bought any in case he jinxed his chances. Food appeared, brought by the Bells, Phoebe and Adam, and Jacquie. And Erin's victory hug was a sweet, simple moment he would remember all his life.

Late in the afternoon, his dad gripped him by the arm and pulled him into the hallway, away from the crowd. "Fahed and I will be leaving. The limo's outside."

Rhys tried to be generous. "I'm glad you came, and could see Imperator win."

Owen nodded. "I'm still selling the horse."

A wave of dizziness struck, so hard and fast that Rhys thought he might fall over. "You said—"

"I know what I said. I changed my mind." He slipped a folded piece of paper from the inside pocket of his jacket. A check. "I've signed the bill of sale. The horse's papers will be in the mail tomorrow."

"When...where is he going?"

His father shrugged. "How should I know? Ask your friend Galen." He winked at Rhys. "She's quite a woman." Without waiting for a reaction, Owen strode down the hall and through the door to the front of the house.

When he thought his legs would hold him up, Rhys went back into the gathering room. Across the room, Galen stood by herself, a glass of champagne in one hand. When she saw him, she smiled and lifted her other hand to wave a piece of paper.

Even at this distance, he recognized the bold slash of Owen Lewellyn's signature on the page.

AROUND MIDNIGHT, Jacquie abandoned the party for the peace and quiet of the barn. Imperator's blue ribbon glinted in the distant light from the house windows. Down the aisle, a white ribbon fluttered on the stall where Mirage was spending the night. Erin had taken fifth place in her own class at the Top Flight trials, an achievement as significant as Rhys's in some ways. They hadn't been sure Mirage could compete, but with Erin home he'd been back to his old self in a matter of days, fit and ready for the ride of his life.

Footsteps at the door of the barn turned her around. There was no mistaking that silhouette. "Rhys."

"I couldn't find you, and decided you must have come out here."

"I needed a little peace and quiet. It's been a crazy weekend."

He nodded. "I'll be glad when things settle down tomorrow. We can get back to ordinary work."

"Ordinary sounds good." The silence was uneasy, but she didn't know what to say to break it. Rhys moved to sit down on the hay bales she herself had once occupied. "You must be tired."

"A little."

"Did your back bother you this weekend?"

"Not much. That massage of yours seems to have made a permanent difference."

"Oh, come on." The memory of that night flooded through her.

"Honestly, I think the…er…mental and emotional massage might have been as important as the actual muscle work."

"Oh."

After another pause, he said, "You've made a big difference in my life, Jacquie. In every possible way."

She wouldn't say "oh" again, so she didn't say anything at all.

"I regret the way I left your house that night. I shouldn't have said what I did."

That, she had to answer. "No, you were right. I wasn't realistic in my expectations, that summer. I was eighteen—what did I know? I thought romance meant happily ever after."

"It should."

"At the right time, in the right place. With people who are free to love." She sighed. "None of that really applied to us that summer."

Rhys stirred. "How about now?"

"Now?" Her voice sounded like a mouse squeak.

"We're free to love." He reached out to take her hand. When he sat back, he drew her nearer. "I think the time is right. And the place. I've written the owners of Fairfield Farm to extend my lease for at least a year."

"You're staying?"

"If you'll have me." He placed her hand on his chest, set his hands on her waist and drew her to stand between his legs. "Finally, wholeheartedly, proudly, I can ask you to marry me. Only fourteen years late."

Jacquie touched his face with her fingertips—his forehead under the dark hair, his temple, the line of his jaw, the slope of his nose, the soft curve of his mouth. "I love you." She leaned forward to place a soft kiss on his lips.

Rhys closed his eyes and smiled. "Ah. I forgot that part. I love you, too. Ever since you were eighteen and 'snippy.'"

"I'm still snippy." Skimming her mouth over his cheek, she went back for another kiss.

"Good. I'm a little sharp-tongued myself, as you

may have noticed.'' Rhys returned the kiss, offered one of his own.

''A time or two.''

''And so…'' The conversation wandered, got lost in the pleasure of touching, tasting, trusting.

Finally Jacquie pulled back to see his eyes. ''I do have one last question.''

''Anything.''

''Would you have turned to me—would you have asked me to marry you—if you'd lost today?''

He met her gaze with only honesty in his own. ''Yes. Only you,'' he said quietly. ''Today…forever.''

''Today and forever,'' she repeated. ''Yes.''

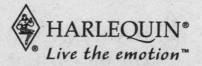

National Bestselling Author

brenda novak

COLD FEET

Despite the cloud of suspicion that followed her father to his grave, Madison Lieberman maintained his innocence...*until* crime writer Caleb Trovato forces her to confront the past once again.

"Readers will quickly be drawn into this well-written, multi-faceted story that is an engrossing, compelling read."
—*Library Journal*

Available February 2004.

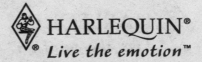

HARLEQUIN®
Live the emotion™

Visit us at www.eHarlequin.com

eHARLEQUIN.com

For **FREE online reading,** visit
www.eHarlequin.com now and enjoy:

Online Reads
Read **Daily** and **Weekly** chapters from
our Internet-exclusive stories by your
favorite authors.

Red-Hot Reads
Turn up the heat with one of our more
sensual online stories!

Interactive Novels
Cast your vote to help decide how these
stories unfold...then stay tuned!

Quick Reads
For shorter romantic reads, try our
collection of Poems, Toasts, & More!

Online Read Library
Miss one of our online reads?
Come here to catch up!

Reading Groups
Discuss, share and rave with other
community members!

For great reading online,
visit www.eHarlequin.com today!

If you enjoyed what you just read,
then we've got an offer you can't resist!

Take 2 bestselling love stories FREE!

Plus get a FREE surprise gift!

Clip this page and mail it to Harlequin Reader Service®

IN U.S.A.	IN CANADA
3010 Walden Ave.	P.O. Box 609
P.O. Box 1867	Fort Erie, Ontario
Buffalo, N.Y. 14240-1867	L2A 5X3

YES! Please send me 2 free Harlequin Superromance® novels and my free surprise gift. After receiving them, if I don't wish to receive anymore, I can return the shipping statement marked cancel. If I don't cancel, I will receive 6 brand-new novels every month, before they're available in stores. In the U.S.A., bill me at the bargain price of $4.47 plus 25¢ shipping and handling per book and applicable sales tax, if any*. In Canada, bill me at the bargain price of $4.99 plus 25¢ shipping and handling per book and applicable taxes**. That's the complete price, and a savings of at least 10% off the cover prices—what a great deal! I understand that accepting the 2 free books and gift places me under no obligation ever to buy any books. I can always return a shipment and cancel at any time. Even if I never buy another book from Harlequin, the 2 free books and gift are mine to keep forever.

135 HDN DNT3
336 HDN DNT4

Name	(PLEASE PRINT)	
Address	Apt.#	
City	State/Prov.	Zip/Postal Code

Forrester Square

LEGACIES . LIES . LOVE .

In February,
RITA® Award-winning author

KRISTIN GABRIEL

**brings you a brand-new
Forrester Square tale...**

THIRD TIME'S THE CHARM

Dana Ulrich's wedding planning business
seemed doomed and the next nuptials were
make or break. So Dana turned to best man
Austin Hawke for help. But if Austin had
his way, it would be Dana walking down
the aisle...toward him!

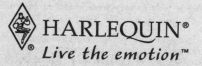

HARLEQUIN®
Live the emotion™

This April 1, anything is possible...

FOOL FOR LOVE

Vicki Lewis Thompson
Stephanie Bond
Judith Arnold

A hilarious NEW anthology in which love gets the last laugh! Who'd ever guess a few amusing pranks could lead to the love of a lifetime for three couples!

Coming to your favorite retail outlet in March 2004— just in time for April Fools' Day!

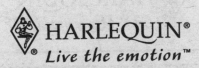

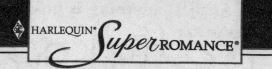

HARLEQUIN *Super*ROMANCE®

**Sea View House in Pilgrim Cove offers
its residents the sea, the sun, the sound
of the surf and the call of the gulls.
But sometimes serenity is only an illusion...**

Pilgrim Cove

Four heartwarming stories by popular author

Linda Barrett

The House
on the Beach

Laura McCloud's come back
to Pilgrim Cove—the source
of her fondest childhood
memories—to pick up the
pieces of her life. The
tranquility of Sea View House
is just what she needs. She
moves in...and finds much
more than she bargained for.

**Available in March 2004,
The House on the Beach
is the first title in this
charming series.**

*Available wherever
Harlequin books are sold.*

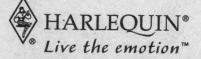

HARLEQUIN®
Live the emotion™

HSRPC1

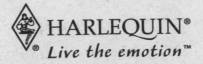